BAD COMPANY

BAD COMPANY

Stories of intrigue, suspense and thrills

COMPILED AND EDITED BY JOANNE HICHENS

PAN MACMILLAN

First published 2008
by Pan Macmillan South Africa
Private Bag x19
Northlands
Johannesburg, 2116

www.panmacmillan.co.za

ISBN 978 1 770 10087 9

Design and typesetting by Triple M Design, Johannesburg
Cover design by Donald Hill of Blue Apple

Printed and bound by Interpak Books, Pietermaritzburg

Contents

Acknowledgements

Most importantly, I'd like to thank contributors for generously sharing their stories without which this anthology would not exist. I'd like especially to thank Richard Kunzmann and Mike Nicol for invaluable help in the early stages, and Margie Orford who, as emails went back and forth, came up with the title for this anthology. *Bad Company* refers not only to the characters in the stories, but also to the company of thriller writers gathered here. It seems fitting thus, that Orford's story *The Meeting* should lead us into this collection.

Thanks to the team at Pan Macmillan, especially to Terry Morris, Publishing Director, for supporting this project, and to Jonathan Williams, working with local imprints, for willingness to sort out whichever problem I threw his way. And thanks to Rene Brophy, Nina Gabriels and Smangele Mathebula for marketing and promotions.

Thanks also, for sound advice, to crime-aficionado's Gerald de Villiers and Joe Muller, and to editor friends Ben Williams, Maire Fisher and Heather Parker Lewis.

And of course, a huge shout-out to David Hewson, International Vice President of ITW (International Thriller Writers) for an enthusiastic response to our collection, and to Lee Child, Emeritus board member of ITW, for taking precious time to write the foreword.

The National Arts Council of South Africa has lent financial support to this project, and for the decision to do so I am also truly grateful.

JOANNE HICHENS
November 2008

Introduction

JOANNE HICHENS

When I was three years old I toppled my six-month-old sister out of her pram. I stole her bottle. I sat in the pram myself. I pinched her butt so she'd have no choice but to crawl. With each progressive year, I never failed to throw a tantrum at her birthday party. In photographs I am sullen-looking in the background, but appeased, clutching a consolation-gift doctor's kit or a Barbie or a tennis racket. This blonde, blue-eyed sister played happily in the yard with her pals till called for dinner, she could make a jelly which would set without skin, she could ski without poles down the slope of PeeWee at Camp Fortune as I was left in her powder, shivering and crying about my frost-bitten toes. This was when we lived in Canada. My sister was easy-going. She had fun. I wore glasses and sulked a lot. I resented her arrival and her permanent presence. Why, when my parents had two sons and *me*, had they wanted another daughter?

Another memory that remains fresh, is gingerly extracting the volume of Hans Christian Andersen's illustrated tales from our bookshelf, this volume with it's cracked blue spine, which I'd leaf through to find the picture of Red Shoes the ballerina with her feet chopped off, her ankles dripping blood as she sat excommunicated at the door of the church. Although this was to my childish mind a totally barbaric punishment for Red Shoes' vanity, I could hardly take my eyes off the image.

I remember too, the number of hours I spent in front of the TV. There was none in South Africa where we'd come from. So while my socially adept sister played soccer and ice hockey with her friends, and Risk and

Monopoly, I retreated increasingly to our basement where I watched *Hill Street Blues* and *Monty Python's Flying Circus* and *Get Smart* and *The World at War*. I loved Charles Bronson movies and James Bond and Dirty Harry, wanting someone to "make my day ..."

As I expose my childhood intensity, and a propensity for the absurd and bizarre, plus a morbid fascination with the underbelly of crime, it is no wonder that as my placid sister grew into a teen dreaming of the princes featured in her historical romances, I looked for reading material that reflected the way I felt – cheated, jealous, furious! Wanting justice. The rough kind especially appealing to me (oh, the things I wanted to do to my sister. And I wanted no white knight, I wanted a man with a gun!) My emotions ran high. I wanted to read stories where the forces of good and evil pulled against each other, and the themes revolved around life and death. Of course, as a well brought-up child I wanted Good to prevail, but I wanted a dose of strong stuff, and what stronger stuff is there than murder and mayhem? I did not read spy-thrillers or war stories (although I loved war comics) but was primarily interested in the kinds of intimate crimes that people perpetrate against one another.

Simply put then, in my personal view, crime-thriller fiction tells stories of the dark side and gives us the opportunity to *face* the dark side – the evil that others do, as well as our own intrinsic darkness – the probability that evil exists in all of us, and that we are each one of us capable of terrible acts.

Indeed crime-thriller fiction is a vehicle for the sort of themes that man has philosophised about for thousands of years; no doubt man will grapple to eternity with the construct of good versus evil. Why do men lie and steal? Why do men commit the primal sin of murder? Why do men take action that is destructive to others' lives as well as ultimately to their own? Is it something more than the desire for wealth, position, revenge, power? Is the "bad guy" (or gal) simply a psychopath on the loose? And how is society to blame? And equally what motivates the "good guy" – the cops, the PIs the journalists, the psychologists – to take a stand against evil and, in many cases, to search out, at great personal risk, the perpetrators of crime – whether it be against an individual or a society – and bring them to justice?

Writing crime-thriller fiction then, and indeed reading it, is an exploration of the age-old dilemmas of being human which encompasses the dangerous territory of our extreme emotions – jealousy, rage, revenge, impotence, fear – and the chains of events that are set rolling when those extreme emotions, linked to motivation, are unleashed.

It is important to note too, that we live in a society increasingly characterised by personal fragmentation, and a loss of values and morals, the result being a world littered with gangs and wrecked marriages and orphans; man is, if not broken, detached and isolated as he may face not only deeply personal problems, but issues such as global warming and the meltdown of capitalist values.

In South Africa in particular, opulence sits side by side with poverty, millionaires live in mansions just across the railway line from squatter camps where indigent thousands subsist in tin shacks; in a land with eleven official languages, home to every religious group, and with the claws of our convoluted past of apartheid still digging in, compounded by the universally felt stresses of global crises and the everyday issues that are apparent in even the most loving relationships, the cracks are bound to show. The centre cannot hold. Crime fiction explores this fragmentation of a contemporary society straining at the seams as it develops.

But whether the crime is a car hijacking in Johannesburg, a mugging in New York, the disappearance of a child from a hotel room in Portugal, the stabbing of an honours student outside a London nightclub, none of us, anywhere in the world, is immune against acts of evil, including murder. And as Jonathan Kellerman once wrote, "the manipulated demise of any human being bears our serious attention, if not always in compassion, at least in horrified pause."

* * *

On a less complex level, crime-thriller fiction, like any fiction, must entertain. It must be sufficiently gripping to keep the reader interested enough to read on. In the words of Jeffrey Deaver, "the story must deliver on the promise of a thrill". On the level of pure reading pleasure, we get a kick out of mystery and suspense, the what-happens-next factor. It's the thriller writer's job to create, as far as possible, stories that pulse with energy, that grab our balls (or at least tickle them), if not our hearts. And this sort of fiction is as much of a word game as any other. The use of satire, ironic twists, black humour, for example, keep the reader turning the pages. We are offered at times a perverse kind of entertainment akin to stopping at an accident scene. We're fascinated by the dead body, and relieved too that it isn't us. And we want to see paramedics and detectives at work, doing their jobs to restore order, if not life.

Bear in mind however, that Good does not always triumph, evil cannot always be rationalised. Sometimes no professional "crime busters" feature at all in crime-thrillers, or their role is minimal. On the market, there are increasingly many compelling stories propelled forward by outsiders confronted by the ugly side of life, particularly in the darker crime fiction and Noir tales. In some stories we are invited into the world of the criminal, we share his mind space as he commits crime openly, and sometimes gets away with it. Indeed, a good deal of contemporary crime fiction centres on the crime and not on the solving of it, and criminals, fraudsters and murderers are not always brought to justice.

As writers, we draw attention to the unforgivable; we draw attention to the pain we most want to ignore in real life; we scratch through the veneer of everyday positivity; but as readers of crime-thriller fiction, above all we want satisfaction, we want a "good read". Whether it's Agatha Christie or Raymond Chandler, or hard-hitting contemporary authors the likes of Elmore Leonard, Vicki Hendricks and Ken Bruen, we want to be kept in suspense.

*   *   *

For many years apartheid cast such a pall over our society that writing considered legitimate was that which reflected the struggle and brought to the attention of readers the system of oppression that had to be toppled. Free at last, writers post-1994 have had the doors open to try their hand at whatever stories they want to write – as it should be – and the last several years have seen a spate of crime-thriller novels published as popular fiction.

Crime-thriller fiction however, is not new in South Africa. Arthur Maimane's short stories, heavily influenced by US pulp, were published in *Drum* magazine during the 1950s; long-time crime-fiction writer June Drummond published a first novel in the late fifties, and is still writing; James McClure hit the crime scene in the '70s, smack between the eyes with his cheeky cop-duo Kramer and Zondi; Wessel Ebersohn created prison psychologist Yudel Gordon in the '80s; and the success of Deon Meyer over the past ten years shows that South African mainstream crime-thriller fiction has been of interest, and selling, here and abroad for a long time.

When it comes to this particular collection, fellow writer Richard

Kunzmann and I bandied about the possibility of a crime-thriller-stories anthology, and thanks to Richard, Pan commissioned me to compile a selection of stories as a showcase of South African crime-thriller fiction, specifically from currently published authors.

As I've gone about the work of compiling the anthology, I have realised there are many authors out there writing in the genre, so this cannot be seen as a definitive collection. Prolific writer Omoseye Bolaji, for instance – who recently received a lifetime achievement award from the Free State Department of Sports, Arts and Culture for his contributions to African Literature – has written a series of novellas featuring sleuth Tebogo Mokoena, and deserves to be featured; Angela Makholwa was unable to contribute due to pressure to complete her new novel; there are a number of true-crime writers, such as Anthony Altbeker and Chris Karsten, currently trying their hand at fiction, and Rob Marsh who does both. And novelists Quintis Van der Merwe, Chanette Paul, Piet Steyn and other popular authors – whom I'm sure will feature in a future collection – write in Afrikaans.

Without being specific about any of the stories (I'm loathe to give the game away), there are several points worth making before you read on. The crimes that the stories in this anthology revolve around are of the more personal kind, as opposed to crimes against humanity, or political crimes. And of the seventeen stories, guns feature in only around a third – which is interesting considering our out-of-control gun culture. Between these covers, there are all sorts of ways of killing.

A large number of the stories feature women and children as victims – which reflects the reality of the rampant abuse of women and children in our country.

Several stories offer closure, which begs the question: is redemption still something we so desperately seek? On what level do we want things to work out? Although a selection of the stories feature capable police, a couple of them touch on apathy and corruption in the ranks of the cops, which rings only too true.

And as our collective rainbow-nation culture – with our unique political and social history – has developed, the question bears asking: do these stories reflect unique tensions in our society? Some most certainly do.

The xenophobic violence of mid-year 2008 rocked South Africa to the core. So it is not surprising that two of the stories are set during this time. Simply by the nature of the diversity – of culture, and experience, and given the extremes in our society that give way to crime – there exists an excess of material to work with. This is manifest in every street-pole news poster, in every tabloid, in almost every conversation at dinner parties, that contemporary South Africa, not only tainted but stained by crime and corruption, is fertile ground for the author looking to write crime-thriller fiction.

As for me? Thanks to a good shrink I came to terms with my feelings of jealousy towards my sister – and although there was quite a bit of hair-pulling, and a punch-up or two, I never resorted to doing real harm. My sister and I are now the greatest friends and allies. I'm still a fan of TV shows – *CSI* and *Law and Order* and *The Wire* – and of course my reading matter – dark and nastier than ever – includes a growing crop of exciting South African thrillers.

In this collection, there is variety to appeal to all tastes; from the more laid-back "mystery" to the roller-coaster "thriller", a "good read" is guaranteed.

FOREWORD

LEE CHILD

I was present at the birth of the new International Thriller Writers organisation, and in the four short years of its existence it has generated much discussion about each of the three words in its name. *Writers* is easy enough to understand – although our members cover the whole span from established superstars to the man or woman who rises at four in the morning to add five hundred words to a debut work-in-progress before heading out to a long day at the factory.

The definition of *Thriller* is more difficult – we know one when we read one, but a holistic definition of the genre is hard to achieve. Obvious bullet points would include great pace, high stakes, danger, peril, resolution, safety – and actual bullets, probably, although not necessarily. But in my view, for thrillers to work, they have to reach backward into the structures of our ancient myths and legends. I just wrote an essay for another ITW publication showing how the legend of Theseus and the Minotaur and Ian Fleming's James Bond novel *Doctor No* are in fact the same story, separated by 3 500 years. Certain stories just work: if they didn't, why would we keep reinventing them over the centuries?

Which is why thrillers sell so well. In all their different shades and flavours – suspense novels, crime fiction, mysteries – they consistently dominate bestseller lists all over the world. They fill the racks in airports, drugstores, and supermarkets. They're found in hotel lounges on all five continents, battered, creased, smeared with suntan oil. They are the world's shared stories, because they arise from the world's shared human history.

Hence *International.* And we're being selfish here. Those of us who love the genre love finding new stuff to read. And those of us who travel to promote our own books are always finding new stuff to read. My friend and fellow author David Hewson went to South Africa to support his excellent Nic Costa series, and e-mailed me from a hotel to rave about the great local stuff he was reading. He told me there was an anthology coming out – the book you are holding right now – and suggested that ITW get behind it. To help the local guys? No! Talent like this doesn't need help. The idea was simply to bring pleasure to our friends and members in America and Europe and Australia and the rest of the world by bringing them something they might not otherwise get a chance to see.

And what a pleasure it will be. This is a sampler of current South African thriller fiction, featuring seventeen authors, some of whom you will know and others you won't – yet. Deon Meyer is probably the best-known internationally – and deservedly so – but he will have his work cut out to maintain that position based on the evidence here. The stories themselves are fascinating in the way that they see universal themes through a uniquely African lens. As everyone knows, South Africa's up-and-down history meant that much of its contemporary culture developed in isolation, but now it has half a generation that has been much more exposed to the world. The stories in this book reflect that evolution. Some resist the pull of American and British tradition only mildly; some subvert it wickedly; and some could have only been written in and about Africa. All are excellent.

And all will influence the rest of us. Global exposure is a two-way street. This is not about authors in the rest of the world helping authors in South Africa. It's about the opposite, just as much. The angles and flavours and insights in these stories will enrich the great river of human narrative. They'll find their way into the mainstream and mix and merge and eventually come back again from unpredictable directions.

As well they should. There was a certain election in America in November 2008 that reminded the world that we don't know Africa as well as we should, and that it has plenty of good stuff yet to explore. If you're a reader, then this anthology is as good a place to start as any.

BAD COMPANY

MARGIE ORFORD

Award-winning journalist, children's author and Fulbright scholar, Margie Orford has authored various non-fiction projects including the groundbreaking archival retrieval project, *Woman Writing Africa* (2003), and *Fabulously Forty and Beyond* (2006).

Orford's crime novels *Like Clockwork* (2006) and *Blood Rose* (2008), featuring the intrepid Clare Hart - documentary film-maker-cum-profiler - have been translated into numerous languages. Watch out for her new novel *Daddy's Girl* (2009).

As a mother of three daughters, Orford is especially concerned about violence against women. She says: "Writing crime parachutes me into the present. It allows me to show rather than tell, to write about HOW South Africa is, and not why. Violence - especially sexual violence - has become so 'normal'. Writing about it makes it 'not-normal' again. Crime-thrillers are very intimate - it is the intimacy of violence - both the experience of it for victim and perpetrator, and the amazing resilience that people have to survive and love, which is wide open in crime fiction."

And true to form, here in her fast-paced story *The Meeting*, Orford explores life's messy complexities.

The Meeting

A CLARE HART SHORT STORY

MARGIE ORFORD

TWENTY MINUTES' DRIVE EAST FROM HER CITY APARTMENT AND Table Mountain was a blue cut-out beneath the bleached summer sky. Clare Hart turned off the freeway, the off-ramp sinking her into Khayelitsha, Cape Town's teeming shadow city sprawling unmapped across the sand dunes south of the airport. The houses, makeshift cubes of corrugated iron and wood, roofed with black plastic, homed half a million people, maybe a million. No one was counting.

The road looped under a bridge where shacks sprouted under the concrete ribs holding the flyover aloft. A woman emptying water into the tub of pink geraniums at her front door raised her hand in greeting. Clare flashed her lights in return. A group of small boys huddled together throwing dice abandoned their game to race alongside her car, falling back one by one. The one who fell back last turned back doing a footballer's victory lap, arms outstretched like wings, to join his companions under the bridge.

The main road, thronged with people and vehicles, was lined with small plywood stores fringed with onions and oranges. On the counters, enamel bowls were piled with tomatoes. Withered apples had been counted out, two or three per bag. Severed sheeps' heads grinned beneath a cloud of buzzing flies while the stallholder haggled with a customer. The wind whipped at women's skirts as they called out to passers-by, luring them with freshly baked vetkoek and offal sizzling above the coals. Men loitering near the bass-thumping taxis bellowed their routes, waiting for enough passengers to warrant a trip.

3

Noise filled every crevice between the houses and pushed through the shatterproof windows of Clare's car as she inched forward. This would be her second meeting with Isaac Molweni. He had called her that morning, saying he had to see her today. Could she come straight after school was dismissed? Could she bring the pictures?

The photographs were on the seat next to her. Isaac's careful directions (*left at the second set of lights, look for the traditional doctor's sign at the cul-de-sac, right where the vendors sell sunglasses, there was the school, opposite Shoprite*) were in the boot, tucked into her bag with the pathologist's report and her tape recorder.

A plump girl in a yellow sundress waited at the traffic light, a vetkoek in her hand. She split it, putting one half whole into her mouth.

The lights turned red. Clare stopped.

The girl strolled across the road. She paused in front of Clare's car to greet a friend walking in the opposite direction, handing the other half of her doughnut to the toddler tied to her back. The child stared at Clare as he bit into it, transfixing her as his eyes widened with pleasure. It was the same small child, the one with the limpid eyes – the bewildered child Clare had held on her lap last week in the Molweni's two-roomed house; Lorna's relatives had crowded quietly in the kitchen; the slouching boys in the street had made way for Clare when she had arrived. Lorna Molweni's son had curled his warm body into Clare's, retreating behind the curtain of her hair to lick the pink icing off his cupcake. There had been fifty people there, when this terrible thing had happened, but nobody heard. Nobody saw this.

Clare had stared at the grainy images laid out amongst the tea things, of the child's mother's plump body. No police photographer had come, Isaac Molweni had explained, so he had taken these pictures with his cellphone. For evidence. So that Dr Hart could help him. Then Isaac had pieced together for Clare what had happened to his sister.

Lorna had her hair braided.
Lorna went to a tavern.
Lorna did not come home.
He, Isaac, had gone to look for Lorna because Lorna had to eat, take her medicine.
He found Lorna naked behind the toilets of the shebeen.
Lorna's eyes were swollen shut.

Lorna's belly had a bloody Aids ribbon knifed onto it.
Lorna's body had been split between her legs.
There had been eight men.
Lorna had breath to say two names. Jackson, Sizwe.
Lorna did not know the other six.

The lights turned green. A minibus taxi swooped in front of Clare, the bass reverberating through her chest. The girl in the yellow dress got in, the door sliding shut on her laughter. The truck driver behind Clare leaned on his hooter and she jerked forward, turning left, away from his gesticulated obscenities. The hand-painted sign pointed down the road offering *Hair Ghana Style. Braids for the Laydees, for the Gents.* Not Dr Khoza's fifty-rand traditional cures for bad luck, impotence and Aids.

There was a little pop below Clare's heart. She had turned too soon and then the road was too narrow to turn back.

She drove on until the tar petered out into an open lot where a recent fire had reduced scores of shacks to blackened stumps and twisted pieces of metal. Ahead of her, shacks crowded around a tangle of tracks. The brightly coloured washing snapping on lines marked one handkerchief of space off from another. Two goats nosed around smouldering rubbish piled against a fence. No cheerful women doing washing here. Clare went left, thinking it would U-turn her back onto the main road.

The road narrowed, slowing her to a crawl.

Clare stopped outside a dilapidated shack to get her bearings. She didn't see anyone except a half-naked child leaning against the doorpost watching her, a thumb plugged into her mouth. A scrawny bitch lay in the dust on the pavement, newborn puppies heaped against her belly. Kwaito thumped its sullen beat from the speaker hooked on the lopsided sign of the Nice Time Tavern. A tattered red umbrella provided a puddle of shade for three men sitting on upturned blue crates, quarts of Black Label on the plastic table. An old woman filling her bucket at the communal tap kept a wary eye on them.

A man unpeeled from a wall across the street, his hands in his pockets, his hat pulled low. Clare calculated how many manoeuvres it would take to turn the car around. How long it would take. Too many. Too long.

Another pop.

In her heart this time.

The door where the child stood slammed shut, the little girl drawn inside by a slender arm. The sharp sound took Clare's eyes off the man for a second.

He was standing at her window, both hands up, palms pink, open against his tight red T-shirt. She looked from his hands to his face, at the thin scar threaded through his left eyebrow, across the rounded cheek. A trace of childhood lingered in his eyes. Clare put him at fifteen, maybe sixteen. He tossed Clare a smile, making a tumbling motion with his hands, motioning her to open up. A vein pulsed in the hollow of his throat. She ignored the machine gun pop pop popping in her heart and cracked open the window.

"You're wrong here, *sisi*," he said.

"I know," said Clare, her mouth dry. The old woman, bent by the weight of the bucket on her head, scurried away down an alley.

"Where are you going?" he asked.

"To meet someone near Shoprite." It was close enough to the truth. Isaac's school was very close by.

"You turned too soon. I show you the way out." His eyes were on the road behind Clare's car.

Clare saw movement in the corner of her eye. One of the men from the shebeen was sauntering towards her down the track. Another of the drinkers stood, drained his beer and placed the bottle on the table, his right hand sliding with practised smoothness towards his trouser pocket.

The boy was at the other side of the car.

Clare opened the door.

The boy was inside. He pressed down the lock with his left elbow. He'd placed the envelope of photographs on his lap, his slender fingers curled around Lorna's name. He angled the sun visor so he could watch the street behind them in the vanity mirror. The smell of him – Vinolia soap, wood smoke, adrenalin – filled the car.

"Drive," said the boy. The men from the shebeen had fanned out. The one on the right broke into a slow trot. He was closing in. "Now!"

Clare slipped the car into first, churning the wheels in the sand. The wheels bit and she breathed out, driving fast between the shacks. The strands of barbed wire in front of each dwelling were so close to the car that the hairs on her arms rose. The man from the shebeen stopped and urinated, aiming at the dog. She slunk off fast, scattering puppies. The other two fell back, returning to their beers outside the shebeen.

"Turn here."

Clare turned. The street was wider. Schoolboys in grey shorts and white shirts, trailing bags behind them, parted to let the car through.

"What's your name?" asked Clare.

"Andile." The boy pointed again. "And here, turn." They were back on the busy main road. Clare wound down her window and the comforting sounds of the bustling street enfolded her. She pulled over and the boy got out. "Two robots." The boy pointed ahead. "You turn left at the shopping centre."

"Thank you, Andile," said Clare.

"You're here for Lorna." It was not a question.

"You knew her?"

"I saw her." Andile traced the loop of the Aids ribbon on the window with his forefinger, his shirt colouring it crimson through the pale dust.

"Lorna?"

"I see them." His voice just above a whisper.

"Jackson, Sizwe?" asked Clare. A taxi throbbed past and his answer was lost.

"The others?"

"You must be careful, *sisi*." He handed her the brown envelope containing Isaac's photographs and took off, his blade of a body disappearing between the fruit stalls. Clare leafed quickly through the enlarged prints till she found the only wide shot of the shebeen.

The Nice Time Tavern.

Clare slid her hands off the steering wheel, wiped her sweaty palms on her jeans and drew a deep breath. She leapt out of her car, activating the alarm at twenty paces. Fifty paces and she had squeezed between the stalls where the boy had disappeared, ignoring the shouts of the hawkers. Behind the little shops, the road forked into two dusty tracks. Clare slowed for a second to orientate herself. To the right a flash of red. She sprinted towards it, turning the corner where Andile had turned. He was leaning over a fence, trying to catch his breath. He took off when he saw her but Clare was fast. She was gaining. At the next corner she was on him, one slim, strong arm coiled hard on his throat, pulling his bony body tight against hers.

"Tell me what you did." Clare's voice was harsh from running. He twisted in her grip and she pulled his left arm high between his shoulder blades. He gasped. The women who had abandoned their stalls to follow pressed in around them, yelling at the boy in Xhosa.

"I helped you, *sisi*," he said.

The crowd was swelling, volleying questions and comments over their heads. In the distance a siren wailed.

"Because of Lorna?" Clare's mouth was close to his ear.

Andile's heart thudded against Clare's chest. "I did nothing."

"I know," she said.

Clare's phone beeped in her back pocket. Two o'clock. She was late for her meeting.

"That'll be Isaac Molweni," she said. "Lorna's brother." Andile stood dead still and she loosened her grip on his neck. "This is your chance."

He nodded. Clare let his arm go and Andile turned to face her, rubbing his shoulder to get the blood flowing again. A small boy darted forward and handed him his hat. Andile pulled it down low, tilting his face up and looked Clare in the eye.

"I will tell Isaac." Andile looked Clare in the eye. "I will tell him what I saw."

DEON MEYER

Deon Meyer worked as a journalist, advertising copywriter, brand consultant and off-road motorcycle event developer before taking up full-time writing in 2008. His first novel was *Dead Before Dying* (1999), and the latest of seven is *Blood Safari* (2008).

"My theory is that all authors have a sort of natural niche for their stories," he says. "Mine just happens to be crime thrillers. I have a sneaking suspicion they are the most fun to write."

About an earlier version of *The Nostradamus Document*, he says: "In 2007, *You/Huis-genoot* magazine asked me for a three part serial – a new challenge for me. The original title of my second novel was 'The Nostradamus Document', but my characters just never allowed me to write what I intended. They literally took the book in another direction. I always thought it would make a cool title, so that's where I started for this story, which is totally different from the one I wanted to write for the novel."

Above all, Meyer, as master story-teller, spins a slick and gripping yarn in *The Nostradamus Document.*

The Nostradamus Document

DEON MEYER

1

THE IMPACT OF THE BULLET PLUCKED HER FROM DETECTIVE SERGEANT Fransman Dekker's embrace.

Natalie October had been standing next to her untidy desk, surrounded by high steel shelves crammed with second-hand car parts. A sensuous woman, she was slowly and purposefully unbuttoning her top, her wry smile an invitation. A challenge. The brown skin of her breasts gleamed – there was no underwear. She stepped towards him and, leaning against him, purred, "You're not bad looking for a cop, Dekker ..."

His hand couldn't resist the bare shoulder, his palm touched it, his mouth dry, not sure if he wanted to push her away or draw her to him. Then the shot rang out. He saw the small round hole above her left eyebrow, saw her sinking from his arms. The shot had come from somewhere behind him. He knew she was dead before she hit the desk and slumped onto the concrete floor. He froze, trying to make sense of what was happening. Then he ran for the door, drawing his firearm from the leather holster on his belt.

Outside the small office building a bullet slammed into the doorframe. Diving to the ground he rolled under a stripped Toyota Corolla, firing in the direction of the shots. He scanned the scrapyard for the shooter. Piled high with row upon row of dismembered vehicles the yard offered plenty of cover.

Lying there, watching, listening, with everything gone eerily quiet, he pulled his cellphone from his pocket to call the Bellville Police Station for backup. He held the phone to his ear, suddenly remembered Natalie

October's half-naked body. He would have to explain that. He killed the call, realising for the first time he was in a mess. To put it mildly. Then he heard a car door slam and an engine roar to life. The sound came from the direction the shots had been fired. He rolled from under the Toyota, ran crouching between the rows of wrecked metal, his firearm ready. A grey BMW X5 skidded wildly between the rows of cars, its back wheels kicking up stones against the metal carcasses.

They were going to get away. Dekker stopped in his tracks, turned and ran to his own car. It was parked outside the office, next to Natalie October's red Chevy Corvette. He wouldn't be able to block their way but he could give chase if he hurried. Glancing towards the exit he saw the Beemer swing through the gates and take a right towards Stikland. Pushing his pistol back into its holster with one hand, he dug for the white Opel's keys with the other. He was about to unlock the door when he saw the photograph. It was stuck to the window with a piece of tape.

A photograph of himself and Natalie October.

He tore it from the window and stared at it uncomprehendingly. It had been taken just now. It showed him standing in Natalie's office, his hand on her bare shoulder. From this angle the desire was clearly etched on his face. There was no disputing it was him. The profile was unmistakably that of Fransman Dekker, complete with his white father's Gaelic nose and broad shoulders, and his coloured mother's wide mouth and black curly hair.

Leaning against the Corvette he heard the Beemer's roar fade away in the distance. He breathed out slowly, trying desperately to stop the pounding in his chest. This was slightly more than a mess: he was in deep shit.

*   *   *

He stood on the spot from where they'd taken the photograph – a narrow space between shelves lined with carburettors and headlights and coils and starter motors. There was an opening just wide enough for the camera lens to have focused on him and the woman. It took him a while to take stock of the implications: they'd lain in wait for him, camera at the ready. Which meant it was more than likely they'd known Natalie October had called the Bellville Police Station and specifically asked to speak to Sergeant Dekker. He could hear her husky voice now: "I'm the owner of Octoberfest Auto Spares and Scrapyard and there's a syndicate here that's trying to flog their stolen cars. I've heard you're a straight cop."

"I am," he'd said.

"Then come alone and I'll give you what I've got."

He should never have come alone. The correct procedure would have been to report the matter to his boss, Superintendent Cliffie Mketsu, then come here with his shift partner. But he hadn't. He'd wanted to solve the case on his own. He'd wanted the credit. Because he was "too driven". That's what Crystal had said this morning.

"You're too driven, Frans. I *am* your wife. I *am* entitled to some of your time. But I never see you." In the two years they'd been married, this was the ugliest argument they'd had. It had left him feeling rejected – another reason why he fell for Natalie October's advances.

He'd entered the makeshift office without even wondering why there was no one else around, only the voluptuous woman who'd baited him from the start.

"Do you have a big gun, Dekker?" she'd asked suggestively while someone was standing behind the shelves with a camera, listening to their every word and waiting for an opportune moment to take the photograph.

Then they'd shot her. While he'd taken cover under the Corolla they'd printed out the photograph and stuck it to his car. It didn't make sense.

Why? Why all this effort? All the planning? For what?

It was a fuck-up. An unfathomable fuck-up.

He looked at the photograph. His hand was shaking. He had to pull himself together. He was Fransman Dekker. He could sort it out.

* * *

On the way to the police station in Voortrekker Road he had an overwhelming urge to hear Crystal's voice. He called her cellphone.

"I can't talk now, Frans," she said, her voice still tight after this morning's argument. She was probably in a meeting. That's all they ever did at Sanlam's advertising department. Hold meetings from nine to five.

"I just wanted to say I'm sorry."

He knew the apology caught her unawares. She was silent for a moment, then she whispered, "I'm also sorry. You know how much I love you." All was forgiven.

"I'll be home early, I promise."

"Good. Thanks, Fransman, thanks for phoning." Then: "I have to go now. A meeting. I'll call you. You're important to me."

"Bye," he said as he pulled up outside the police station. He would leave work at five today, come what may. He needed to feel Crystal's body against his.

Someone was hammering on the passenger window. Startled, Dekker looked up. The large shape of his shift partner, Inspector Mbali Kaleni, filled the window. Leaning over, he opened the door for her and she heaved herself into the car.

"You've been talking on the phone while driving." She squinted and wagged her finger at him. "I saw you."

Dekker said nothing. Only two more weeks before his next partner arrived.

"Let's go. Anonymous call. Someone shot a woman at a scrapyard in La Belle Street," Mbali said, looking at him as if it were his fault.

*   *   *

The problem with Mbali Kaleni was she irritated the hell out of everyone. She had the bad habit of suddenly appearing out of nowhere, like a bad omen, usually at the worst possible moment. A know-it-all, overweight Zulu and outspoken feminist, she did everything strictly by the book, abided by every fucking statute, law and ordinance. The smell of KFC permanently hung around her desk although no one ever actually saw her eating the takeaways.

But, Dekker hated to admit, she was a good detective. Not an instinctive one, like him. She was methodical and slow, but she missed nothing. Like now, with the tyre tracks next to the Corvette. Dekker's tracks.

"Here," she said to the two guys from Forensics, stabbing the air with her fat forefinger. "I want prints of these tracks."

She waddled in the direction of the makeshift office, her eyes scanning the ground.

Had he picked up all the cartridge shells after he'd fired from underneath the Corolla?

Dekker realised he'd not yet reloaded his firearm. He felt sick. What else had he forgotten?

Before leaving the scrapyard he'd wiped his prints in Natalie October's office. But he knew the area was covered with his DNA. Hair, flakes of skin and microscopic pools of liquid – an invisible trail everyone left behind wherever they went.

"Come on, *Frons*man," Mbali Kaleni barked, then cackled loudly. She knew he hated the nickname, a send-up of his driving ambition and his scowling dedication to the job. No one dared call him Fronsman to his face. Except Mbali Kaleni. Shaking his head he followed her into the office.

The police photographer was clicking away, taking pictures of Natalie October's body from every angle.

"Hurry up," Mbali snapped, treading carefully around the body. She pulled out the victim's chair and sat down at the desk, surveying the untidy mess of paperwork.

Then Dekker saw it. An A4 sheet of paper with his initials in huge capitals. FD. And a telephone number. Suppressing a rising sense of panic, he tried to read it upside down. How had he missed it? At what number had Natalie October called him? If she'd called his cell he was done for.

Then he remembered: she'd called him on the station number, the telephone on his desk had rung and …

"Have a look over here," one of the forensics guys said.

"What?" Mbali asked irritably.

"Bullet hole."

Mbali heaved herself out of the chair with a grunt and waddled to the door. Dekker quickly scanned the number on the page. It was the office number. He had to get rid of it. Make it disappear. But had Mbali seen it? Would she miss it?

Mbali was standing at the window peering at the spot the forensics guy had found. Grabbing his chance Dekker turned his body so it was between the sheet of paper and Mbali.

He took it and stuffed it under his jacket. Then he went over to Mbali and looked at the small hole in the window.

"Not necessarily new," he said. "It could be an old hole."

Mbali sniffed contemptuously. "Look at this," she said and walked over to the desk. Dekker still had the paper uncomfortably pinned underneath his jacket. He had to get out of the office and destroy it.

Mbali stood in the exact spot and in the same position as Natalie October when she'd been shot. Then she turned to Dekker. "If she was standing here, then that hole lines up with her wound."

"But we don't know where she was standing," Dekker said. Then his cellphone rang. Excusing himself he walked out of the office, pressing the sheet of paper to his body with his one hand and pulling the phone from his jacket pocket with the other. No number, just the word *Unknown* on the cellphone screen. He pushed the answer button.

"Dekker."

"Did you like the photograph?" A man's voice, sounding jovial, as if he were an old friend.

"What photograph?" he asked hoarsely.

"I can have another one delivered to refresh your memory. And one marked for the attention of Inspector Mbali Kaleni."

"Oh, that picture." He tried to sound calm. Then he realised he'd released the pressure on the piece of paper underneath his jacket and it had fluttered to the ground. Turning, he saw Mbali bending to pick it up.

"There's something I'd like you to do for me," the voice on the phone said. "Unless you want to lose your pretty wife and your job."

2

Mbali Kaleni was bending down to pick up the damning piece of evidence.

"I'm listening," Dekker said, his eyes on Mbali who grunted as she straightened up and held out the sheet of paper to him without looking at it.

"You dropped this," she said.

"Thanks," he mouthed. He took the sheet of paper and crumpled it.

"You're wondering why we chose you. Right, Dekker?" the voice on the phone asked.

"It's rude to take personal calls on the job," Mbali said, walking back to the murder scene.

"Yes," Dekker said, to the voice on the phone and Mbali.

"Well, you see, bru: it's really your boss's fault." The self-conscious way the voice said "bru" indicated it belonged to a whitey. Lead number two. The first had been the big grey X5 in which they'd sped away from the murder scene.

"Oh?"

"What was the first thing Cliffie Mketsu did when he took over at Bellville?"

"Tell me."

"He moved the exhibit lock-up to the detectives' office and started controlling access. Only the detectives can get in now. Here's my problem: I've got something in there. Something you don't even know you've got. Or at least not yet. And I want it back. Without attracting any attention.

Nice and quiet. And you're the man for the job because you can get into the lock-up."

"There are seven other detectives who also have access."

"But only one of them is Fransman Dekker."

"So?"

"A birdie told me you want to become commissioner. Told me your ambition is burning white, like a well-tuned engine. And that comes from being poor. I hear Fransman Dekker is still trying to escape Atlantis' squatter camps. And the shame of your mom and the French— "

"Enough!" Dekker realised he'd raised his voice. His hand holding the cellphone was damp with perspiration. "What do you want?" he asked, lowering his voice.

"My thinking is you'll do anything to protect what you have – your career, your marriage … Which is why I'm sure I can depend on you …"

*   *   *

Dekker first made sure his hands were no longer shaking. Then he walked back to the office. Inspector Kaleni was sitting on the crumpled bonnet of a faded tan Nissan 1400 Sport. She was questioning two scrapyard workers.

"Are you still working for us, *Frons*man?" she asked, interrupting her interrogation. Before he could say anything she turned back to the workers in their oil-stained grey overalls. "Where have you two been?"

"October told us to take a walk. She was expecting a policeman."

"A policeman?"

"She told us to go to the Hypermarket because a policeman from Bellville was on his way. She told us to be back by two."

"What time did you leave here?"

"About nine."

Dekker realised he'd have to intervene, sharpish. "Now why would she not want the police to see you?"

"I don't know. She's the boss …" the one overall said defensively.

Mbali Kaleni shook her head, puzzled. "A policeman from Bellville? Are you sure?"

"That's what she said."

"Did she want to report a crime?"

The two overalls shrugged.

"Trouble? Anything?"

"Don't know."

Kaleni stared at the two men, as if the intensity of her accusing gaze would make them change their story. Turning to Dekker she said, "Get her telephone records from Telkom. And find out what cellphone company she used. Let's check if she spoke to anyone at the station."

Natalie October had called the office switchboard number. He was sure …

"Are you listening, Dekker?"

"I'm listening. I also want to check if she has a criminal record. Perhaps it was a parole officer who came around this morning." That was the best he could come up with for now.

"Perhaps," Inspector Kaleni sighed, heaving herself off the bonnet. "Give your names and addresses to the constable," she told the two overalls. "Then you can go."

*   *   *

There were eight desks in the detectives' open-plan office. Dekker's stood on its own against the southern wall, the only one not touching sides with the others. As he sat down to study the faxed copy of Natalie October's criminal record, his cellphone rang. *Unknown*. He knew who it was.

"Dekker." He noticed Mbali Kaleni, the only other detective in the office, approaching his desk with a file.

"It's time we told you how to fix things," the voice said.

"I can't talk now," Dekker said.

"That's right, he's got work to do," Mbali said, breathing over him.

"I can talk now, bru. So you can listen. Get a pen and write: Case number 2008/11/23/37B." The voice slowly read out the number. Dekker concentrated. He couldn't risk taking it down because Mbali was standing right next to him.

"Have you got it?"

"Could you repeat it?"

The voice impatiently repeated the number and Dekker memorised it. Mbali sighed next to him, her dimpled forearms crossed across her chest.

"Right. The exhibit lock-up: I believe you keep the stuff for every case in separate boxes. There are several things in the box for this case – firearms, cartridge shells, a shirt with blood – but what I'm really after is a little black book, one of those in which you write addresses. It has the letters ND on the front. Just take the book. Put it in your pocket and leave. That's all. My guys will meet you somewhere. Then you give it to them and the business with Natalie October and the photograph disappears. You carry on with your life, I with mine."

"ND?"

"It's an abbreviation."

"For what?"

"It's an inside joke, you won't understand."

"Try me."

"The 'Nostradamus Document'. Now do we have a deal?"

"Deal," Dekker said.

"I'll be in touch." Then the phone went dead.

He looked up at Mbali. She slapped the October file down in front of him. "You never got the Telkom records."

"I'm on it. I got her criminal record meanwhile."

"Let me guess – she was in for car theft. Part of a syndicate."

"Close enough. She got a suspended sentence in 1999. The old vehicle theft unit caught her dealing in stolen goods. She had a used car lot in Voortrekker Road and the engine and chassis numbers of two cars on her showroom floor didn't match."

Mbali nodded. "I'm telling you, the whole thing smells of organised crime. And there's a cop involved."

"Oh?"

"I spoke to Telkom. Ms October called our switchboard. Just after nine. Spoke to a cop."

"Who?" Had his voice betrayed him, Dekker wondered?

"That's what I'm about to find out," Mbali said. Tapping with her forefinger on the file, she said, "Just make sure you file it in the right place. You know I like to keep my stuff in order."

After she'd closed the door Dekker sat motionless trying to get his breathing under control. What were the chances the Bellville charge office would remember a woman had called just after nine asking to speak to Fransman Dekker?

Slim. But you never knew, that was the damned trouble. It took only one bright young constable with a memory like an elephant.

Shoving the fax with Natalie October's criminal record into the file he walked to the notice board where the case numbers of the past three months were listed alongside the names of the respective investigating officers. He ran his finger down the list, his heart pounding. He found the case number – 2008/11/23/37B – and the name next to it. Inspector Mbali Kaleni.

He swore. Why couldn't it have been someone else?

He quickly strode over to the filing cabinet against the wall, found the right drawer and opened it. No case file. It had to be on her desk.

He was alone in the large office. She would probably be gone for another ten minutes. He walked over to her desk. The case files were stacked in three neat piles. He flipped through the first lot and soon found the docket he was looking for. Paging feverishly through the contents he found the charge sheet. A car hijacking gone wrong: on 23 November Vincent van der Westhuizen, a 35-year-old male from Table View, had tried to hijack a Jeep Grand Cherokee Laredo in Kenridge. Fortunately the owner of the Jeep, a Mrs Regina Kemp, kept a Beretta Vertec on her lap while waiting for the automatic gate at her house to open. She'd shot Van der Westhuizen, who had three previous convictions for car theft, point blank in the chest. His life had been saved on the operating table of a private clinic and he was currently recovering under heavy police guard.

Dekker paged through the list of exhibits. It wasn't long. A silver .45 Smith & Wesson Model 457S firearm, ammunition, the cartridge shells from Mrs Kemp's Beretta, the Beretta itself, one blood-stained blue short-sleeved shirt, car keys for a 2006 Ford Ranger 2.5 Diesel, a leather wallet with R136,51 in cash, a bank card and card licence in the name of Vincent van der Westhuizen. And a black address book.

Hearing footsteps outside the door he quickly put the file back and turned around. The door opened and Vusumusi Ndabeni, the only Xhosa detective at Bellville, came into the office, whistling cheerfully.

"Howzit, Fransman."

"Hi, Vusi." The adrenaline was pumping. He took a deep breath and said, "I have to go into the exhibit room." That was one of Superintendent Cliffie Mketsu's regulations: access to the exhibit lock-up was permitted only if two detectives keyed in the code. Last year someone had stolen cocaine with a street value of R70 000 from the old storeroom. So the Commissioner had appointed Mketsu to get the place in shape. He'd hand-picked his detectives: Dekker, Kaleni, Ndabeni and four others, chosen for their integrity and work ethic.

And now he'd been forced to resort to this.

"Sure, partner," Ndabeni said and walked with him to the heavy steel door. They each keyed in a code. The light above the door changed to green. Ndabeni turned and walked back to his desk. Dekker pulled open the door and switched on the neon lights inside. The walls were lined with wooden shelves, another row down the centre of the room. The shelves were stacked with cardboard boxes, all neatly arranged in date order.

Dekker glanced at his watch. The fat inspector would be back in five minutes. More or less. He walked down one row, but he was going too fast to read the numbers. He stopped, forcing himself to stay calm. Get the box, find the book and get out. He closed his eyes as if praying. Then he scanned the boxes again, much slower this time, carefully reading each label for the case number, 2008/11/23/37B. He found the right one on the bottom shelf against the back wall. Ignoring the handling card on which he was supposed to enter his name and the time and date, he pulled out the box, and lifted the lid. The little black book was right at the bottom. He took it, put back the lid and pushed the box back on the shelf.

"What do you think you're doing, Dekker?"

Inspector Mbali Kaleni's large frame was silhouetted in the doorway. All he could think of was whether his hand was big enough to conceal the little black book.

3

"Hell, Mbali, you gave me a fright."

"It's your guilty conscience," she said. "What are you looking for?"

He hesitated before replying, "Case 2008/11/23/37B. It's one of yours, the Vincent van der Westhuizen car hijacking. I … I wanted to look at the firearm." The half-truth ensured his voice remained even. He walked out the storeroom but Mbali didn't budge.

"Why?" she barked.

Six hours of tension caused him to go on the offensive, perhaps because it was his only recourse, perhaps because he had the little black book in his pocket and the worst was over.

"Why do you think, Mbali? Have you noticed any similarities with the October shooting? Like car theft?"

She looked as if she'd been mortally wounded by his dripping sarcasm.

"You can explain it to the super," she said after a martyred pause and shut the storeroom door. "He wants to see you."

"About what?"

"You'll see," Mbali said, making it sound like a threat.

*   *   *

Dekker knew when it came to Superintendent Cliffie Mketsu, appearances were deceptive. He was a man of physical averages, not too short or too tall, not too fat or too thin, and with premature grey flecking his temples. He spoke in half-completed sentences and his hooded eyes created the impression of a sleepwalker. But behind this façade was one of the sharpest brains in the business. It was common knowledge no one had ever achieved higher marks than Mketsu in Unisa's master's degree in policing. Now rumours were doing the rounds he'd been earmarked to become the next commissioner, and that the Australian police force had offered him a million bucks a year.

Which is why Dekker felt an uneasy sense of apprehension when the supe fixed his dark gaze on him from behind his desk and asked, "What's up?"

"Supe?" He and Mbali Kaleni were sitting opposite Mketsu.

"The October matter …"

Dekker tried to suppress the sick feeling in his gut. How much did they know?

"Inspector Kaleni says … uh …" started Mketsu, "uh … you … your support in the October matter has been … uh …" His voice trailed off and he made the familiar gesture that implied they knew what he meant.

"Inadequate," Mbali finished the superintendent's sentence for him.

"Exactly," Mketsu confirmed.

"You're on the phone all the time. Busy with other things. Or you're dipping into my files and exhibits." Turning to Mketsu, she continued, "The latest, Supe, is he thinks there's a link between the October matter and my car hijacking in November."

Dekker felt relief wash over him. They know nothing. "Supe," he said confidently, "October was part of a syndicate. Her record proves it. So I looked into the activities of vehicle theft syndicates in our area …"

"And what about the telephone call?" Mbali asked triumphantly, like someone playing a trump card.

"What telephone call?"

"The charge office says a woman called this morning and asked to speak to you. About nine."

Dekker felt his throat constrict, then took a shot in the dark. "And what about you, Mbali? How many people asked to speak to you?"

"Only my mom."

"So a woman called and asked to speak to you."

"That's what I said. My mom."

Mketsu sighed loudly. "You're like my kids."

A guilty silence descended over the office. Mketsu sighed again. "We must …" he said, searching for the right word, " … cooperate."

"Yes, Supe," Mbali and Dekker said in unison.

"This job is tough enough as it is …"

"Yes, Supe."

"Right," Mketsu said, and again made the familiar gesture.

* * *

"Why don't you like me?" Dekker asked Mbali as they walked back to the office.

She surveyed him in silence. When they got to the entrance she held on to the doorframe. "Because you're blind," she said, catching her breath as her mighty bosom heaved up and down.

"Blind?"

Mbali headed for the lift even though it was only one floor up to their office.

"Yes, blind, Fransman. Blind," she said, pressing the lift button.

Before he could respond, his cellphone rang. Shaking his head he headed for the stairs. "Dekker," he said.

"Have you got the book?"

"It's hard. I can't attract any attention. I have to find a reason to go into the lock-up."

"When?"

"Tomorrow morning."

"I'm a patient man, but I'm telling you now, I want that book in my hand by tomorrow morning at ten or else I'll have your photograph delivered to your boss and that fat policewoman."

The line went dead and Dekker gripped the phone. Suppressing an urge to fling it against the wall he wondered what he'd done to deserve this fuck-up.

"You're too driven," he remembered an angry Crystal telling him earlier. And this morning the man's voice on the cellphone had said: "They tell me your ambition is burning white, like a well-tuned engine." So what was wrong with that? Why shouldn't he work hard and get on in life? Or did they expect him to stay in a squatter camp in Atlantis for the rest of

his life, like his mother, and blame someone else for his lot in life. Is that
what they wanted?

The lift doors opened and Mbali pushed out.

"Blind?" he asked again.

"You see only yourself," she said and walked through the door.

*   *   *

He left the office at five, determined to get home early as he'd promised
Crystal. He'd bought her a bunch of flowers and she hugged him when she
saw them. It was a perfect evening, so they ate outside in the small garden
of their townhouse. After their argument this morning and the relief of
making up they couldn't keep their hands off each other. "Do you think I
see only myself?" he asked.

"For now you're going to see only me," she said playfully, leading him
to the bedroom.

Afterwards, lying close to him, her small hand on his chest, she said, "I
think you sometimes see other people in terms of how useful they are to
you."

*   *   *

During the night, Crystal asleep, he got up and fetched the little black
book. Sitting at the kitchen table he paged through the book. The pages
were filled with indecipherable abbreviations, tables and notes. The only
inscriptions he could make out were the addresses.

DCN1:

MBCL7. Wh. 79 Conradie, Wlglgen

JGC8 Bl. 21 Oleander, Parklnds

MBM7 Gr. 17 Seagull, Mlkbs

He stared at the entries, trying to make sense of them. The owner of the
voice on the cellphone had been prepared to have Natalie October killed
and blackmail a policeman to get the book back. It had to be worth a fortune. And it had to mean something. But what? He'd better make photocopies of the book before the morning. But he couldn't risk being spotted
with the book. There was only one alternative. He got up and fetched a pen
and paper. Sitting down he knew he had a long night ahead.

*   *   *

"Wait at the pedestrian crossing on Voortrekker, opposite Edgars. At ten on the dot a car will stop next to you. My man will use the code word."

"Which is?"

"You'll know it when you hear it. Hand over the book and walk away. If it's the right book and there are no comebacks, you'll never hear from me again."

"And the photograph?"

"It's digital, bru. There's only one copy and that's on my laptop. If I get the book I'll delete the picture."

He knew he was powerless. "You'll just have to trust me, bru," the voice said.

*   *   *

There were four of them in the Mercedes SUV: two whites and two coloureds. The guy sitting in the passenger seat next to the driver held out his hand and said, "Nostradamus". He was young and wearing a cocky hat. Dekker gave him the book and the Benz drove off. As he memorised the registration number he knew he was wasting his time. Saw the sticker on the back window. *Daimler Chrysler, N1 City*. He watched the vehicle disappear around a corner. There was something else that bothered him but he couldn't put his finger on it. He walked over to the CNA and bought an identical little black book.

Choosing a quiet corner in the Bellville Library he took out the sheets of paper on which he'd duplicated the information from the book and started the tedious process of copying it into the new one. He was halfway through the process when his cellphone rang. *Mbali* it said on the screen.

"Dekker."

"I have to see you. It's urgent. Where are you?"

"I'm following up a lead. I'll be along as soon as I'm done," he said and ended the call. She rang back immediately but he killed the call and focused on the task at hand.

Tables, abbreviations, addresses. What did it all mean?

He painstakingly copied the data into the book, then burnt his notes in the library's toilets and called Crystal from his car.

"Hi," she said. He was pleased to hear her sounding so happy. "I can't talk too long, I have to go into a meeting.'

"Who's Nostradamus?"

"Was. He died five hundred years ago."

"Who was he?"

"A chemist and a prophet. Predicted the future. Why?"

"I'll tell you later. I have to run."

As he turned on the engine his phone rang. Mbali again.

"I'm on my way."

"Where's my little book?" She sounded angry, very angry.

"Your what?"

"The little black book you took out of my exhibit box."

"In my pocket."

"I'm waiting for you in the supe's office," she said and Dekker realised he'd better solve the case. Now. Before he got back to the office. It was his last chance.

*   *   *

He stopped at the police station. Nothing made sense and he knew he'd have to lie and that would mean his end because lies had short legs. Perhaps he'd get off with a warning. Or perhaps Mketsu would demote him to the uniformed division. Perhaps he should tell the truth. No, then he'd lose everything. As he walked past a row of parked cars his eye caught the sticker on the rear window of a rusty Toyota. Kulu Motors.

He pushed open the door. His mind was a blank. He chose the stairs. Kulu Motors. As if they couldn't spell Kudu. Or Zulu. Like in Mbali Kaleni, his Zulu nemesis.

Mketsu's secretary looked sombre. She indicated for him to go in. He took the forged little black book from his pocket and opened the door. A grim-faced Superintendent Mketsu and Mbali were waiting for him. Then it hit him: the sticker on the back of the Mercedes SUV.

Daimler Chrysler, N1 City.

It was a sticker for a dealer, like the Kulu Motors sticker he'd just seen outside.

"I have it," he said. His head was spinning. Sitting down at the desk he opened the Nostradamus Document.

"What?" Mbali didn't even try to hide the aggression in her voice. Dekker ran his finger down the tables.

DCN1:

MBCL7. Wh. 79 Conradie, Wlglgen

JGC8 Bl. 21 Oleander, Parklnds

MBM7 Gr. 17 Seagull, Mlkbs

"Look," he said. "DCN1 is Daimler Chrysler in N1 City. The MBCL7 is a CL-series Benz. I think it's a 2007 model. The Wh stands for white and the address indicates the owner. JGC8 is a Jeep Grand Cherokee, 2008 model—" He was talking too fast. The adrenaline and relief had parched his mouth. But he had their attention.

"This is the Nostradamus Document. Don't ask me how I know, but this little book makes predictions. It predicts who'll be hijacked next. Look, it's only expensive cars – Mercs, BMWs, Audis, Volvos. The syndicate some-how knows who's buying these cars; these must be the addresses of the new owners. For all the Cape dealers in expensive cars. It's all here, right down to the model number and colour. They somehow get the informa-tion, and pass it on to the hijackers. And somewhere Natalie October fits into the picture."

*　*　*

Mbali Kaleni had it all pieced together by the next afternoon. She slowly and methodically eliminated all the possibilities until she homed in on the company that researched client satisfaction in the automotive industry. Every sale entered into a national database, every new owner called up to be asked questions about service levels and the quality of the vehicle. And every byte of data passed on to a syndicate.

They swooped on the company. Dekker was with her when she read the database programmer his rights.

Three hours later the programmer gave them the name of the head of the syndicate. When they arrested him at his Plattekloof home, Dekker recognised the voice from the cellphone calls. White guy, rich, mid-forties, who stared at Dekker. If looks could kill.

The media were waiting outside. "It's your case, Mbali. You speak to them," Dekker said

The bulky inspector squinted again, eyeing him suspiciously. "That's new," she said.

"I still have work to do," he said, tapping the laptop he held firmly under his arm.

RICHARD KUNZMANN

Richard Kunzmann is the author of three highly acclaimed police thrillers set in South Africa. His first novel *Bloody Harvests* (2006), was shortlisted for the Crime Writers Association's J.C.W. Creasy Award for Best New Novel. Publication of *Salamander Cotton* and *Dead-End Road* followed soon afterward.

Born in Windhoek, Namibia, in 1976, he moved to South Africa with his family just in time for colour television. Asked why he writes crime, he says, "Any good story is about human extremes, which normally also involves some sort of criminal behaviour. I've been watching gangster movies since I was old enough to sneak out of my bedroom at night and switch on the TV. Writing thrilling stories was a natural progression and, besides, it keeps me out of trouble."

Not only is his story *If Nothing Else* riveting as part examination of violence, part parody of crime writing, but he uses his experience and knowledge in the field of psychology to its best advantage to pack his work with authentic detail.

If Nothing Else

RICHARD KUNZMANN

IT WAS A DESPERATE DEATH TO LOOK AT: LIVING ROOM BRIC-A-BRAC strewn about, muddy handprints tracked across the walls, an elderly woman lying spreadeagled and face down on the carpet. A leg was stuck up at an odd angle against the footstool of a massage chair, you know, the ones that telesales companies only ever sell to lonely widows. I'd expected an odour in the room, but clearly this kill was fresh. Standing there, it felt like I'd hidden away in this 62-year-old's cupboard and was watching her undress. This was about as close as you or I would ever get to someone without having blood ties or sharing their bed. It was both a great intimacy and a great disappointment, if I think about all the fuss that's made about our deaths.

"You're not going to puke in here, are you?" Mike Vosloo looked expectantly at me from where he squatted next to the body. His latex-covered hands hung limply between his muscular thighs and he had heavy bags under his rheumy eyes. "If it's chunks you're gonna blow, out."

A police officer for eighteen years, he held the rank of captain, but could just as easily have been a leg-breaker. It wasn't just his body – flabby and amorphous, yet rock solid underneath all the padding – it was the way he stared at you that was imposing. He seemed to never blink. I'd heard of people calling him The Gargoyle before we were introduced, and I still couldn't tell whether it was because of the atrocity of his appearance or that stony gaze. I'd have loved to tell you that behind his expression burnt an immutable intelligence, because isn't that what we all expect to hear

29

about homicide detectives? But really, he looked like a fool who'd fallen into the job and couldn't get out.

"Hey, Sam. Snap— "

"I'm all right. Just taking it in."

"You sure? You're looking a little green around the gills." He indicated his own jowls to emphasise the point.

It wasn't that I was nauseous. I felt excited to be part of something forbidden. My heart was pounding and sweat beaded on my palms and top lip. I'd finally crossed the line to look beyond death's veil. Normally, people died in hospitals or far-off wars, some backstreet maybe. They died sensationally on TV all the time, but there was always the acting to insulate you. Rarely are we treated to the spectacle of what is guaranteed to one day happen to all of us. Modern society robs us of a unique experience on a daily basis, and this is why I wanted to relish the moment.

"It's nothing like I expected," I said.

A smile crossed Vosloo's lips. "What were you hoping for? Some chick with a nice arse and pair of tits you could bury your face in? It hardly ever happens that way."

It was a distasteful comment and I couldn't help but turn up my nose. "No. But I did hope for a mystery. A smoking gun, a bloodied knife. This is so … mundane."

"Mundane?" He looked stupefied.

"I'd hoped for a residue of what happened in the room. Details I could really sink my teeth into."

"Residue?"

Vosloo turned his attention back to the woman. Her safari-green skirt was hiked up to her thighs, revealing the blue varicose veins at the back of her knees. She still had on her muddy gardening gloves, which must have left the desperate streaks on the walls as she tried to evade her attacker.

"Residue," he repeated in a patronising tone I didn't like.

Vosloo shook his head and took the woman by the chin. Gently he raised her limp head to take a closer look at the telephone wire twisted around her neck and throat. It was only then that I saw the half-opened blood-shot eyes, the swollen purple tongue protruding from thin blue lips. The excitement I'd felt a moment ago lurched and my stomach clenched.

"Tell me," Vosloo said grimly, "if you can't see the story written all over this room, what the fuck are you doing calling yourself a crime writer?"

I threw open the door to the pick-up and chucked my new notebook and camera on the passenger seat. They landed amidst a collection of props: handcuffs, a ball-peen hammer and a screwdriver.

"Hey, Sam, come on. I was only joking."

The Gargoyle lumbered towards me, down the same garden path the woman must have been tending when the killer struck. Behind Vosloo, I could see a handful of technicians and police officers sniggering at my expense.

"Don't take it so hard," he said with a straight face. "We're always kidding around with each other. I'm not treating you any different."

He was dismissive, like he was talking to a spoilt child. It only made me angrier.

"Your head office gave you orders to help me with my research, did it not?"

Vosloo sighed. "If you say so."

"I've got a copy of that email in my bureau."

"Look, there's no reason for you to get into a huff like this." Vosloo pushed the car door closed. "I'm ready to help, but I can't have you taking photos of a crime scene."

"Why not? I signed a confidentiality agreement."

"I remember."

"Well then?"

Vosloo scratched his rumpled forehead. "What the hell do you want photos of that dead lady for? Isn't it enough to have seen all that?"

"Captain, if I wanted to imagine every thing about what you do, I would have stayed home and come up with the sort of inaccuracies your lot has a good laugh at. I'm interested in writing about the real deal, if nothing else."

"It strikes me as … what's the word?"

"Macabre."

"Thank you."

"My point is that your work is interesting to me and the people who read my books. And to give them a decent impression of what you do, I must expose myself to that grim reality also."

Vosloo shuffled where he stood. "Sir, you don't want to invite all this into your life. Trust me."

"How about you let me be the judge of that?" Vosloo glanced away but I pressed on. "It took me four months to negotiate this opportunity with the police service, and now you want to tell me I can't do the research?"

He held up both his hands in appeasement. "I didn't say you can't do your work. Crime writers obviously also need their bread and butter. But besides stating the obvious – that it's against police policy to allow unauthorised photos of a crime scene – I want you to think of her dignity."

His sarcasm incensed me. "What dignity? You ask me if I've come to look at her, hoping for a nice piece of arse and then you talk to me about her honour? She's nothing to me."

The words slipped out before I realised what I was saying.

"Surely you don't mean that, sir." Vosloo grew cold. "How would you like it if that was your mother, and some pencil-pusher took pictures that might land up on the Internet? No, I won't allow it."

I'd put myself on the back foot and he knew it. As if to underline the point, he hawked loudly and spat on the driveway between us.

"Fine, no photos." I got into the car and started the engine. But I wasn't finished with Vosloo yet and opened the window. "Tell me one thing, though. Do you think it was a serial killer who got to her? I mean, nothing was taken from the house, so she must have been the target."

Vosloo scratched his head. "What is it with everyone and serial killers? We've got an average of fifty killings a day in this country, and hardly any of those murders are perpetrated by what you call a serial killer. Why don't you think of something more real to write about?"

I waited.

Vosloo shook his head at what he must have thought was my absolute ignorance. "No, I don't think it was a serial killer. At this stage we can only guess that nothing's been taken from the house. Until we've had family members through here, we won't know for sure. If you ask me, it was some strung-out bastard looking for quick money who panicked when our granny walked in on him."

He put meaty hands on the door, but before he could say anything else, his eyes fixed on the tools lying openly on the passenger seat.

"What the hell is all that?"

I glanced at the gleaming weapons. "Finally! I've been driving around with that stuff lying in the open all week, in the hope of getting stopped and asked about it."

"You didn't answer my question." Now Vosloo looked downright furious.

"I read about how Ted Bundy got off with a traffic fine, even when his murder weapons were displayed openly in the car. Now I know why that happens."

"What are you saying?"

"You're a bunch of arseholes, if nothing else," I said and drove off.

That night I couldn't sleep. I felt feverish and the damp sheets were cloying on my skin. Every time I was on the verge of falling asleep, that woman would come to me. The way her body had unnaturally arched backwards when the policeman tilted her head back. The dyed hair which had been caught in the telephone wire wrung around her neck. Any other thoughts I might have had were crowded out by those memories. I sat up and switched on the bedside reading light, but it did nothing to dispel the brutal imagery in my head.

She was nothing to me, I'd said. Ha! In just a few hours she'd become everything to me. I'd gone out looking for murder and now she wouldn't let go of me.

The only way I could rid myself of those images, I decided, was by writing about them. Capturing on the page what I felt at that moment would not only be a release, but the words I so desperately needed to bring to life would also be impregnated with a seed of authenticity.

The mahogany bureau at which I wrote stood by the window of the study. I sat down and for a while watched the wind blow outside. The ancient evergreen pine trees that hid my home from the rest of this chaotic country creaked and sighed. I felt comfortably sequestered in this large sandstone Herbert Baker, built on the Westcliff of Johannesburg in the time of the gold rush, when the north of the city was still covered in planted forests that fed the city's insatiable mines with timber.

Louring over my work area was a framed imprint of Hieronymus Bosch's *The Temptation of Saint Anthony*. I smiled at the familiar parallel between that hellish imagery and the horrors that existed beyond the perimeter of my sanctum. I could identify with that lonely martyr, maintaining his beliefs in the face of never-ending evil. In the triptych, demons torture a saint humbled by the weight of an unearthly world, but really, those images are a metaphor for the decay of a society's moral fibre. It is an ancient interpretation of the modern apocalyptic times that have descended upon this generation. *The Temptation of Saint Anthony*. How many of us, I wondered, were tempted on a daily basis to lash out as violently as the rapists and murderers? And how many of us wondered what it felt like to be like them.

When my mind turned abruptly to Mike Vosloo and his suggestion that I might actually be a contributor to the decay – a demon from the triptych, if you will – anger rose up inside me. How could he suggest that I might sell those photos or display them on the Internet? I wanted them to enhance my memory of the facts, nothing else.

And yet, could I really aspire to the pinnacle of my profession if I did not at least explore such temptation? How could I truly distinguish myself in the field and write with authority? Did we all have a serial killer in us, I wondered? Did I? How might I wake him? Was he already awake, that I had such an interest in crime?

A shudder ran down my spine. There were lines you could cross and others you couldn't, and to think further down this avenue opened doors better left firmly locked.

A black fountain pen and a virginal sheaf of A4 lined paper were laid out on the desk before me. I concentrated on these items until the marauding energies inside me were brought into tight focus. Only then did I reach out, uncap the pen and begin to write.

When I emerged from the study just before dawn, I felt exhausted but content with the work I had managed. I even thought I should thank Captain Vosloo for giving rise to such conflicting feelings in me. He might have been more grotesque than anything my friend Bosch ever painted, but he was certainly helping me along the right path. Next time I saw him, I would strike a more conciliatory tone.

That day kept getting postponed, however, and a week later I had to excuse myself yet again from doing the rounds with Mike Vosloo. A forensic psychologist who had specialised in studying the country's most notorious sexual offenders, Dr Desirée Jacobs, had finally acquiesced to meeting me at the university where she was a guest lecturer. How could I resist?

A short woman answered the door by cautiously peering around its edge.

"Mr Sam Engels?" She was attractive, though her smile showed two front teeth that overlapped and her brown hair was tied back in a bland ponytail.

"Dr Jacobs, thank you for finally seeing me."

She waved me inside. I could see her fingernails had been gnawed to the skin, and a silver bracelet with those silly good luck charms encircled her wrist. "It's been a busy term," she said. "Please, sit and tell me what exactly I can do for you."

I made myself comfortable and came straight to the point. "I want to know more about the serial killers you've studied."

She smiled suspiciously and seated herself across from me. Her desk was cluttered with used tissues and dog-eared exam papers.

"I gathered," she said. "But doesn't everyone?"

"I'm writing a book."

"Again, isn't everyone?"

This wasn't going where I wanted it to, and I involuntarily shifted in my chair. "Is this a bad time for you?"

Somewhat surprised at having caused offence so easily, she offered me an embarrassed laugh. "No, it isn't. I'm just a bit weary of people, and that includes authors, who want to know more about murderers."

"Why is that?"

"It's about motive, Mr Engels. I wonder why anyone would want to willingly expose him or herself to such an unwholesome subject, from which many professionals try very hard to protect ordinary citizens like you."

"Why do you feel the need to make that decision for me, though?"

"Isn't this what we all want, to live safer lives without fear of violence?"

"Not necessarily," I said. "Without violence and without *fear* of violence are two very different things. People like you have created a safer world, yes, but it is also one in which death and violence have become alien to us as human beings. And the moment we became estranged from our dark side, it also became a threatening unknown. By rejecting violence we're simultaneously internalising a fear of it."

"That's an interesting idea." She studied me with large hazel eyes. "But I can't advocate people getting to know their own dangerousness."

I leaned forward in my chair and looked directly at her for a long time. It made her uncomfortable but she tried to hide it.

"Will you tell me their secret: how do they turn their childhood fears into actions that inspire fear?"

"Hurting someone is easy, Mr Engels. It's kindness that's difficult." She reached for a pencil and ran it between her fingers. "Why such a morbid fascination?"

"You know why."

She was growing more nervous. "I'm afraid I don't."

"It's for the same reason you first started to study serial killers, except I neither have the competence nor the confidence to tackle a complex subject like psychology. Besides, I enjoy making a person like you look good in a story."

At this she laughed and I laughed along with her.

"Please allow me to buy you lunch," I said.

She glanced at her watch. "But I have to prepare a talk for tonight."

"It's only this evening and you've done it a hundred times before, I'm sure."

"Yes, you are."

"Excuse me?"

"Sure of yourself," she said. Then, "All right, I'll come."

She took a light jacket from a stand in the corner and glanced back at me with a bright smile. "I read you up on the Internet before agreeing to this interview, you know."

"And what did it say?"

"Are you sure you can handle it?"

"Why not?"

"One blogger called you an eccentric recluse and arrogant pig. Another called you a nightmare worse than any of the characters you've ever conjured up."

"And did you read any of the actual reviews?"

"No. I'm more interested in the person. I've read enough murder scenes and personal interviews with perpetrators to last me a lifetime. Why would I bother with fiction that imitates life?"

"Fair enough," I said.

"And why is it that there aren't any photos of you online?" She looked me up and down. "You look pretty presentable."

I arched an eyebrow at the flirtatious comment, but inside I froze. Why did I suddenly feel like I was under investigation?

"Because I'm an eccentric recluse?" I offered cautiously.

At this she laughed a little too loudly. "OK, Mr Engels. You keep your secrets and I'll keep mine."

"Please, I'm Sam." I took her hand with her palm facing downward, and my thumb gently brushed across her index finger knuckle.

She blushed crimson at this and plucked away her hand. The smile on her face remained steady, however. "And I'm married. Pleased to meet you."

The afternoon progressed well. I had successfully coaxed her into sharing a bottle of Merlot with me, over two salmon salads prepared with mascarpone cheese and dill. Her unfortunate choice of wine to go with the fish, not mine. By the end of the meal, I knew exactly what I needed from her. I also felt surprisingly drawn to a Mrs Jacobs who it turned out, was very susceptible to alcohol.

"I still don't get something," I said as I paid the bill. "You're telling me they are often bed-wetters, and they have a penchant for cruelty to animals and lighting fires."

"Yes."

"But then, aren't we all serial killers waiting to happen? To be honest, I wet my bed when I was a kid, and I nearly set the house on fire on a few occasions. Not while wetting my bed, though. Then there was the sadistic joy of tearing the wings off a fly in kindergarten, which I still remember clearly. You also say these killers have sadistic fantasies they want to act out in the real world, but let's face it, don't we all have kinky thoughts about domination and submission?"

Her cheeks glowed red with the wine and she had a goofy smile on her face. Already she'd told me she was thinking of leaving her husband. She'd come to this university specifically to get away from him and the people they both knew. There was hardly anyone who would miss her, she said, if she disappeared tomorrow.

Desirée, as she now insisted on being called, toasted me. "You're right. Most of us have done something similar, especially boys, but was that behaviour repeated? Did it generally get worse? As for your last question … well, all things within reason." She gave me a meaningful appraisal when she said this.

It was my turn to toast her.

"Sooner or later that initial antisocial behaviour is phased out by our interaction with a relatively stable home and community," she continued. "We come to see it as unacceptable and we begin to *feel* it is wrong. Guilt is a powerful force."

"But isn't guilt artificially created in us by society?"

"Can you call it artificial when we're social beings?" she replied. "When our identities extend into society as we grow up, society simultaneously extends into us."

This provoked some thought in me, and I didn't speak on the subject again until we were safely ensconced in my car. A ferocious highveld thunderstorm broke just as we exited the restaurant and we were forced to sprint across an abandoned parking lot. By the time we reached the vehicle, our legs were sopping wet from running through puddles. Even the omnipresent car guards had sought refuge and no one was begging for money. The scene was almost romantic.

"So it's at the point when society invades us that violence becomes an enemy to be feared? There is a dilemma right there, wouldn't you say? We are violated by a force we cannot resist, in order to change our perceptions about violence." My mind raced with ideas faster than I could digest them. "But serial killers, they don't submit to those social mores. They transcend that cultural abuse and remain free to do what they want."

"You're making a lot of assumptions—" she started, but I refused to let her interrupt me.

"They are empowering themselves in a way the rest of us will never understand. We're worse off than them, because we remain meek in the face of socialisation. The moment we realise violence is the antithesis of social living is also the point at which we begin to fear ourselves. In other words, we undermine our potential as powerful human beings for the sake of communal living." Was this Eden's apple, I excitedly wondered, the very point at which the few realised the power to take life rested within them – not God, not society, but them? I tried to imagine what it must feel like to sense that power within myself.

But Desirée Jacobs had lost interest in my monologue. She lurched slightly where she sat watching the rain pound against the window. The car was already fogging up.

"Desirée?"

She turned her gaze on me and I was surprised by the defiance burning there.

"Don't you sometimes wish society would go to hell and we could do more of the things we wanted?" Every trace of her earlier self-consciousness had been erased.

I considered that she might have had too much to drink, and that her advances had little to do with her attraction to me. She most likely hated her husband and wanted to hurt him. Maybe she even wanted to hurt herself for hating him, who knows. On the other hand, she was a good-looking woman in her academic way, and she had been flirting with me all afternoon.

I began to look about, but she stopped me with a hand on my cheek.

"Don't have second thoughts," she whispered. "Act on your instincts."

I smiled and said playfully, "Forcible, aren't we?"

She returned the smile. "Downright impassioned."

"And what of Mr Jacobs?"

"Screw Mr Jacobs." She laid an open palm on my chest. "Now, are you going to practise what you preach, or is your bark worse than your bite?"

Temptation, Saint Anthony. What lines can you cross, and which are forever forbidden? And can you ever judge these things before crossing them?

In no time, we were groping each other like two teenagers. I locked the doors with the centralised locking system and manoeuvred her onto her back beneath me. It was a tight fit but I managed. My lips found hers and they tasted of wine and lipstick. I ran one hand up her thigh and flanks. Her body was a lot firmer than it looked. She started biting at my bottom lip and tongue, and soon I could taste blood too.

"You said a stressor usually sets off a serial killer."

I could hear the irritation in her voice. "What?"

"What makes us kill?" I mumbled urgently against her neck. "I mean, them."

"Usually a sexual experience gone horribly wrong." She giggled. "You're not going to kill me, are you?"

"I might." I had her ear lobe between my front teeth and felt an overwhelming urge to tear it off. "Depending on whether I can get it up or not."

She reached between my legs. "No," she said with an exaggerated sigh of relief. "I think I'm safe."

What is temptation, Saint Anthony? And when is the world taking advantage of you, or you taking advantage of the world?

She pulled me towards her and bit my neck so hard I cried out. I tried to sit up, but she clung to me with surprisingly strong arms and legs.

"Hit me," she whispered. "As hard as you want. Across the face."

I sat up and took a hurried look around. But the car had fogged up completely in the incessant rain and it was impossible to tell if anyone could see us. I met her eyes. She looked vulnerable where she lay, pinned under my knees. Her lips had bruised and swollen from the rough kissing, and her skirt was hiked up to her knees, like that old woman's had been. There was something exhilarating about the association. An immense feeling of power came over me, knowing that she could be killed as easily as that victim.

"Did you hear what I said?" She shimmied up on her elbows until her head rested against the side window. "I want you to hit me. You talk about violence like it's something we should enjoy. So show me."

Vulnerable she looked, but predatory also. There was an urgency coming off her, like hot musk. Who was I to argue the point? I slapped her. She cried out and buried her face in the crook of her elbow. I tore away her arm and backhanded her across the other cheek. It stung my hand, but it felt better than I imagined it would.

"Is this what you want?" I shouted.

I was surprised by how easily the anger came. The release of pent-up frustration and the sexual tension between us quickly turned into an intoxicating pleasure I had never experienced before. Was this a return to Eden, or would I follow in Cain's footsteps?

"Answer me!"

"Yes," she said timidly. She had tears in her eyes and her make-up had smudged. Humiliated, she looked all the more attractive. I wanted to possess her, to enhance my memory of this moment, if nothing else.

I grabbed the front of the good doctor's white shirt and tore it open. Her back arched and a hungry moan escaped her lips. When a hand bunched the hair on my neck I impatiently batted it away. Her exposed stomach felt warm under my fingers. I imagined drinking of that life force, imbibing it like it was Holy Communion. I sank my teeth into the soft white skin, and felt her inhale sharply.

"No," she said through clenched teeth. "No biting."

I bit her again, to let her know I was in control, and when she tried to push me away, I grabbed her by the wrists and pressed them up against the glass above her head.

I glowered down at her. "You're mine now."

"No biting," she repeated. "The bruises won't be gone by the time I need to fly back."

"Back to your husband," I sneered. "I take it this isn't your first time, then, fucking a stranger?"

"He's still my husband."

"We'll see if you make it back."

Her body tensed under me, the lust in her eyes flickered, but she didn't ask me for clarification. To ask would have been to break the fantasy. The moment's authenticity would have been transmuted into a mere re-enactment, and so her silence suited me perfectly. I bent forward and bit her breast through the material of her bra.

She cried out in pain. "I said, *no!*"

Desirée Jacobs struggled against me but I held firm. It was relatively easy because I was already on top of her and there was little room to manoeuvre. She was pinned down good. It was then that I started to laugh. What an exulted state to be in! There I was, experiencing first-hand what I had wanted to write about – the intimacy only killer and victim share, and the rest of us could only guess at. I had crossed yet another line, but did I dare go even further? The opportunity to explore this new reality was too good to miss. How could one re-enact this? How could you have someone simply retell the experience? No! This was the authenticity I yearned for. This was what I had wanted for myself: to control the demon, to control the world. By claiming this moment, I would embrace the violence inside me, and thereby the brutality manifest in the greater world. I would reject society's intrusion of me and free myself from the unknown.

"Let go of me!" The naked terror in her voice only spurred me on.

I took hold of both her wrists in one hand, while the other reached for the cubbyhole where I had stored the handcuffs and screwdriver.

I had, however, underestimated her strength and desperation. She quickly tore free from my flimsy single-handed hold, and with an almighty heave, pushed herself into a sitting position. Before I could regain control, she had kicked out with her legs and sent me sprawling against my side of the car. Next, instead of simply unlocking the driver's door and fleeing, she lunged for the glove compartment, intent on retrieving the weapon she thought I had hidden there. The flap sprang free and spilled the screwdriver into her hand; the handcuffs and hammer fell into the footwell.

Desirée Jacobs' eyes widened at the sight of these items, and I don't think there was any guessing as to what they might have been used for, given the circumstances. Her fist tightened around the screwdriver.

"Wait!"

I lunged for the weapon, but it was probably the stupidest thing I could have done given the circumstances.

She responded by plunging the weapon deep into my abdomen. And when I started kicking and punching to get away from her, she drove the screwdriver into my chest, where it stayed.

"Christ, you stabbed me!" I screamed the obvious and clutched at my stomach where blood was already seeping into my shirt.

She looked dazed as she sat back on her side of the car. I smeared blood across the foggy windshield as I sat up. I took hold of the tool embedded in my chest and yanked hard.

For all my bloody research, I hadn't covered the practical bits on hand-to-hand combat, like: you aren't supposed to remove sharp objects buried in your body. The screwdriver came loose and white light flashed across my sight. The pain was extraordinary and I screamed out. Immediately, I could feel blood filling up my punctured lung.

When I came to, I saw the good doctor running across the waterlogged parking lot, back towards the restaurant. "I'm going to sue you, bitch!"

That was the last I remember.

It might have made for an interesting story if I had died at that point. It would have spared me the messy details that followed, particularly in the tabloids. But life hardly ever turns out that way, does it? Nice clean endings only belong to books. The thing is, screwdrivers aren't very dangerous, unless you use them repeatedly. Especially so when there's a private clinic nearby and you have a healthy medical aid to boot.

It was a week after the incident that Captain Mike Vosloo lumbered into my private room. He greeted me and immediately took an interest in the food that I had left untouched on the trolley at the bottom of the bed. I knew I was in deep trouble when I spotted my notebooks under his arm, texts which were meant to be safely tucked away in my study.

"Any of this good?" he asked.

"What do you want?"

He popped some grapes into his mouth as he made himself comfortable.

"Not bad for a crime writer, this. Attempted murder. Sexual assault. The prosecutor might add abduction, too, if he can make it stick. Tell me, how stupid are you, to try all that with a woman who regularly works with the police?"

"I didn't try to kill her."

"Yeah?"

"It was research."

"And the bruises all over her face? How do you explain that? Next you're going to tell me she asked for it."

"She did." As I said it, I knew how ridiculous it sounded.

I'd worked out this conversation long before, but now that it was actually spoken out loud, it sounded even worse than I'd imagined it. I already knew what he was going to say next: 'I've got these diaries, and they're pretty sick, I have to tell you. I know you're going to tell me they were the thoughts of your characters, but please, spare me the BS. You know what this is all going to sound like in court? I'll tell you. Sick man gets involved in hobby that lets his sick fantasies loose. Sick man isn't happy with his success. He wants to take it further, as they always do, because it gets him off. So he reckons he's real smart and says to himself, let me do this in front of the cops. Let me show them that I think they're arseholes, if I may quote you, sir."

I waited for his acerbic comment, but he sat there staring at me the way only a gargoyle can stare. When he had finished all the grapes, he got up and patted me on the leg.

"You think you're special, Mr Engels, but you're about as mundane as they come." He paused for effect. "If nothing else."

DAVID DISON

David Dison is best known as a specialist defamation and media lawyer, and co-founder of the *Weekly Mail*. He fought numerous anti-censorship cases and, throughout the eighties, he represented hundreds of detainees and trialists, most prominently in the Delmas Treason Trial. Author of numerous papers and articles on media and civil rights law, he currently holds the position of MD of Media and Broadcasting Consultants (Pty) Ltd.

His acclaimed first novel, *Death in the New Republic* (2007), features the tormented investigator Nossel, who dashes around Joburg on a murder case, continually fascinated by its dual nature.

"My character, Nossel, is able to delve into the inner workings of the criminal justice system in a way that I hope exposes the reader to the workings of our strange and exciting society, and its people. I've been a fan of detective fiction since my teens. And the genre is growing on my wife, my muse and first editor."

Nossel will be back in the sequel, *The Good Nigerian*, and features here in *Louis Botha Avenue*, set against a backdrop of South Africa's recent turmoil of xenophobia.

Louis Botha Avenue

DAVID DISON

NOSSEL EMERGED CONTENTED FROM THE CONVENIENCE STORE AT THE BP garage in Orange Grove. His solitary coffee date with the weekly pulp media had preserved his sanity for years, and it had not failed him today. There was no need to pull up his collar as the Highveld sun had already broken the midwinter chill. He sloped across the forecourt towards his waiting Defender.

Not even the upheavals in his beloved, but lately beleaguered, city could have deterred Nossel from his time-honoured Sunday morning trek down Louis Botha Avenue, the old northern artery of Johannesburg. So when it was still icy, an hour ago, he'd crept out of home, spluttered the Defender to a start, glided the vehicle through the curves on Death Bend, past the Victory Theatre, through the old Gallagher's Corner – usually bright and gaudy with Nigerian and Congolese wares – now disturbingly bare, into petrol bay no. 1. He'd tossed the keys to Ephraim the old faithful, his regular petrol attendant, then grabbed the weekly offering at the news-stand outside the convenience store, ready for his Sunday morning orgy of cappuccino and weekly tabloids in the inner sanctum.

And even though the news had been grisly, as it had been for weeks, the ritual had soothed Nossel's troubled mind, the anonymity of the store providing the refuge he needed. The predominant content of the tabloids had been much the same fare spewed out by the media ever since the troubles began.

Xenophobic killing spree spreads to the Cape

Burning man was Mozambican
Refugees seek safety in cop stations
Tutu's xeno talk

None of it gave a clue as to the origin of the sudden upsurge. Of course the columnists had theorised about relative deprivation and perceptions of favouritism in the allocation of land and homes for shack dwellers, who were split along South African and foreign African lines. But Nossel had suspected other forces at play here. The viciousness of the attacks on the foreigners had brought back twenty-year-old memories of a gratuitous, group violence that Nossel had thought banished from the city forever. He had wondered at times what had happened with all that violence. And here it was again, foiling all the cheap pundits, including him, who had grown complacent after years of political peace in the new republic. This time the group violence had emerged in a new guise – xenophobia! For Nossel, the word had lost all its meaning, a convenient media buzzword for the worried citizenry to cling on to.

He had found the usual fare of sensationalised stories of graft and greed and corruption far less troubling, a joy to read compared to the pornography of the reportage on the allegedly xenophobic attacks. The papers revelled in their near-absolute freedom of expression, and boy did they hand it out in spades. Where else in Africa would the members of the ruling elite be subjected to such widely published excoriation and exposure of their excesses?

But now, the ritual completed with an aggregated payment to the cashier secure behind her bullet-proofed console in the convenience store for petrol, coffee, croissant and papers, he quickened his pace across the forecourt as he saw Ephraim gesticulating with a woman bearing two large hawker carrier bags on each of her scrawny shoulders. Ephraim was shooing her away from the Defender, his remonstrations accentuated for Nossel's benefit.

"I told this *makwerekwere* woman from Mozambique to go but she said she must wait for you."

"That's fine, Ephraim. Here's your tip. Leave her alone," Nossel admonished the man.

Ephraim slunk off, and Nossel looked into the eyes of the Mozambican woman, embarrassed.

Her nomadic get-up, her baggage and her deeply etched exhaustion spoke volumes. He knew she would struggle with English so he tried his Gauteng Tswana.

"*O tswa kae, mme?*" Where have you come from, mother?

"You don't have to talk to me in your Joburg Tsotsi taal, sir. I can speak English."

Relieved, Nossel asked her what she wanted.

"I am a refugee from Alexandra Township. I want you to take me to Alexandra Police Station down this road, at the other end of this Louis Botha Avenue. I watched you park this car here this morning, I saw you drinking your coffee and reading. I said to myself, Maria Qotane, here is a man who will help you with your journey to find your family."

She looked deeply into Nossel's eyes, her grief and despair penetrating Nossel's blurred consciousness. When the response came it was clipped, out of character for the laconic Nossel, who shook her hand, and said: "I am Nossel, Mrs Qotane, and I will drive you to Alexandra Police Station."

"Thank you, Mr Nossel, but please do not call me Mrs Qotane."

"Whatever," Nossel sighed as he ushered her into the Defender, relieving her of the enormous carrier bags full of her worldly possessions. He hauled them into the boot. As he drove off the forecourt, negotiating his way through the taxis on to the northbound concourse of Louis Botha Avenue, he noticed that his wave to the scowling Ephraim was not returned.

They drove in silence past the old white suburbs of Joburg, barricaded behind high walls and electric fences, as they had been for decades. No squatter camps here, mused Nossel. When they got to Highlands Park football ground, Maria Qotane sighed, commencing with her inevitable narrative.

"This is where my husband would take my boy, on a Sunday morning, for soccer. They would be so happy when they came back; it was a joy to behold, all those boys from the townships and the suburbs in their bright jerseys."

Nossel imagined the scene. He thought of how a stray bullet had killed the father of one of those boys at Highlands Park, while watching his boy play the game at this premier soccer stable of the north. A father who was, by all accounts, one of the gentlest and kindest business mavens of Joburg.

"What does your husband do, Maria?"

"We have a spaza shop in the township. We made a good living from it until the troubles."

"Is there no way back to the township for you, Maria?"

"I am too scared to go back. We hid in our friends' house, the three of us, until Wednesday, but then all the men in the camp were told to come out, and my husband and son insisted that I leave for my own safety. I hear that many of them made their way to Alex Police Station, but I cannot get near there on foot. I have been sleeping for days in doorways here on Louis Botha waiting to find a way to get in to the place."

Nossel had read that the township police stations had become places of refuge for xenophobia victims. What a reversal of roles for the former apartheid outposts, he mused. They were nearing Alex now, barbecue ovens braaing tough meat on the side of the road, and little children kicking balls. The police station was on the other side, at the end of a circular sweep across the motorway through the southern edge of the formal township.

"But why couldn't you get into the police station, Maria?"

"You will see soon, Mr Nossel, when we get through the taxi rank."

And indeed as they skirted the township's western edge, as grimy as ever, Nossel saw the barriers. Police were manning a double roadblock with all the requisite paraphernalia: double booms, armoured vehicles, guard boxes, scores of cops in fatigues looking fearsome. It felt like a twenty-year time warp.

"And what happened when you tried to get through here, Maria?"

"They said it was full. They said my refugee ID paper – here it is, Mr Nossel – said I was unmarried. And when I explained to them that I was not married under the Mozambican civil law, that I am his common-law wife, they said that's not our problem, and they refused. Even though I begged and pleaded with them."

Because he was in a time warp, Nossel was not disheartened by the news. Something about the time warp suggested to him that his vehicle and his status and his whiteness and his cunning would get him through the barricades, into the police station. He was back in the eighties, bullshitting his way through the barriers; that was when he had been at his best.

He was polite with the myriad of officials at each stop, metropolitan, national and Department of Foreign Affairs, cajoling, dreedling and draydling as his late grandfather used to remark about the whining smouses who came to his door. And what a smous act Nossel put on:

"I am a private detective, *ke moagente ntate mme*, this poor lady needs to find out what happened to her husband and her son, Mozambicans who were caught up in the xenophobia …"

On and on and on he prattled and whined, laughing and joking and stroking the officials' egos. He had the impression that each lot let him through to shut him up, just like the old days, crying and moaning on the edge of the township in order to bore one's way across the barricades.

When they got through to the police station Nossel was treated to a sight he had never seen in Joburg before – a police station surrounded by a tented village, flying the flags of UNICEF, the Red Cross, Gift of the Givers, the TAC, Habonim and the DFA.

Alexandra Township Police Station had become a refugee camp!

Maria smiled for the first time on their journey, beaming and thanking him profusely, but he shrugged her off.

"Do not be too thankful, Maria," he intoned gravely, "you still have to find them. I will wait for you, here."

"No, Mr Nossel, they must be here," she said as she alighted and looked pensively towards the entrance of the tented village, on the western side of the charge office. Hundreds of refugees were milling about, queuing up at various tables manned by the good members of the non-governmental organisations, waiting patiently for assistance. "You have done enough, sir. Thank you once again but you may go. I will find them now," she said, as she took her worldly possessions from him and strode down to the tented village.

"Please, God, let her be right," Nossel sighed to himself as he parked the Defender next to a row of 4x4s belonging, no doubt, to the good and kind NGOs working here.

He walked toward the old Alex cop shop, almost lost within the gaudy tented village. Professional curiosity drove him to find out how the boys in blue were handling this onslaught.

Inside, the sight that met him was gratifying. Teams of cops were gathered around four different workstations, some manning two-way radios, others laptops, and others processing refugee witnesses. And at the back, in the glass cage, poring over a video monitor on an elaborate edit suite was his old friend Nxumalo, head of the Special Unit.

He motioned to Nossel to come over.

"Nossel, you dog. What are you sniffing around here for?"

Nossel explained his mundane Sunday-morning mission.

"Well," sighed the Special Unit Chief, "you're just in time to watch the most horrific piece of footage to emerge from this township ever. Not all your fancy psychological evidence in the world – and I know you private eyes love this psycho evidence these days – will mitigate this crime."

The edit suite assistant rewound in a speedy cacophony. As he watched the tape begin to run, Nossel sensed with a sinking heart that none of his past cases could have prepared him for this.

The grainy footage showed how the gang built a fire with burning tyres in the Alexandra squatter camp. The ritual chanting reached a crescendo as their leader summoned up a bound and beaten man, who they struggled to place on the fire, while fighting off a young boy who tried to hold on to him, striking him away with their sjamboks and pangas. As Nossel watched, he knew that the screaming and the burning of the man, for what seemed like aeons before he finally succumbed, would be etched on his consciousness forever. Nossel swallowed hard. He imagined the charred smell of burning human flesh. Flashes of burning bodies and tyres from the eighties arose in his troubled mind.

"Who got the footage?" Nossel quizzed Nxumalo, talking to relieve the bile that was rising in his throat, as much as to sate his morbid curiosity.

"A freelance cameraman. The gang took his equipment, but we recovered it from Alex hostel. They should have smashed it to erase the images, but greed overtook them. We have them now. We think they killed his son as well."

A host of questions about their motives and paymasters occurred to him but there was a more important, dreadful one that trumped them all.

"Do you know who the burning man was?"

Nossel's heart thudded as Nxumalo intoned the chilling words: "A Mozambican spaza shop owner, Moses Qotane. We are searching for his wife."

Nossel got up and ran, Nxumalo hollering after him.

He ran through the gate of the makeshift tented village, through the queues and the gatherings and the handing-out points, scouring the faces of the refugees.

And then he saw her, on her knees, with a group of women. She was moaning quietly, intoning the sounds of grief, and they were trying to comfort her.

As he approached her, she looked up, her face transformed, frighteningly, with the look of a wounded animal; as the women drew a protective ring around her she glared at him and waved him away as if to say, "Stay away from me, you mesenger of death!"

Nxumalo led him away.

The world had turned on its head, the kindness of civil society, the generosity of the public at odds with the anguish of the frightened faces around him, all amid the smell of plunder, petty jealousies and resentment.

Nossel climbed into his Defender and sped home to his other reality, to the comfort of his loved ones safe and secure in their boomed-off road with their 24-hour security service patrolling. The dogs barked their joyful greeting as he drove through the electric gate; his wife would be cooking lunch, his son waiting for their promised soccer practice. He felt the heaviness in his heart lifting as he closed the front door. He smelt the roast cooking in the oven, heard the beautiful melancholic tones of Leonard Cohen lamenting about the sisters of mercy.

JASSY MACKENZIE

Born in Zimbabwe (then Rhodesia), Mackenzie, the second youngest of five daughters, moved with her family to South Africa when she was eight years old. Books and reading were considered so important that television was banned from the house.

She lives in Kyalami, a suburb. of Johannesburg, with her partner, plus two horses and two cats, and admits to getting a rush from living in Joburg, where high levels of crime, although frightening, provide a fertile field of inspiration for an up-and-coming thriller writer. Mackenzie is currently editor of *HJ*, a hair and beauty magazine, with an acclaimed first novel, *Random Violence* (2008), to her credit.

Self-confessed thriller and mystery addict, she says, "Reading crime fiction is an adrenaline rush. It allows you to be the detective, to try and guess the identity of the killer and anticipate the twists in the plot. Writing crime fiction is as much fun as reading it – except it takes longer."

The prose style of crime-thrillers is often crisp, the pace racy, as in Jassy Mackenzie's *The Beginning*.

The Beginning

JASSY MACKENZIE

KATE RAN UP THE WINDING PATH THAT LED AWAY FROM TOWN. THE ground was stony and hard, made treacherous by swathes of loose gravel, dotted with tall clumps of veld grass and the occasional shrub.

Her hair, wet with sweat, was bunched up under a baseball cap. A kitbag bounced on her shoulder blades, the friction creating another pool of sweat in the small of her back.

She ran alone. It was two o'clock on a cloudless Sunday afternoon. Yesterday, temperatures had peaked at forty degrees. Today felt even hotter. People with any sense were indoors, their fans powered up to maximum, enduring the sweltering heat as they waited for the afternoon to cool into evening.

In a wire-fenced paddock, two chestnut ponies dozed together under a tree, tails swishing. They pricked up their ears briefly as she passed, and then lowered their heads again.

The forest loomed ahead of her.

Kate slowed, stopped, glanced back. Nobody was following. Behind her, the path snaked down to the valley, where the tin roofs of the town shimmered in a distant haze of heat. All she heard was the trill of cicadas and the occasional stamp of the ponies' hooves.

She walked into the forest. It was cooler here, gloomy and dank under the thick canopy of leaves. Her sweat turned clammy on her skin, and she shivered.

Her head whipped round as she saw a flicker of movement to her right.

She stared at the yellow crime-scene tape that flapped between two tree trunks.

Her heart banged in her chest, as loud and urgent as a drum.

Kate slipped her backpack off her shoulders and rummaged inside. Her fingers closed around the solid handle of a rolling pin. The smooth, curved wood felt reassuringly heavy in her grasp. She held it for a moment, then replaced it in the bag and hoisted it onto her shoulders again.

Two weeks earlier, an eighteen-year-old girl had been murdered in this forest, right there in the place now marked by the yellow tape that gleamed so incongruously bright among the dark trees. Kate had known the girl, blonde, beautiful Celeste Schoeman. She was in Kate's matric class.

Celeste had come to this forest in the evening – why, nobody knew. Bird watching, some folk thought, although she hadn't had binoculars or a bird book with her. Meeting a boyfriend, others guessed, although no boyfriend was seen, and nobody had come forward to help the police with their enquiries after her body had been discovered the next morning, propped against a tree trunk, her skull shattered from the repeated blows inflicted by the chunk of sandstone that lay next to her.

The crime had rocked the town to its foundations. At Celeste's funeral, her parents had begged anyone with information on their daughter's death to come forward. A ten thousand rand reward was offered, sponsored by Dirk Grobler, the wealthiest farmer in the district.

No information had surfaced, only rumours. Some people said in hushed tones that Celeste was murdered by one of the migrant labourers who were in town for the cherry-picking season. Possibly even a tour-ist or backpacker, or one of those oddballs from the hippie retreat in the neighbouring valley. Others voiced their suspicions about the town's only black residents – Mrs Molumi and her son Jacob. Twenty-one-year-old Jacob was tall and quiet, hard-muscled, his dark face stern and unsmiling. He could easily have crushed the girl's skull with a rock. Perhaps she had refused his advances. Nobody knew, because nobody had seen Jacob – or questioned him – since the murder. He had disappeared.

Everywhere she went in town, Kate heard the whispers. She heard them outside the church, in the local tearoom, in the town's second-hand book-store, in the Internet café run by old Ouma Pieters.

The police were investigating. Two detectives had travelled all the way from Bloemfontein, and were staying at the town's only guesthouse. The sandstone used for the murder had yielded no evidence, nor any clues.

It occurred naturally in the area, and there were pieces and chunks of it strewn throughout the forest.

The detectives were interviewing suspects and hunting for Jacob Molumi.

Since the murder, none of the townsfolk had been into the forest. Dogs were kept indoors and in yards to keep watch. Ponies remained unridden, and lovers' trysts were cancelled. In the hottest summer on record, this cool, peaceful haven had become a no-go area.

Or had it? Looking closely, Kate saw faint footprints tracked into the dirt.

She circled the taped-off area, treading carefully, staying in the shelter of the thicker trees. The tape surrounded a tall Australian bluegum, its bark ghostly pale in the gloom.

This was the tree where Celeste's bloodstained body had been found, half-naked with her white blouse ripped away, and stiff with rigor mortis, ants swarming in her hair.

Or so the stories went.

Kate breathed deeply. She took a cautious step forward. Leaves rustled loudly ahead of her and she froze.

An annoyed squawk, a flap of wings. Just two grey loeries having an argument.

Then another rustle, this one from the other side of the tree.

Kate stood stock-still. Then, cautiously, she turned towards the sound.

Rustle, rustle, scrunch, scrunch. Someone was approaching, his footsteps loud and confident.

A tall, blonde man wearing jeans and a red T-shirt came into view. He lifted the crime-scene tape, ducked underneath, and strode over to the bluegum tree. He stood with his back to the trunk and scanned the surrounding forest. Then he tensed. He stared in Kate's direction and his hand dropped to a leather pouch on his belt.

"*Wie's daar?*" he called. Who's there?

Kate exhaled slowly. It was Wouter, the handsome eldest son of wealthy Dirk Grobler. Every girl in town between the ages of fifteen and twenty-five fancied up their hair and wore their push-up bra when they knew Wouter was going to be at a town social. He'd never paid Kate much attention. She was too skinny and too English, she guessed, and she wasn't blonde enough to show up on Wouter Grobler's radar.

Kate crept out of the cover of the trees and into the blue laser beams of

Wouter's eyes.

"Just me," she said, approaching him cautiously.

Wouter stared at her for a long moment, then relaxed.

"*Jislaaik*. You surprised me, Kate." He smiled, showing sparkling white teeth. "What's up? You look scared to death. I don't blame you. This forest is creepy." His Afrikaans accent was strong, but not unattractive.

"I am scared," she replied. "I didn't want to come here on my own, but I had to."

"Why?"

Kate hesitated. "I've been getting some weird letters. Hand-delivered to my postbox. I don't know who sent them."

Wouter stared at her, his expression a blend of confusion and fear.

"You serious? I've been getting them, too. What do yours say?"

"I brought one with me." She turned round and indicated a small zip-up pocket on her backpack. "It's in there. Can you take it out for me please?"

Wouter moved behind her. She twisted her head to watch him. He raised his hand and she flinched, but all he did was remove a leaf stuck in the fluffy brown scrunchie that held her hair back. Then he unzipped the pocket and removed the envelope. He opened it. Inside was a single page. On it, laser-printed on white A4 paper in big black capital letters, was, I KILLED CELESTE SCHOEMAN.

"That was the first one. I got others, too," Kate said. "I didn't bring them, but they told me to be here in the forest this Sunday at 2.00 p.m. And to come alone."

Wouter frowned as he read the note. "I got the same letters. I didn't bring them with me though. I threw them away."

He held the paper out to her.

Kate shook her head. "Please keep it. I don't want it back. It's too upsetting. I didn't want to touch any of them after the first one arrived. I wish I'd thrown mine away too."

"I know how you feel," Wouter said, looking down at the page again.

"Do you think the murderer wrote it?" she asked.

Another rustle in the trees. They both spun round.

Nothing there. Just more quarrelsome birds.

"I think so," Wouter replied. "Looks like it was printed at Ouma Pieters' shop. You see, it's got that fuzzy grey line in the middle of the page from her old laser jet. My notes had that too."

Kate craned her neck to see. "You're right."

Wouter replaced the page in the envelope, folded it, and stuffed it into the pocket of his jeans.

"So why would this person have written these letters?" Kate asked.

Wouter shrugged. "I don't know. To confess, perhaps. Or else …" His voice tailed off into silence.

"I don't feel safe here." Kate glanced behind her again. "Standing right where Celeste was killed. What if the murderer is watching us, Wouter?"

Wouter's hand strayed to the leather pouch on his belt. Looking more closely, Kate saw the black handle of a knife protruding from the pouch.

"Maybe we should wait somewhere nearby," she suggested. "Somewhere where we could see him, but he couldn't see us."

Wouter considered for a moment and then nodded.

Kate ducked under the tape again, feeling the plastic brush against her cap. She walked a short distance through the woods until she reached a tall tree with a smooth trunk. One of its branches had recently broken. It had fallen to the ground in a spray of leaves, the wood raw and splintered at the breaking point.

"We could hide behind here," Kate suggested, indicating the fallen branch.

"Good idea."

They crouched down in the shelter of the pale green leaves and waited. Kate stayed behind Wouter, shielded by his bulk. She could feel his body warmth. His deodorant smelled pleasant but unfamiliar. Expensive, Kate thought. She probably reeked of sweat after her run in the heat. She edged away from him.

"It must be at least half past two by now. Maybe he isn't coming," Wouter said.

"Who is he?" Kate asked. "Who do you think killed Celeste?"

"I know who did," Wouter said. "The whole town knows. It's Jacob Molumi, of course."

"You sure? Why do you say that?" she asked.

"He works for my dad, remember."

Kate frowned. "I thought he was studying accounting in Bloemfontein."

Wouter shook his head. "It's holidays now. In the holidays he works for us, doing repairs and maintenance on the farm. I never trusted him. That guy's a psychopath. A serial killer if I ever saw one." Wouter's hand crept to his knife again. "My dad thinks so, too."

"You're not the only people who suspect him," Kate said.

"Those notes were sent by somebody in this town, somebody who uses that Internet café. Ouma Pieters doesn't let strangers in. She thinks they'll put viruses on her computer and visit sex sites. So it has to be Molumi. I was wondering if he sent me the notes because he knows that I know. I think he's trying to get me back here so he can kill me, too. That's why I brought a knife with me." He touched the black handle again. "To be prepared."

"I'm glad you're here," Kate said

Wouter reached back and spread his big warm hand over hers.

"I'll look after you, Kate. You don't need to worry." He turned and looked her up and down as if he'd never seen her before. "When we're finished here, you can come with me to Ficksburg. We'll take my father's new Isuzu and have some fun. Dad lets me use it. He doesn't even mind if I only bring it back in the morning." He smiled, squeezing her hand harder. His fingers slid between hers.

Kate was surprised at the strength of his grip, the roughness of his skin, the arrogance of his offer. She'd never realised until now how cold his blue eyes were.

They were silent for a minute. Above them, a bird cawed.

Kate wanted to ask Wouter why he hadn't taken his notes to the police. Perhaps they could have lifted fingerprints from the paper and traced the killer. She didn't ask the question, though. Instead, she freed her hand from his grasp and rummaged in her rucksack. Her fingers brushed against the wooden handle of the rolling pin.

"Do you want some Coke?" she asked.

"Ja, thank you. It's hot today, isn't it?"

She handed him a plastic bottle and he stretched round to take it from her.

"I've been running," she said. "Open it slowly or it'll spray all over your clothes."

Wouter eased the screw top open. It made a series of tiny hisses.

Kate grabbed the handle of the rolling pin, dug in the rucksack, and found the other handle. The two handles weren't attached to a rolling pin any more. They were joined together by a piece of thick wire slightly short-er than Kate's arm.

Jacob Molumi had made the weapon for her. He'd taken the rolling pin apart, the one she'd taken from her mother's kitchen drawer, and drilled holes through the handles and wrapped the wire through each hole several times. It stretched between the handles in a round silver loop. Her hands were slick with sweat, but the dry wood provided a good grip.

While Wouter was peering down at the Coke bottle, Kate slipped the wire over his head and yanked it as tight as she could around his neck.

Wouter dropped the bottle. He made a gagging noise and his hands flew to his throat, but the wire was too deeply embedded for him to pull it free. He flung himself from side to side, convulsing.

Once, when she was younger, Kate's dad had taken her fishing and she'd hooked a massive barbel. The fish had almost pulled her out of the boat. She remembered how it had fought her, bucking and struggling as she clutched the rod in a death grip.

Wouter's struggles reminded her of the fish. He flailed back and forth, tried to kick her, tried to wrench himself free. He reached back and grabbed at her face. Kate twisted her head away, screwed her eyes shut and carried on pulling.

Then Wouter's hands dropped to his sides and his fingers closed around the hilt of his knife. Kate tugged the makeshift garrotte even harder, her arms trembling with the effort, her teeth clenched so tightly she thought they might break.

Before he could remove the knife from the pouch, Wouter's body sagged and his head lolled sideways. He slumped to the ground.

Kate fell with him. He was so big and heavy she had no choice. She held the wire taut around his neck for another minute in case he was playing dead, but he wasn't.

Panting, her limbs quivering, Kate scrambled to her feet and stared down at the body of the man she'd just murdered. Her palms felt tender and bruised. She rubbed a trickle of sweat off her forehead.

Then she went to work. She replaced the garrotte in the rucksack, and pulled out a coil of nylon rope, thin but strong. Jacob had stolen it from the Groblers' farm shed just before he went into hiding.

Kate knotted the rope in a noose around Wouter's neck, trying not to look at his purple, bloated face and bulging eyes. The wire had cut into the skin under his chin. She pulled the noose tight and tugged at the knot with all her strength, forcing the nylon rope deep into the wound.

Then she tied the other end of the rope around the fallen tree branch. She pulled it as tight as she could and, for good measure, sawed the rope back and forth along the top of the branch until it left a scar.

Then she stepped back and surveyed her handiwork.

It told a sad story. A troubled young man walks into the forest, climbs a tree, knots a rope around his neck and hangs himself from a high branch. The branch soon breaks under the weight of his body, but by then the man is already dead.

And why does he commit this terrible act?

The printed note in his pocket. I KILLED CELESTE SCHOEMAN. A confession. A suicide note of sorts. Not totally convincing, but the police would discover that Wouter's prints were the only ones on the paper. Every time she had touched it, she had worn cotton gloves.

Kate had broken the branch herself the day before. She'd needed a broken branch because she wasn't strong enough to haul Wouter up a tree on her own, and Jacob couldn't help her because he was in hiding. He'd gone to Bloemfontein where he was staying with a university friend. If the police bothered to catch up with him after Wouter's body was found, they'd find Jacob had a cast-iron alibi for the day of his death.

The notes that Kate had slipped into Wouter's postbox had been similar to the ones that she had told him she had received, apart from one small but significant difference.

Instead of I KILLED CELESTE SCHOEMAN, the first note to Wouter had read, I KNOW YOU KILLED CELESTE SCHOEMAN.

No wonder he had never taken that note to the police. No wonder he'd brought a knife with him when he arrived for the rendezvous with the man who knew he had killed Celeste Schoeman.

Jacob Molumi had been taking a shortcut home through the forest two weeks earlier when he'd heard the sounds of a fight. A woman's voice had risen, shouting insults at somebody. A man, Jacob guessed, from the explicit and highly personal nature of the insults. Then she'd screamed. Jacob had run to help, and seen Wouter hurrying away from Celeste's lifeless body. Worst of all, he suspected that Wouter had seen him too.

Not many people knew Kate and Jacob were lovers. They had kept it a secret, small-town life in the Free State being what it is. She didn't want to become the target of the town's curiosity, or the subject of the townsfolk's vicious gossip.

After Jacob had discovered Celeste's body, he'd called Kate immediately. Should he report the crime? If so, who would believe his word over Wouter's? Who would believe the town's golden boy was a killer?

Kate had agreed it would be unwise to inform the police.

Together, they had devised this plan.

The Coke bottle lay where Wouter had dropped it. Kate picked it up and gulped the cold, sweet liquid before replacing it in her bag. She felt calmer now, and oddly elated. She'd done it. She had killed him.

She glanced around the area one last time. Then she continued along the path that would take her all the way through the forest and on a wide circular route back to the town.

Tomorrow, life would continue as normal. School, studying. Jacob would be back next week. Her matric exams were looming. After that she'd have to decide on her future career. All her teachers said she had potential. They'd told her she was a clever girl, that she could do anything she put her mind to.

When she'd called Jacob yesterday, he had mentioned a situation he'd heard about in nearby Ficksburg. A young woman, recently married, was being pushed around by her husband. More than that. Her family feared he might beat her to death, would pay money to sort out the problem. Good money. Jacob thought they should do the job. They would discuss it when he returned.

Kate broke into a jog, smiling as she left the forest's chilly depths and ran along the path in sunshine.

DIALE TLHOLWE

Tlholwe started a Law degree at the University of Fort Hare in 1980 but his studies were interrupted by the student upheavals of the time. He then worked as a production clerk at a metal company, a teacher, and as a local government liaison officer for a consultancy company, before turning to writing.

Although he holds a diploma in journalism from the *Star* Newspaper's Argus Journalism Cadet School, from the time he wrote a prize-winning play while still at high school, Tlholwe has wanted to write fiction. His short story *Gaufi* (Near), written in Setswana, was published in the anthology *Walala Wasala* (2004); his first novel is *Ancient Rites* (2008), described as a "bewitching detective story unraveling ancient African rites."

Tlholwe says: "I hate the random crime and violence in our country, and writing about it gives some of it at least some meaning and context. And the bad guys don't always win."

In *Anger Mismanagement*, the disgruntled and on-edge ex-cop Tau typifies the anti-hero of much of contemporary detective fiction.

Anger Mismanagement

DIALE TLHOLWE

TOMMY DRUMMED HIS FINGERS AGAINST THE DASHBOARD.

"Stop that," Tau barked.

"Whatever you say, *Malume.*"

"It's irritating, distracting."

"I'm bored. Don't you agree this job is tedious, Sergeant?"

"We saw him go in; we have to wait for him to come out."

Truth was, Tau himself was bored to tears, and on top of that he was stuck with this apathetic partner whom he disliked intensely. He had a bad feeling about this job. Always did about these last-minute scrambled jobs. But he could not be picky in these hard times. Where were the openings for a disgraced cop with few other marketable talents or skills? They didn't exist, that's where.

This made him angry. Angry and afraid. Angry that he was now forced to consort with third-rate scum like this Tommy. Afraid of this anger and what it might lead to just as it had led to other disasters in the past. And this blasted Tommy knew this like he knew everything about him, taking sly verbal jabs at him, calling him Sergeant with exaggerated politeness that just stopped short of being an open sneer.

He, Tau, on the other hand, knew next to nothing about his so-called "partner" for the night, this cocky upstart.

"I'm not a sergeant, Tommy. I've told you that twice already tonight."

"Oh yes, you did. I forgot. But that's me, slow. Even as a boy at school I could never remember ..."

63

"Let's skip the history lesson."

"Right, Ser … sorry." That infuriating sly crooked smile again.

Something was finally happening down the road from where they were parked. A car had turned the corner and stopped in the driveway of the house they were watching. A big expensive triple-storey house in a suburb which he, Tau, could never afford to buy in. Couldn't afford a house, couldn't even afford a bloody garden shed. A woman, followed by a small boy, got out of the Peugeot Sport and walked to the front door and opened it without knocking and went inside.

"My piss …" Tommy exhaled sharply but quietly.

Ex-sergeant Tau turned to look at him. "What! right now? You want to …"

"No! Watch the house, damn it, and don't shout."

Tau felt something hot and bitter rise to his throat and he choked it back before it could escape through his dry lips. He had not been a policeman for fifteen years without learning to recognise a red light or a dangerous man. And this long, lean and loose-limbed Tommy was both. Tommy glared at him, but Tau did not notice, did not want to notice.

He turned his attention to the house and inwardly cursed Tommy, and his own bad luck. This Tomcat would get what was *coming* to him some day, but this was not the day, the time nor the place. Tau needed the money from this stupid nothing job. Following some nouveau-riche foreigner around. God! How he was always in need of money. To save his house, his marriage and the façade of respectability and solvency that was so important to his wife and two brats. Their pretentious fatuousness often left him trembling and he had to rush to the bathroom to dry heave over the basin and dab his cold sweat-streaked face with a damp towel. Today's children! How did they get to be like this and so young too? His wife, when did she turn into the mean-faced foul-mouthed witch she was today? How he hated them sometimes. With their always open, grasping, soft little paws, seeking every advantage. He looked at his own large, scarred right hand and cracked the big knuckles with a series of loud pops.

The front door of the house opened and a man stepped out. He turned his head to talk to some unseen person inside before walking to the car in the driveway, the Peugeot the woman had arrived in.

"It's him," Tau said.

"Yeah. The piss. Where's he going?"

"Well, he's going somewhere," Tau observed as the interior lights came on in the car ahead of them. "I hope it's not going to be a long night. My wife …"

The passenger door clicked open and Tommy was suddenly out there in the night walking towards the car and their target. This was against all their orders. Follow but don't approach. Easy job, easy money, no problems and here was the idiot Tommy messing it all up, his gun in plain view sticking out of his pants.

Tau opened the door and jumped out and in a few flying strides was next to Tommy.

"What are you up to, Tommy? Get the hell back here."

Tommy snarled at him, his mouth twisting above dark, depthless eyeholes in an iron-hard face.

"Cool it, *Malume*," Tommy ordered, "and go back to the car."

Once again, that very annoying and patronising label: *malume* – uncle. Popularly and indiscriminately pasted onto those ineffectual older men occupying that indeterminate colourless space between being no longer young or strong enough to be feared, but not yet old or powerful enough to be revered. From a fake sergeant to a false uncle in a few minutes and back again. It was going to be a long night, Tau sighed, feeling suddenly clear headed, knowing that he and Tommy had some reckoning to do at the end of it.

"Okay then, Tommy, I say nothing. The boss said you're the team leader," Tau gave up and walked away. But Tommy, swearing softly, had got the message, and followed him back to their Toyota.

The foreigner they were merely supposed to be following was now standing alongside the open door of the Peugeot. The interior light spilled out and painted him in uneven broken angles of shadow and light. He climbed into the car still oblivious to the watching men; after all, there was constant motion on the road and the pavements. Tau and Tommy were too far away, enclosed once again inside metal and glass and could have been anything or anyone at that distance. Tau wound down his window to let in a measure of cool air.

He thought it better, for now, not to remonstrate with Tommy. If the whole thing blew up because the foreign African man had seen them, spotted them on his tail, it was Tommy who would have to do the explaining, or the dying; whichever, Tau didn't care. Some said, his wife included, that he had no initiative and real guts, another thing that had kept the promotions beyond his reach, but he'd just laughed at them. How many blue-uniformed warriors with initiative had he buried while he remained large and alive? He laughed now, to cover his anger, always so close to initiating something bloody and painful.

The front door of the house opened again, flooding the front yard with a brighter, more evenly spread island of light with the African man in the car caught almost in dead centre.

The small boy, the brat who'd arrived with the woman and looked around six years old to Tau, stepped out of the house and started to run towards the road. The job *was* about to go wrong. He exulted, though not for the reason he's anticipated.

"Pa!" The boy sang out happily, and started to run towards the African gentleman in his car – and the busy road.

The foreigner hesitated and then shouted at the boy. But another voice seemed to have pre-empted him; a voice much nearer to Tau. "Get back in the house, boy!" Tau heard from some source. Tau looked this way and that and even spun around but could see nothing.

Who had spoken? Tau was confused. Tommy seemed unconcerned, distant with his half-closed bored eyes. Tau pushed the whole thing away and did not discuss his concerns with Tommy the idiot. Another sneering jest would probably be the response from Tommy, about *Malume* losing his nerve, seeing and hearing things, too old and used up to focus on the job at hand.

The boy hesitated in disappointed uncertainty and then obeyed the voice. He went back into the house. The door closed behind him. Tommy told Tau to start their car, get on the man's tail as the Peugeot in front of them fired up.

The destination was one of those dilapidated warehouses that skulk under the flying highways that pass overhead. Warehouses that don't store anything, except the defeated and ragged denizens of the city sewers who flee like blinded bats at the faintest tremor of light.

The foreigner got out of his car and with swift steps entered a dark alley. Tommy, suddenly wide awake, was already out and on his tail before Tau could react. He got out of the Toyota and made to follow them but Tommy waved him away with his gun. Tau thought this was unacceptable. He flexed his hands, the knuckles tightening. He would not allow himself to be bossed around by this pipsqueak. An idea was dawning in his frenzied mind. He waited for a few minutes, then entered the dank alley.

It was a long alley and Tau wondered if he had waited too long and would not find which side door the two had slipped through. It was not difficult to figure out as it was the only door left ajar. A steel door left recklessly open for any passing tramp seeking shelter to walk in through. Overconfidence gone mad leading to stupid mistakes like this, he thought, and laughed soundlessly at Tommy's coming surprise when he, Tau, crashed his party. He slid in and saw another door ahead, streaks of light showing at the edges. And of course the irritating bantering voice of Tommy could be clearly heard through its worn thinness.

"Where's the baking powder?" Tommy said.

"I tell you man, there's going to be bigee bigee trouble," the African voice protested.

"You are the one who is in bigee bigee trouble," Tommy taunted.

"I donte do tings thisi way …"

"Your way is not my way and my way is the right way tonight," Tommy said.

"Your boss willi note be happy."

"That's my bigee problem, not yours. Come, produce. The boss wants to know where you keep the powder."

"He didn't telli me there's a change of plan. I always make the exchange at the house."

"Hey, *Mobutu*, listen up …"

"I'm not a *mobutu*."

"I don't care. I'm not Home Affairs. Your real name, if you have one, means cold piss to me."

Tau trembled closer to the door and with stiff fingers pushed gently against it. It was not locked or even properly closed and it inched forward. What was this if not a sign? He nearly tittered. A plan of usurpation and replacement, dim and formless, but a plan all the same: Tommy was going to be the latest of the golden city's lawless marauders – who'd complicated Tau's life long enough – to feel the weight of his iron justice.

Tommy said, 'Now where's the goods? Or do I have to blow your brains out and then search myself?'

"In that cupboard there is a safe," the African whimpered. "Here are the keys. Be careful with the gun."

"This? Nonsense. A real gun is an AK. And is this the best hiding place you could find? Oh my neighbour's dog's piss," Tommy exclaimed. "I like the money!"

"Leave the money, please. Iti isi note mine. It belongs to other people. Bad people."

"Bad people? I'm bad people. I'm the one with the gun now, aren't I?"

"Your Constitution says ..."

"Oh my holy piss, don't start about the great Constitution. I spit and shit on it."

"The man outside. He willi ..."

"He willi do nothing because he willi know nothing." Tommy was in a frisky mood. "He is a fool, and he will do what I tell him. The boss gets the powder as always, I get the money and you get the bullet ..."

Tau banged the door open just as Tommy leaned forward and shot the foreigner in the head.

"He willi do nothing. He is a fool," Tau mimicked Tommy, as Tommy, with his engorged thrill-kill eyes, turned around. Tommy never stood a chance, got the bullet right in his heart. If Tau was nothing else he was an excellent shot with numerous police prizes and awards to confirm it. And Tommy had learned this too late.

What an easy score! To shut up that woman who was his wife he now made up his mind to divorce as soon as he got properly organised. It was amazing how everything now seemed so clear, and even preordained.

Tau went to the cupboard, packed everything into the bags in there, the drugs and the money, a semi-automatic that was no help to the foreigner and even some boxes of ammo, as best and as fast as he could. He left everything else as it was. It was not his indaba. It would be somebody else's bigee biggee problem when the bodies were discovered. He hurried back to the car and stashed the bags in the boot under some dirty rags and a pile of discarded clothes.

He carefully attempted to park the car exactly where it had been earlier and settled himself for a long, uncomfortable and pointless vigil. But he could use the time to get his story straight though he was finding it hard to control his erratic thoughts. He must say that he never left this spot. Tommy's orders. No! He had gone with Tommy after the foreigner and they had lost him. Tommy had ... No! He had ... he had ... what had happened was ...

His cellphone rang and he jumped.

"Is that you, Tau?'

"Yes," he answered the voice that always gave him orders.

"Get out of the car and come up into the house."

His head was now feeling rather heavy and disconnected to anything.

"The boss is here and wants to meet and talk to you."

At last! Tau felt himself immediately reconnected to a higher reality, excited and reckless. The crunch was here and now and he didn't have to wait all night with his mounting fears and multiplying doubts. He got out, locked the car door and strode towards the house. He was in control now and did not fear any so-called boss. They were all the same, little men who had been in the right places at the right times to grab their chance. That's why they hid behind stupid thugs like that extinct Tommy.

The door was ajar; of course it was, what else, he thought, still gripped by the strange bungee-jumping joy.

He walked in and was met by a young man who seemed somehow familiar (but how?). The young man stood in a beautifully decorated room with a thick white flawless carpet that would have sent Tau's wife into an incoherent rapture. But its luxuriousness only made him tremble with self-righteous resentment and he failed to see anything else.

"Where is he?" Tau asked.

"First, your car keys," the polite young man said with an outstretched hand.

"Who are you?" Tau asked.

"He is my nephew, Lefu." A distinctly familiar voice announced from the top of the stairway leading to the upper floors. The owner of the voice was coming down like a high priest from an altar, condescending to walk among his prostrate adorers and devotees.

Tau did not want to recognise him, but he did.

It was Captain Direko. From his old station. It was like coming home and finding an empty house with everybody gone and no one left to explain the absence.

"Give Lefu your keys," the voice of authority commanded.

As the young man leaned over to take them from Tau, a blind reckless and impulsive resistance made him snatch his hand away. A futile groan of defiance was all he could manage when his arm was twisted and almost wrenched from his shoulder and a fast combination blow to the neck and abdomen sent him sprawling to meet the carpet. He felt a shattering explosion at his face, as the young man's boot connected with his nose and broke it.

"Lefu is a police instructor who teaches unarmed combat, and a lieutenant with many service awards for excellence. After your time of course, Tau, or you would have known him and not tried any funny tricks. He's a fierce and loyal family guard dog. A fine young man in all respects, if a little idealistic, but he'll grow out of that. I helped smooth his way into the service at a time when it was difficult to get in and recruitment was stalled by the bungling comrades," the fatherly voice explained. His mouth was the twisted sneer of a man remembering old humiliations and injuries to his pride but refusing to acknowledge them even to himself. A secretly angry man, the most dangerous and unpredictable of all angry men

Tau began to speak, suddenly uncertain, trying to explain the state of affairs, but the young man kicked him in the mouth, then searched him quickly and expertly. He removed his gun and threw it carelessly onto one side and retrieved the car keys which had fallen onto the floor.

"I'll go get the packages from the car, *Malume*," Lefu said and walked to the door.

"Do that, nephew. I need a few minutes' private talk with the sergeant here."

"Yes, *Malume*."

The door clicked shut. Tau tried to order his thoughts and get his plan back on the rails. But what was it? There had been so many in his life … and none of them had worked out as intended. His nose was blocked with clotted blood and mucus and a swift, rising bile left him gasping for breath. He wanted to spew the whole rotten mess into the smiling old face hanging over his. If he could only harness his strength and propel his anger back into his veins before the young man returned.

"The woman who was here with the small boy … where is she?" he asked to stall for time.

"A poor Angolan woman in a strange unfriendly land, she is just a courier and," he consulted his watch, "is already on her way to Brazil via Angola. So many poor women, so many slippery men, she doesn't know who the father of her child is, of course. Her little boy is therefore confused, running out of the house the way he did," Direko sighed in resigned gloom, "although he is a wonderful cover for her."

The captain's cellphone must have vibrated in his pocket. He pulled it out, listened and the turned to Tau with a smile. "My nephew confirms the money and the package are in the car. Rather stupid of you not to dump them somewhere before returning here, don't you think?"

"It was Lefu's voice I heard shouting at the boy earlier, wasn't it?" Tau said. "I should have taken heed, the voice coming from nowhere, like some sort of omen of trouble to come."

"My nephew has an unfortunate sentimental streak. He will outgrow it. Yes, he was watching you from the bushes, ready to step in, and he was worried about the boy. He has been following you all night, of course. You and Tommy were so intent on baiting each other you didn't pay proper attention, you never thought of looking behind you. That's one of the things that made you unsuitable detective material, Sergeant. 'Lacking in basic intelligence', I think one of the examiners once reported to me. Lefu saw Tommy leaving the car. Saw the two of you in disagreement. It was then that he phoned me and I came to personally take charge of a rapidly deteriorating situation."

The insults so casually spoken triggered Tau's anger in all its bitter glory.

"I accepted my dismissal because I was ashamed that I had let you down. I did not want to see the disappointment in your eyes every day."

"And did you know I am now a commissioner? Though I'm not a freedom struggle hero so they want me out, the useless incompetent idlers!" Direko raised a fist and punched the air. He lowered it, got his voice under control once more. "Early retirement is long and hard and is very expensive these days, as you know. It's almost like your forced retirement. That's why I tried to help you out."

"You were always hard on thieves and corrupt cops. When did you cross the line and join them?"

The boss shrugged and turned away and looked out of the partly drawn curtain, as if contemplating the night and reading his cues in it.

"Everyone steals, don't they? Crossing the line? Where is this line and who draws it? The comrades? They did not struggle to stay poor. Remember that? You killed Tommy, I'll give you that, he was impertinent and undisciplined. I saved him from being arrested a few times. He was made of unstable clay. You tried so hard to stay honest, didn't you? Remember that time you beat up a suspect who wanted to give you money – thousands! And you came to me to cry about it. I felt for you and eventually I reached out and showed you the way out of your troubles. But we've been through this already."

"Captain ..."

"All you got for it was a dismissal."

"Boss."

"And your victim is free and rich with everyone standing up for him. Your minister of justice gave him *your* tax money as compensation. But for you its jail for life, if you are lucky."

In that moment, Tau went for his gun which seemed impossibly far away and too small, a speck of soot on the rich white carpet. His fingers touched it and still the captain did not turn. Tau gripped it finally and brought it around and made to put the barrel against his own head when the captain whirled around in a motion that seemed incongruously slow, almost ballet-like, and shot Tau first, in the chest.

"A renegade cop," the captain explained sadly as Lefu ran in and looked sadly down at the choking Tau. "He left dead bodies lying all over the city. And this is probably a revenge killing by someone who was faster on the draw than he ever was. He was always unlucky. There was an American comic book when I was young about an unlucky man, Sad Sack. He reminded me of him the first time I met him."

Tau coughed only once. The words were wet and slippery in his mouth and his tongue could not form them properly. All the same he knew his record, tarnished and tattered as it was, had been good overall. He had been a good cop once. God! How he had tried to be one. It was his temper always got in the way of the promotions. Cascading dark shrouds pressed in on his mind, shattered his thoughts into countless sparks that faded before he was hardly even aware of them.

"Let's go, Lefu," Direko said. "We'll put through an anonymous call to the local police at that public phone on the next block. Be careful where you step ... You don't want to spoil your nice new shoes."

"Yes, *Malume*, my shoes. And watch yours too," Lefu said as he pulled out his service pistol. "Though the place you are going, you won't need those shiny leather shoes. Drop your gun, *Malume*! I'm placing you under arrest. All that you did here is on tape. I was never on your side. I hoped all the rumours that infuriated my aunt about you were not true." Lefu stopped and exhaled a huge burst of air, shook his head in disappointment.

"After all I've done for you!" spat Direko.

"You finally crossed the line into murder. The others will soon be here. You can hear the sirens, can't you?"

The screeching wail, then the spinning, pretty and many-coloured lights flooded the room.

"You ..." the commissioner's voice started, accusing, then faltered and faded.

With a deep remote sigh, Tau dropped into a dark and final silence.

ANDREW BROWN

Andrew Brown works as an advocate in the Cape High Court and is a reservist on the South African police force, as well as being a family man, and writer with the prestigious *Sunday Times* Fiction Award to his credit for crime-thriller *Coldsleep Lullaby* (2006). *Street Blues: the experiences of a reluctant policeman* (2008) is Brown's non-fiction account of his nights on duty as a police reservist. He describes his decision to join the reservists as both an act of commitment to transforming South Africa and a cathartic move to quell his own demons. Active duty has taken him from the tree-lined avenues of Rosebank to the squalor of Joe Slovo squatter camp in Langa, all the time gaining invaluable insight into crime, as well as first-hand experience with transgressors and the police who pursue them.

On writing crime fiction, Brown says, "The writer can explore his or her own fantasies, the darkest sides of human behaviour, without fear of sanction. Although predominantly plot-driven, the genre provides opportunities to develop interesting – and sometimes bizarre – characters, and to explore intense inter-personal relationships." As he does in *Occam's Razor*.

Occam's Razor

ANDREW BROWN

"HOW WOULD YOU COMMIT THE PERFECT MURDER, DOCTOR?"
The question might have seemed mischievous in another setting, but the accompanying cold stare established the solemnity of the speaker. Detective Inspector Daniel Mentor had a grizzled, irritable manner about him, constantly flicking ash off the burning end of his cigarette, perpetually ensuring that only the glowing ember showed. Flakes of ash collected in the folds and cracks of his faded jacket, staining the leather like mould. His chunky fingers rolled the cheap ballpoint pen back and forth across his palm. His voice was rough and guttural, and the stark linoleum floor and bare walls made the cold room echo slightly as he spoke. Outside the wind swirled and pushed against the windows.

Dr Riaan Kotze shook his head and pointedly wafted his open hand at the curling grey-blue smoke that drifted towards him. In contrast to the policeman's tired attire, he was neatly dressed in pleated grey trousers and an off-white polo fleece jersey. His skin retained a youthful glow and tension, and his thick hair was swept back confidently. He sat with his back straight up in the uncomfortable chair, his one leg placed carefully across the other and his free foot bouncing lightly up and down. The detective had left the door open and other police officers unashamedly looked into the room as they strolled past. The cursory stares, the distracting movement of the pen, the constant drift of cigarette smoke in his direction, all added to his sense of detachment. The specialist anaesthetist's ambivalence at agreeing to the meeting grew.

"I'd kill 'em in the hospital," the policeman said, coughing wetly onto the back of his hand, the cigarette wandering dangerously close to the pock-marked skin on his forehead. Dr Kotze winced involuntarily. "Yeah, I'd take 'em out in the ward of a hospital. Just like your hospital, Doctor. Nothing obvious, no violence, just play with the dials, you know, tweak a monitor, fiddle with the meds. Then I'd blame it on the doctors, or the nurses. Sue them for millions. Escape scot-free. The perfect murder." The policeman's delivery was deadpan and it was impossible to assess whether he was being serious or not.

"With respect, Detective Inspector." Dr Kotze formulated the words carefully in his mouth, like polished billiard balls that dropped heavily off his tongue and rolled determinedly across the dirty desk. "I don't know who these people are whose lives you plan to terminate by 'twiddling a dial' or 'tweaking a monitor', but I assure you that certainly does not take place in my ward. And certainly no amount of tweaking or fiddling could have resulted in Mrs Anderson's death. Her death was an unexpected tragedy, sir, and one which my profession most sincerely regrets. But I do not understand why you seem to adopt the view that someone *must* necessarily be responsible for her demise." The doctor paused, still bristling, before concluding: "Bad things do sometimes happen to good people, especially in hospitals."

Mrs Sylvia Anderson had been the heir to the fortunes of Titran Investment, a Black Economic Empowerment company started by her father, Herbert Acker, in association with certain well-connected political figures. Amongst those involved in Titran were the deputy minister of defence and the incumbent mayor. The company had concentrated on lucrative state tenders, operating as a middleman between subcontractors with less credible BEE credentials and the government. Titran had exploded onto the share market, heaping fortune upon its equity holders. Acker was an astute businessman and he had already anticipated the massive flow of wealth into his estate: he had set up trusts and off-shore investments in the name of his children, Sylvia included. Of all his children, Sylvia had been the only one to feel any qualms about the unsolicited success accruing to her; her response was to utilise her time and boundless energy to promote charitable organisations. At the relatively young age of forty-one, Sylvia, as the benefactor of several high-profile charities, had made millions: although she had undertaken the work in her personal name, her largesse, inevitably associated with the Titran empire, was a positive association that Titran nurtured. The media regularly carried photographs of Sylvia, cool and reserved, warmly clutched by one beaming political figure or another.

Sylvia had married in her early thirties; her husband, Jonathan, was then an impassioned playwright whose play, *The Fire-Eater*, had just finished a successful run at the prestigious Theatre House and had been on its way to London. The darling of the artistic community, Jonathan Anderson was, at the time, a mixture of boyish good looks and dark unresolved temperament. He was prone to bouts of grey depression, interspersed with eruptions of grandiose creativity, at one moment unable to attend even a small family social occasion, and the next holding forth with sweeping arms and burning eyes amongst a large gathering of adoring strangers. Sylvia had been captivated by his passion and emotion, marrying him in spite of her father's obvious displeasure.

Jonathan had spent their married years clawing vainly at his spiralling career, desperately trying to find a handhold to stop its decline and pull it back into the spotlight. After the acclaim of *The Fire-Eater*, his plays were met with patient silence, then disappointed criticism. After three works had been staged and closed early, playing for weeks to half-empty halls, the theatres and play companies stopped automatically agreeing to fund his work, asking first to see the scripts. Then they had started to reject his plays, until nearly a decade after *The Fire-Eater*, Jonathan was left crawling in the literary desert, unable to find anyone prepared to take on his increasingly obtuse works. The strain on their marriage had been palpable and Jonathan, with every perceived failure, became further withdrawn and taciturn, while Sylvia threw herself with vigour into her charity work.

Then, one unassuming April morning, Sylvia consulted her gynaecologist for a regular check-up. He sent her for an ultrasound the same day: the scan report indicated the presence of an unusually large cyst on her left ovary. Further scans had followed the next day. These showed an over-developed cyst, suggesting a possible malignancy. Within only a week of having first visited her doctor, Sylvia was booked into a private hospital for the removal of the ovary under general anaesthetic, the surgery scheduled for the Monday. The operation itself was uneventful and the cyst had turned out to be large but benign. Dr Kotze was the attending anaesthetist. Sylvia experienced pain in the recovery room as the anaesthetic had started to wear off: Dr Kotze recommended that she remain overnight in the general ward to recover fully. When doing their rounds the following morning at 5.00 a.m., the nursing staff found her dead in her bed.

Public reaction to her death was immediate and unforgiving. Jonathan awoke from his self-engrossed slumber, distraught and angry, turning his blazing emotional focus onto the cause of his wife's death. In a unique photograph, he was seen standing alongside his father-in-law, calling for an investigation into the conduct of the hospital. Political figures called for immediate sanctions to be imposed; the health minister was asked to provide a report to the provincial cabinet on the state of private hospital care. The minister of police quickly announced that criminal charges would be investigated.

"But tell me, Doctor, if no one is to blame, why is the hospital entering into a secret settlement with Mr Anderson? That tells me they think their nurses were at fault, in some way."

"Inspector, I am not privy to the internal workings of the hospital. They obviously felt that for some reason they were at risk." Dr Kotze knew he was answering too stiffly, and that as an expert called upon to assist the police he ought to be more collegial and relaxed. He tried again to engage the detective, leaning forward slightly. "It is the responsibility of the nursing staff to monitor the intake of medication, Inspector. I am responsible as the anaesthetist for post-operative pain care: the nursing staff must administer and monitor the medication that I prescribe. I prescribed twenty Doxyfene tablets for Mrs Anderson's pain. Doxyfene is a standard analgesic for post-operative pain: each tablet contains 65 mg of propoxyphene, which is the active analgesic."

Dr Kotze paused to see if the detective wanted to make any notes. The policeman continued to observe him coolly. "According to the prescription chart, four of those tablets were administered by the nursing staff as I had prescribed, namely four-hourly. After Mrs Anderson's tragic death, the packet of tablets was found in the drawer beside her bed – that in itself was unusual, as the medication is usually kept at the nurses' station. Be that as it may, only six tablets remained, with the balance of ten unaccounted for. The post-mortem pathology indicates a raised level of propoxyphene in the femoral blood sample taken from the body. This suggests that Mrs Anderson took too many tablets during the course of the night in an attempt to alleviate her pain herself." Dr Kotze lowered his voice and made eye contact with the detective. "Personally, I think that the outcome is a little harsh on the nursing staff, but the protocols require that medication be monitored and that patient access to medication be restricted, even to mundane pain medication such as Doxyfene."

Without warning, the detective let the cigarette drop onto the floor and placed his heavy heel over it. The room filled with a sooty smell as the cigarette was extinguished. The anaesthetist watched as the big man immediately lifted the pen to his mouth, chewing on the crushed end with strong bites. Neither of them spoke as the policeman became engrossed in pulling a small spur of broken plastic off the end, tugging at it with his incisors. The box of cigarettes was positioned halfway between them on the table. Dr Kotze gently nudged the box closer to the fidgeting officer.

"Ta, thanks." The detective snatched the box up with surprising deftness and lit a cigarette, drawing in the smoke as if it was his first of the day. "Terrible habit … but fucked if I can stop." Dr Kotze nodded sympathetically, his eyes starting to water from the fog in the small room.

"It's more Mr Anderson I'm interested in," the policeman said unexpectedly, leaning in his chair and staring back evenly.

"Oh." Dr Kotze stroked his chin in puzzlement. "I hadn't realised that was a line in the investigation at all. I wasn't asked to comment on that in my report, you know."

"Yeah, I know. We're keeping it quiet for now. With the media and all, you know." The commissioner – an overweight man who sweated when he talked – had called Mentor into the provincial offices in the city. "Mr Acker wants the husband checked out, doesn't like the smell he gets from the man," his rotund superior had hissed, rolling his eyes while he wiped his glistening cheeks. The detective resented the order.

"So, Doctor, just take me through the medical records again." The toneless voice displayed no interest in the task. The anaesthetist could not decide whether the flat affect was indicative of fatigue or an intellectual dullness. Perhaps both, he thought, as he nodded, still trying to appear agreeable. He pulled the sheaf of papers from the brown envelope, briefly paging through the records until he found the right starting point in the documents.

"Okay, let's see. Mrs Anderson arrived in the ward at 17h05 after surgery. She had been under anaesthesia for forty minutes; I'd used Sufentinol during the anaesthetic and I'd given Omnopon and Kytril intra-operatively. She spent twenty minutes in the recovery room: there she was given morphine before she was wheeled back to the ward. That's a fairly quick recovery period. The medication is standard stuff. I stopped by after six o'clock to check on her before leaving the hospital. She was still a little drowsy at that stage but she was able to communicate adequately with me. You know, respond to simple questions, provide information on her pain levels etcetera." The policeman nodded, barely perceptibly, but said nothing.

"According to the nursing notes," the doctor continued, "Jonathan Anderson remained in attendance at his wife's side from her return from theatre. The nursing staff reported that Mr Anderson had assisted the patient in drinking some juice, but save for that she did not eat or drink anything further."

"Where had the juice come from?"

"If memory serves me correctly, Inspector, Mr Anderson had brought some juice with him. I recall him asking me, when I saw the patient at six, if it was alright to do so." The policeman made a note on his pad and gestured for the anaesthetist to continue. "Okay. Urine output through the catheter was normal. Her blood pressure was taken once, on shift change at 19h00: 120 over 75 was on the low side, but not enough on its own to raise any alarms. Mr Anderson remained on after visiting hours had ended ..." Dr Kotze turned over the page of nursing records. "And at 20h45 the nursing staff asked him to leave so that they could prepare the ward for the night. It is recorded that Mr Anderson was annoyed at the request, had argued with the staff until the matron was called. She then escorted him from his sleeping wife's bedside.

"Thereafter monitoring of the patient seems to have been intermittent, with the nurses recording that the patient continued to sleep. That kind of intermittent observation is not unusual in the general ward, by the way, Inspector." The policeman grunted. Dr Kotze could not tell whether it was a cynical expression or not. "At about 22h00 that evening, I returned to the hospital to check on another patient who had had a rather stormy time in surgery. I happened to stop by at Mrs Anderson. I made a note in the nursing records at that time that if Mrs Anderson was sleeping, she ought not to be disturbed. The last relevant nursing entry was at one o'clock, when a nursing assistant noted that the patient was sleeping comfortably on her side. As you saw in my report, Inspector, it is my view that given the post-mortem and rigor interval, the probabilities are that the patient was already dead at this stage, having died somewhere around eleven or twelve o'clock in the evening. That in itself is not as strange as it might sound," the doctor added cautiously. "Someone who has died peacefully in their sleep may well appear, in a darkened ward, to be comfortably asleep. One can't blame the nursing staff for this."

Detective Inspector Mentor rubbed his chin thoughtfully, scanning through his untidy notes. "We are grateful for your help, Dr Kotze. I assure you that we do not intend to make any hasty decision in this matter. I just need your help on one or two aspects further." The policeman's manner remained vaguely threatening, despite his assuring words. He appeared to be drawing small spirals on the page in front of him. "I think we are agreed that cause of death was most likely a reaction to the raised level of the drug propoxyphene in the deceased's blood."

Dr Kotze viewed the detective with renewed interest. "Yes and no, Inspector. The propoxyphene level in the blood found at post-mortem is consistent with the patient having taken approximately fourteen tablets, possibly more. This concentration of propoxyphene would not usually be fatal for a person of her weight and health." Detective Inspector Mentor turned over the page and started slowly scanning through a typed document. Dr Kotze craned forward without success to see whose report the policeman was reading.

"However," he continued obediently, "the effects of the propoxyphene may have been exacerbated by the remnants of the opiates and anaesthetic drugs that were administered during the surgery – in particular, the morphine derivatives given during surgery and in recovery, which are central nervous system depressants. The probable cause of death was a fatal combination of the effects of all these drugs, repressing her respiratory function to a point where she became hypoxaemic. Death would have been slow and insidious."

The detective dropped the report onto the table. Reading upside down, Dr Kotze thought he recognised the letterhead of a colleague of his. "But Doctor," the detective said loudly, forcing him to look up quickly, "you are surely not suggesting that it was your anaesthetic drugs that killed this woman?"

"Good God, no, of course not!" Dr Kotze felt that he had protested too vehemently and chuckled lightly to neutralise any semblance of anxiety. "All anaesthetic drugs are potentially lethal, Inspector, but the idea is to bring the patient out of theatre alive, if at all possible." The policeman did not smile back. "But your point is well made. The anaesthetic drugs did not cause Mrs Anderson's demise. The probable cause of death is the heightened level of propoxyphene in her blood." A policewoman walked past the open door, their eyes briefly meeting. The anaesthetist continued to feel unsettled. He wondered if he could ask the detective to close the door.

"Precisely. And you suggest, it seems, Doctor, that Mrs Anderson took her own life by swallowing an overdose of tablets, while lying recovering from surgery intended to prolong her life."

"No, no, no!" Kotze's face reddened with emotion. "Good grief, man. You can't go around suggesting that kind of thing. Imagine if the media got hold of that." Detective Inspector Mentor smiled thinly for the first time, like the glint of a sword as it is pulled from its scabbard. "I have no idea how the extra propoxyphene ended up in her system. There are many possibilities. The most logical explanation, however, seems *to me* to be that she took them while she was in pain, not realising the disastrous effect that this could have."

He examined the detective closely, concerned that the man still seemed hostile and distant. "Have you heard of Occam's razor, Inspector? Not the weapon, the maxim." He laughed lightly, but the policeman's eyes narrowed with apparent malevolence. "Well, Occam's razor essentially comes down to this: the simplest solution is usually the right one. In other words, don't complicate things with speculation or assumption. Stick to the simple facts that you have and the most straightforward answer is probably the right one. In a nutshell, that's Occam's razor. It can be applied in medical conundrums and I would think that it applies equally to your … line of work—"

The policeman interrupted him, ignoring his philosophical diversion. "Are you aware, Doctor Kotze, that Mr and Mrs Anderson were having marital difficulties?"

"Yes, I am." The anaesthetist sighed resignedly to himself. "I have been a friend of the family over the years and, although we are not close, I do see them at social functions from time to time. I am aware that the marriage had experienced some problems over the years. Quite what the nature of these problems was, I can't say."

"Well, are you aware that Mrs Anderson had served divorce papers on her husband?"

"No, I'm not aware of that," he answered, shaking his head and watching the detective, annoyed. "How could I be?"

"Yes, I have a copy here," the policeman replied, ignoring the question. He tapped the disordered pile of papers on the desk, raising his eyebrows. "She insisted that he should be excluded from benefiting from her estate. Their pre-marriage contract indicated that she had brought all the wealth into the marriage and he had contributed almost nothing. He stood to lose everything, Doctor, everything." The thin smile widened slightly, displaying the tips of his yellowed teeth. "And the allegations were extensive. She accused him of emotional abuse, a lack of affection, alcohol dependency …" He held his hand up theatrically, indicating that there was more to come … "And even affairs … of a homosexual nature."

"I was unaware of this," Kotze threw back tersely. "But how people choose to live their lives really does not concern me. I fail to see what this has to do with anything."

"Well, yes and no, as you like to say, Doctor." The small round ember glowed as he drew on the filter tip. "The man was on the verge of losing his luxurious lifestyle. He would have been publicly humiliated and financially broken. Yet, despite the viciousness of his wife's attack on him in these court papers, he is the loving husband, doting on her after a minor surgical procedure. Faithfully filling her glass with juice."

"Perhaps he was trying to make up to her. How do I know, Inspector? Do you want me to say that he could have killed her? Yes, he could have. Medically it is possible. He could have broken open the Doxyfene tablets into the juice and got her to drink it. He could have physically held her down on the bed and forced the tablets down her throat. These things are possible. I don't know the man well, and maybe he did exactly that." A jangling pop tune intruded, filling the room with a surreal techno beat. The policeman delved into his jacket pocket, unapologetically producing his vibrating cellphone. He pushed the buttons with heavy fingers, jamming them down on the small buttons until the phone stopped ringing and the screen went blank. He put it on the table and looked up at the doctor, as if questioning why he had stopped talking. Dr Kotze cleared his throat and proceeded: "But I am a doctor and a scientist: I deal with matters of logic and probability. Many things are possible, Inspector, but only a few explanations are probable. The probabilities are strongly against such a scenario."

"Ah, well, now we are getting somewhere perhaps. Why do you say that?"

"Well, it is highly unlikely that in a general ward anyone would be able to force tablets down an unwilling patient's throat. This means that the capsules must've been opened and the contents dissolved. This is easy enough to do, but the dissolved propoxyphene would then have to be administered either – as you suggest – in a drink, or injected directly into the bloodstream." The detective's eyes widened noticeably and he sat forward and made a note in the corner of the report. He nodded for the doctor to continue.

"Propoxyphene is an extremely bitter substance and for that reason, when taken orally, it is contained in a capsule. It is unlikely that a patient would not object to the bitter taste of any drink tainted by that quantity of the drug. That leaves the possibility of injection." Dr Kotze folded his arms. His voice had returned to an even metre, like a lecturer guiding new students through basic concepts. "And the problem with *that* theory, Inspector, is that death would be almost instantaneous." The policeman frowned, stamping out his cigarette and immediately reaching for the box.

"You see, Inspector, the effect of that dosage of propoxyphene taken through the stomach is utterly different from that administered directly into the bloodstream. The effect of the drug is far slower as it makes its way across the stomach wall: This results in a slow combining effect, the gradual suppression of respiration and a mounting hypoxia. The patient would drift into sleep and not wake up. However, if that concentration of drug were administered directly by injection, the effect is likely to be far more catastrophic. The full impact of the drug will be felt immediately, and the patient will experience a sudden collapse, lapsing into a coma followed shortly thereafter by death." Dr Kotze sensed he had gained the upper hand and he had a triumphant look on his face as he ended. "So if your scenario were to be true, then Mrs Anderson would have been dead soon after Mr Anderson had left the ward. Within half an hour, no more."

"And she wasn't?"

Dr Kotze was unsure whether the question was rhetorical or not. "No, sir, she was not. May I show you in the records again?" The detective did not respond. Dr Kotze picked up the bundle of hospital records and thumbed through the photocopies, quickly finding the entry. "There, you see, the patient's spouse left the ward at 20h45. And I personally saw the patient at around ten o'clock and she was very much alive." Dr Kotze pushed the records back along the desk, opened to the relevant page, and stood up to keep his finger on the relevant entry.

"That's the nursing entry in which you instructed that Mrs Anderson not be disturbed during the night if she was sleeping."

"Yes, it's a fairly standard instruction and I don't normally write it in. I did this time because, after I'd seen my other patient, I stopped in at her bed. She was drowsy but not asleep. I spoke to her and she indicated that she still had some pain. I checked her charts and saw that she had taken two tablets of propoxyphene only one hour previously. I advised her that she couldn't have any more at that stage, and that she should try and sleep. She seemed almost ready to drift off and I was concerned that the nurses might wake her on their next shift. Sleep is a very important part of the healing process, Inspector."

"So you gave the instruction and wrote it in the nursing records. How long were you with her?"

"Oh, I don't know. Not long." Dr Kotze sat back in his chair. "We were alone in the ward. I asked her a few questions, looked at her chart and left. I wasn't really there to see her at all, as I said. Quite fortuitously I stopped by, because now we know that she was alive at ten o'clock."

"The pathologist put the time of death at somewhere between ten o'clock and two in the morning."

Dr Kotze tensed at the insinuation. "I accept, Inspector, that the drowsiness that I saw at ten that evening may well have been the onset of a drug interaction. I have spent many hours pondering whether I ought not to have recognised the early stages of hypoxia. But I am comfortable that it is not something I could ever have been expected to diagnose in the circumstances. I hope you are not implying that I acted in any way improperly."

"Relax, Doctor. You're here to help me. Nothing more than that." The voice was stern and still inexplicably threatening. "So, either it was a slow drug interaction caused mainly by the intake of too many tablets, whether accidentally or otherwise, or it was a rapid interaction due to the direct administration of the drug shortly before death. The slow route means that she got the propoxyphene in capsule form sometime earlier in the evening, and the fast route means that she got a lethal injection sometime between ten and two in the morning."

"That is pretty much it. And of those two scenarios ... well, the first one seems likely and the second one seems ludicrous. No one sneaks into a hospital in the middle of the night with a syringe and needle to bump off a patient. I mean, members of the public would be obvious at that time of night. It's only nurses and doctors around then."

"So you're telling me that Mr Anderson could not have killed his wife: If he had, she would not have been alive at ten when you saw her?"

Dr Kotze nodded. "I'm afraid so, Inspector. Occam's razor. The facts just don't work out."

"And so Mr Anderson will inherit her estate, receive the life insurance policies *and* be paid out by the hospital."

"Detective Inspector, just because someone benefits hugely from an-other's death, does not mean that they wished it on that person, or that they are not genuinely distraught by their demise. Jonathan and Sylvia may have been having some difficulties, maybe they even had become acrimonious towards one another … but there is no reason to believe that Jonathan wished her ill. With respect to you, Inspector, I think this is one file that ought to be closed. I don't think there is a criminal prosecution here, not even against the nurses." Kotze felt as if he had said all that he could; he sensed that the detective had come to accept his argument.

Detective Inspector Mentor sighed and pushed his papers further onto the table. He tipped the empty box of cigarettes upside down, then crum-pled it up and threw it inaccurately in the direction of the wire dustbin. "I will talk to the commissioner and convey your views, Doctor." The police-man stood up, his chair grating noisily on the floor. "Thank you for your time."

Dr Kotze packed the records back into the envelope before standing. He stretched his hand out over the table. "It's a pleasure, Inspector. Let me know if you require anything further." The policeman's grip was surpris-ingly firm and dry. Despite the thanks, the man's eyes remained remote.

Dr Kotze walked out of the office into the chilly corridor outside and was momentarily uncertain as to which way to turn. "To your right," came the gruff voice from behind him. He mumbled his thanks and walked swiftly down to the end of the passageway. The walls were lined with cork notice boards covered with yellowed and fading notices and posters. The place smelled of detergent and musty damp. The brown swing doors led out into the tarred courtyard filled with parked police vans and damaged private vehicles. The anaesthetist averted his eyes from one violently crushed in the front, the driver's seat squashed beneath the bonnet and engine.

He turned into the road outside. A silver Corvette was parked behind his Range Rover. Jonathan Anderson stood next to the low-slung sports car: his long thick overcoat and unkempt black hair added to his brooding appearance.

"Nice car," Dr Kotze said lightly as he walked up to him. "I didn't expect to see you here."

"My wife bought it for me," Anderson said dryly, answering the first comment and ignoring the second.

Dr Kotze brushed past him, heading for his own car. The two men's fingers met, briefly intertwining in a delicate but sensual hook that pulled apart even as they touched. The blush of a smile crossed the doctor's lips.

"Occam's razor."

Dr Kotze's smile faded as he heard the guttural voice of the detective coming from the station entrance just to his left. "It only applies, Doctor, once you have all the facts."

TRACEY FARREN

Tracey Farren is a full-time writer with a psychology honours degree and some years of experience as a freelance journalist. With a forte for delving into disturbing issues, she says, "I found myself haunted by the human drama that I witnessed. The newspaper reports could not accommodate the texture and charge of these stories, so I turned to fiction to express the emotional reality of some of these themes."

Farren had several hard-hitting short stories published before turning her hand to her first novel, *Whiplash,* a gritty narrative about a street prostitute who launches into a dangerous battle to turn her life around. Apart from raising two teenagers, and surfing the waves on weekends in Cape Town, she's in the process of writing a second novel, a psychological thriller titled *Snake in the Grass*.

Read on for Farren's deliciously gut-wrenching tale, *Chop Shop*.

Chop Shop

TRACEY FARREN

JOCK AND RANDALL SMOKE OUTSIDE THE DOOR. RANDALL TELLS JOCK about the new Toyota. I listen while I'm falling sleep. "I punched the kid's mother out of the seat. I put the gun on the kid in the back and said, 'Get out!' She tried but the fuckin' child lock was on. This black guy started shooting for my fuckin' head. I whacked it into reverse. Sorry about the back bumper. Man, I belted down the N1 at two-forty."

I'm nearly asleep and Randall says, "I'm not saying kill her, Jock. I'm not saying that." I open my eyes wide. I stand on the bed and peep through the window. I can see Randall's black peak cap. "She's seen nothing. Just dump her on the driveway next to Isaac's Butchery."

"How old?" Jocks asks.

"Eight, maybe nine. A laaitie."

When Randall goes, Jock drives the Toyota to the block and tackle. It's got three legs and a chain and a big metal hook. The men get a strap around the engine. They get the hook into it. The winch makes the heavy engine light. One man stops the swaying. One man pulls the chain. While they are busy in the front, Jock opens the boot. He picks the girl up in his arms but he doesn't put her in the bakkie to dump her. He brings her in like a baby. He puts her on the bed.

She is in a yellow and white school dress. She smells like wee. She has got one sock and one shoe on. The other grey sock is tied around her eyes. Her hands and feet are tied with wire. There is blood in the lines. Jock rolls her onto her back. He strokes her legs. He strokes her ribs. He doesn't touch them, but I see him staring. Her flat chest makes him sexy. He says nicely to her, "Be quiet or else I will tie up your mouth."

To me he says, "Make sure she shuts up."

He goes back to work in the yard. She whispers, "Is there someone here?"

I don't breathe. "Help me," she begs. She cries for a while. She has brown skin and thin legs. She has long fingers and a long neck. I have white skin and I am fat. I have big cheeks, and big breasts that grew last year. They are the problem. They are white and they wobble. He doesn't touch them. He shuts his eyes tight and turns his face away like he has got arc-eye from welding. He also has fat cheeks and he even has breasts. He laughs at his own breasts, but he hates mine. He said he took me because we look like family. I could be his daughter.

I wait until she is asleep, then I get into bed next to her. When she sleeps her lips twitch. Her vein jumps inside her neck. I can smell toffee too, not just wee. She is in Jock's place against the wall. When he comes to bed one of us will have to get out. Jock doesn't work in the day. He makes sex with me and sleeps and cooks for us. Eggs and mash. We live in the middle of factories. In the day there are trucks and cars and clanks and crashes and men shouting, shouting. Men laughing loud. When they go home and the gates go clang crash, then Randall and the others bring stolen cars. Jock drives them straight to the block and tackle. I've watched how he does it. D for drive. R for reverse. They think I'm Jock's child because of our fat cheeks and fat breasts. But I am his wife.

I don't try to get out anymore. There are people out there who like to hurt girls. Sometimes I wish I could see over the walls, but they are miles up. Jock doesn't want the cops to find his chop shop.

On Sundays there is a church next door. An angry man shouts at the people. "Every week you people come to me whining, I am so broke, I don't have anything extra. For God's sake. I mean it. For God's sake. No one is going to appear out of nowhere and hold your hand. Grow up! Earn money! Give money! Tithe to your church. Grow the house of God."

The people speak back softly like sad children, "Thank you, Pastor. Yes, Jesus. Hallelujah."

Tithe is the same as tide. When the sea washes out and washes in on the beach. The sea is bigger than the sky I think. The sea is more water than I have ever seen. It makes me sad to see it on TV. Sometimes I think I can hear waves at night. I asked Jock if there was a sea in Milnerton. He said that there isn't. He asked, "Are you sure you don't want to kill yourself?"

He doesn't care if I'm sad. He just doesn't want me to die.

The singing wakes me. It's the new girl singing a soft song about glory. "Is that a school song?"

She jumps and twists to me. Her wires bleed. "Will you help me?"

"Uh-uh. I can't. Do you know this song?" I sing my favourite song about chasing pavements. In the day I climb in the cars and listen to the CDs that come in stolen cars. I know it's childish to pretend, but I lie on the backseat and dream that I have a mom and a dad. I have lunch in my lunchbox. I sit at a desk. My teacher wears pink lipstick. I even dream that the boys hurt me because I am new. It's okay because there is always someone to stick up for me. Sometimes it's a nice boy with brown eyes, like the guy Tertius in *Think Free* on TV. It's a programme about happy children who are leaders. They climb mountains and save people in the sea. My singing puts us back to sleep. We sleep together, the new girl and me.

Jock takes her sock off in the morning. She has sock patterns in her skin. Her face is not straight. She blinks in the sun. Jock takes her to the toilet. She says, "Go out. Go out."

He bangs the door and shouts through it. "Did I hurt you? Did I?" He looks angry at me. "I don't hurt kids."

When she is finished, Jock carries her to the carpet. He makes her sit and watch him doing it to me. He says, "This is how we do it here. Later I will do this with you."

She turns her face and cries and cries. "Watch!" he shouts. "Or I won't take you back home!"

But I know he won't. I know she is his new wife.

Afterwards, Jock asks nicely, "What's your name, little girl?" She doesn't answer. Jock looks sad, like he's sorry he made her watch. Before he sleeps Jock says to me, "Shut up in here. No one must know."

While Jock's sleeping she stares at me like I'm not a child anymore. She stares at me like I'm Jock's old whore.

Jock used to promise he would build me a car when I'm big. Yesterday I knelt at his fat stomach. "When I grow up will you make me a beautiful car?"

He shrugged.

"What colour can I have?"

"What colour do you want?" But he was tired of me.

"This colour pink." I pulled up my shirt to show him my nipples. He covered his eyes to stop the arc-eye. "Watch it, you little whore. You're getting too old." He pushed me off the bed. I slid right onto the carpet.

I watch TV. The new girl watches me. I watch a programme called *Sing for Africa*. The children sing with mikes. The audience vote for the best child. When they've all sung I say, "I like the girl with the black hair."

The new girl doesn't answer. That girl with the black hair *does* win. She goes up to fetch her voucher. I say to the new girl, "She looks just like you."

Jock snores and says, "No Daddy," in his sleep. He always does it. He farts and scratches his chest. Jock has three cigarette burns on his mouth and lots on his bum. His stepfather thought he was the devil. Long ago I asked, "Why did he think that?"

Jock shouted like a devil, "Stop messing your food! Stop pissing on the seat! You are not a baby!" Jock started crying.

"Is that *his* voice?" I asked.

"I can still hear it. I was three. He wouldn't let my mom help me."

I patted Jock on the head. He asked, "Have I ever hurt you, Snoekie?"

I patted him on the head.

"You don't want to kill yourself, do you, Snoekie?"

"Uh-uh," I said.

He always asks because of his wife in the yard.

His first wife killed herself with a whole box of pills. He buried her in the yard where the block and tackle is. Jock never leaves pills anywhere. He keeps them in his pockets with his keys. Sometimes I get sick from making sex. He gets me medicine and gives me pills from his pocket. He used to say, "Poor child." Now that my breasts are fat, he still gets me pills. But now he says, "Poor little whore."

There's an engine speeding, then the bang of the garage bolts. I wake him up. "The men are here."

"Ah shit, no. I slept too long." He gives the new girl water. She messes everywhere. He feeds her bananas. He takes her to the toilet then puts her on the bed. He rubs her ribs. "We'll do it in the morning."

He says to me, "Shut up in here. No one must know."

I sing the chasing pavements song again. But she doesn't sing school songs, she starts to talk soft and sad like the people with the angry pastor. But she doesn't say, "Thank you, Jesus. Hallelujah." She says, "Is he your father?"

"Not my real one. We just have fat cheeks."

DAY 9

Breakfast

cottage cheese with cantaloupe sprinkled with 1 tbsp sesame seeds

1 slice whole grain toast, with a dab of **extra-virgin coconut oil**

Rooibos, green, black, or herbal tea or **coffee**

Appetizer

celery stalk with 1 tbsp almond butter

Lunch

*1 cup Sunshine Soup

½ whole-wheat pita stuffed with 2 oz white **turkey** meat, lettuce, tomato, light mayonnaise, and mustard

ice tea with lemon or seltzer water with lemon

Appetizer

1 fresh fruit

Dinner

6 oz grilled halibut steak

broccoli

steamed snow peas

tossed salad

Dessert

1 cup mixed berries with 2 tbsp non-fat frozen whipped topping

DAY 10

Breakfast

1 cup low-fat sugar-free **yogurt**

fresh fruit

1 sesame Ryvita Crisp Cracker

Rooibos, green, black, or herbal tea or **coffee**

Appetizer

7 to 10 cherry tomatoes stuffed with low-fat **cottage cheese**

Lunch

*Terrific **Tuna** Casserole OR shrimp or **tuna** salad: toss mixed greens with tomatoes, cucumber, red onion topped with tuna and 1 can baby shrimp and **olive oil** and balsamic vinegar to taste or 2 tbsp prepared low-sugar dressing

1 small whole grain roll

ice tea

Appetizer

½ cup four bean salad

Dinner

*Crispy Oven-Fried **Chicken** or Vegetarian Burger

steamed broccoli

broiled tomatoes

¾ cup couscous or quinoa

Dessert

1 cup Jell-O with 2 tbsp non-fat frozen whipped topping

"Like Tertius on *Think Free*?" She nods. She likes Tertius too!

Then she says, "You can share my mom."

A happiness starts hurting me. I think of myself with a school dress and a mom. It's me in my daydream. I lie with her in the bed. I pat her head. "Do you have another sister?"

She says, "No." She asks, "Can you cut these wires?"

"Uh-uh. I can't." I think and think. I ask, "Are you sure they don't chop girls?"

"Look at me. I've never been chopped." She starts crying again. "But please don't let him put that ..."

"I won't." I won't let him do it to my sister.

I think and think. I make lots of plans. I am a leader. But my plans make me scared and that makes me fall asleep.

"Shelly." I think it's my granny's voice. But it's my new sister, staring at the sun through the window. "He's coming soon."

I go into the garage to the men. They are putting a new number plate on my new mother's Toyota. The men look at my breasts. "Can we have Rice Crispies?" I ask.

"Has your kid got a friend here?" They are worried because of the chop shop. Jock's eyes go black and tight. They squeeze my head like a vice. He says, "No, man. The Rice Crispies are for me." Jock's smile is angry. He hates me.

Me and Jeanette crunch Rice Crispies. The sun shines on the black oil on the walls.

"Don't let him ..."

"I won't."

Jock hates me for letting the men know she's here. He does it with me instead of Jeanette. This time she lies on her face so she can't see us. She crushes her crooked nose into the carpet. I listen to the church people sing and play their organ, like on TV. The angry preacher starts again, "We come with a new week of sins. And we expect him to turn a blind eye. We should be ashamed. We must apologise to God."

"Sorry. Sorry," the soft, sad voices say.

When Jock is finished I say, "Sorry, Jock." That makes him fall asleep.

I get Jock's long-nosed pliers. I cut the wire off her hands and her feet. The blood is dry on the wire. I slide my hand under Jock and slip it into his pocket. I feel for the keys. Jock jumps up, "What? What?"

My first plan didn't work. I pretend that I woke him on purpose. "Jock, wake up!"

"What?"

"There's a voice. I can hear it. Come and listen."

"What?"

"In the yard. Come and listen."

"It's just the church."

"No. It's her."

I put my ear against the black sand. The hook on the winch hangs in the sky. He doesn't lie on the ground, but he bends close and listens. He grabs for my neck, "I'm sick of your teasing you little …" He wants to say "whore", but I twist up and pull his arm hard. He falls to his knees. I jump up and pull on the hook. The thick chain speeds. I force the hook into his mouth. I pull it up with two hands. The huge metal hook slides through his soft mouth. I feel it hook into hard bone. I jump on the chain and pull it down, pull it down. Jock's spinning and screaming and trying to pull the hook out.

"Help me!" I shout.

Jeannette hangs on the chain with me. We pull it down, pull it down until only Jock's toes are touching the black sand. The hook comes out through his nose. Blood pours out like engine oil out the sump. He is gobbling and gurgling red oil. I stand at the garage. "Get up on my shoulders." She tries, but we both fall over. I start giggling but my sister starts to cry. She climbs back on and holds onto the garage wall. She can't reach the roof. We fall again. Jock is trying to pull himself up the chain. I get into the red car. I put the gear stick in R. I turn the engine on. It rides slowly backwards. It bangs into Jock's bakkie. I push the gear stick to D. I turn the steering wheel left. I sink down and shove my foot on the accelerator. The car swings. It smashes into the new truck that came last night. It tears along the garage wall. Bricks fall on me, one hits my head. I shove both feet on the brake.

She is crouched in the corner on a pile of tyres. "Come!" I climb onto the roof of the car. I'm still too low. "Bring tyres." We do it together. We roll the tyres along the bonnet, up the windscreen, onto the roof. We pile them up. Me and Jeannette. I don't want to look, but I can't help it. He is still hanging onto the chain with his hands. The hook comes out of his nose like he's a big fish. The hook gives him a terrible smile. But it makes his face crooked, not straight. He is gurgling and gobbling like the girl in *Slasher*. I climb up the tyres. They start to sway, but she holds them straight. I climb onto the roof. The tyres stand still for her. She is light and young. I hold my hand out. I pull her up. The roof scrapes blood on her school dress. We stand up together under the sky.

I was wrong. The sky is bigger than the sea. But the sea *is* more water than I have ever seen. There *is* a sea in Milnerton!

Jeannette screams at the church people. She waves at them through their window. "Rape! Rape!" She knows which word to use to get the people to run and see.

When I look back the blood is coming out of his ears.

But Jeanette said she will be my sister.

She said she will share her mother with me.

MIKE NICOL

Over the years Nicol, a journalist and writer, has penned a number of books – both fiction and non-fiction and two volumes of poetry. Among his most recent titles are the crime novels, *Payback* (2008) featuring security contractors Mace Bishop and Pylon Buso, and *Out to Score* (co-authored with Joanne Hichens) (2006), featuring the PIs Mullet Mendes and Vincent Saldana.

A self-confessed latecomer to crime fiction, Nicol says, "After spurning it for most of my life in favour of highbrow literature, I saw the light at the turning of the millennium and now I read nothing but crime novels – the bloodier the better. High body counts are essential." He's been known to donate to charity the crime novels where no one dies.

When not reading, writing or compiling the blog Crime Beat (http://crimebeat.book. co.za) (with Barbara Erasmus) he spends time listening to country rock – the sound track, he believes, of most good crime novels.

In *The Fixer* we are treated to a slice of Nicol's slick and complex work.

The Fixer

MIKE NICOL

00h32

"I have seen horn," VP Shunt said, adjusting the Bluetooth headpiece, "from Kenya, Tanzania, Zambia, Zimbabwe, Namibia, even in photographs from Angola before the war when they had horn. Horn from KZN and KNP, but I have not seen horn like this, Mr Fong. Not ever. Not this size. This is a size you do not see in the wild anymore. I measure this horn at ninety centimetres. That is a lot of horn.

"The other thing, Mr Fong, is you do not see horn like this in Cape Town. I have never seen horn like this in Cape Town. There are none of these animals anywhere near Cape Town any longer. Not for centuries. So while we may be a port city, we do not handle horn. Johannesburg, yes. OR Tambo International, yes. But not Cape Town. This is an opportunity. Aphrodisiac brought to your door."

VP Shunt listened, not looking at the man sitting on the other side of his desk, the one who had introduced himself as Willie. Not glancing at the other one, Sal, with a pistol, leaning against the door.

"No," said VP Shunt, "I am sure your new girls are of a very high quality, Mr Fong. They are improving all the time. But no, I am happy with Geraldine. After six months I have a relationship with Geraldine. Even as we speak, Mr Fong, Geraldine is at home in our bed waiting for me. There is a light on in our bedroom and a light on in the hall and the apartment is armed. If she could hear, she could hear the sea. Not that it is loud tonight, but even when it is not loud you can hear the sea in my apartment. Hearing the sea is important when you live in a port city. Unlike you, I could not live in Durbanville. Hearing the sea is why I bought that apartment.

"So that is where Geraldine is, Mr Fong, warm and patient, wearing a teddy I bought at your shop. Red. Lacy. Extremely sexy. Like all your products, Mr Fong. Now, as you can gather, I have taken a liking to Geraldine. I like the feel of her, the touch of her. I like the silkiness of her hair. No matter how good your new dolls are, no matter that they are at the forefront of Chinese craft, I am happy with Geraldine. I say thanks for that, Mr Fong.

"Similarly I cannot accept your suggestion of a twosome. I am not a Zulu, Mr Fong. I am a monogamist. A dedicated man. As a man with an imagination I can visualise certain situations where this would offer advantages but I fail to see how two dolls like Geraldine would participate in such a relationship. So thank you, Mr Fong, but no thank you.

"Now, Mr Fong, about this other matter."

VP Shunt listened. Aligned a notepad against the side of his laptop on the desk. Arranged three pencils side by side at ninety degrees to the bottom of the notepad. Glanced at the men, long enough for eye contact with shiny skull Willie other side of his desk.

"Yes, it is twelve forty in the night. Yes, this is inconvenient. These are matters out of my hands, Mr Fong. To answer your questions, no, I do not know the gentlemen who have come to see me."

He glanced at Willie and Sal. They held his gaze.

"I am here because I was asked to meet with them by a person known to me. An important political figure known to me. No, I cannot reveal the identity of this person either."

VP Shunt dropped his eyes.

"What I can tell you is that he is a person of influence. He is the sort of man who can phone me at midnight and receive my full attention. When this man speaks I listen. Because when this man speaks I am being paid a considerable sum to listen. So I listen.

"But that is not the only reason I listen, Mr Fong. I listen because I do not want to get hurt. I listen because I prefer to look down on the sea. I do not wish to look up at the sky from the depths. I do not like the thought of drifting on the floor of a kelp forest with a lead belt around my waist. You know the lead belts that scuba divers wear? Those belts. They are heavy. When you are wearing one you cannot swim up from the bottom of a kelp forest. As my younger colleagues say, *no way, José*. So I listen. And because I listened I find myself in my office at forty-three minutes after midnight with two men I do not know and a suitcase with a rhinoceros horn inside."

"What sort of suitcase?

"A big rigid suitcase. Colour brown. It has small wheels at the one end and a handle at the other. On a carousel at Cape Town International or Tokyo's Narita or Shanghai Pudong for that matter, no one would suspect that inside such a suitcase was the horn of a rhinoceros. They might suspect it carried suits, shirts, shoes, socks, underwear, a toiletry bag, a box of emergency medicines, perhaps even a number of gifts for clients. Local items: rooibos tea, small beaded wire animals, the daring might even have packed biltong.

"What I am saying, Mr Fong, is that the suitcase is innocuous. It does not draw attention to itself. No one wheeling it across the concourse of a departure terminal would cause anyone to be suspicious. So, if we were to give you this suitcase you would simply be a man with a suitcase. A traveller going to catch a plane.

"This said, we could also meet you in a car park for the transaction. At Mouille Point lighthouse, for instance. At Constantia Mall. Hout Bay in the beach parking. In an all-night garage. Gardens, say. Or Canal Walk. Alternatively we could do this in a street. Long Street. Kloof Nek outside Café Paradiso. Lower Main Road, Observatory. It does not matter where we do this. What matters most is when. When has to be in the next few hours.

"Mr Fong, one moment. One moment, please. I cannot tell you that. Absolutely not. He is in government, the cabinet, I will tell you that. But you will have to take my word on trust. I can reveal no further details. Believe me, I am talking *very* important person."

VP Shunt stared at the ceiling. He kept his eyes off the two men watching him: Willie crouched forward in the chair his fingers knotted; Sal with the gun held at his side.

"Now, to the matter. What my clients are talking, Mr Fong, is US$50 000. We are talking R375 000 as at the exchange rate on my bank's website. This, I realise, is a lot of money at twelve forty-six in the morning but this is a big horn. I am a lawyer. I know what is legal and what is illegal. What I am dealing with here is illegal. But that is not the point. The point here is a request from a client to expedite a sale as a matter of extreme urgency. Under the circumstances, given the players involved, I

can live with this. I will sleep easy with Geraldine. In eight or nine hours
we will breakfast together, she and I, with the doors open to the sea and
this telephone call will be one I did not have. So I have to ask you, are
you interested in this proposition?"

He listened.

"I am pleased, Mr Fong. I can give you thirty minutes to raise the
finance. Get back to me quickly, Mr Fong."

00h52

VP Shunt disconnected. The man at the door, Sal, folded his arms, the
silenced muzzle of the pistol resting on his shoulder. Willie, opposite,
shifted in his seat to get comfortable, crossed his legs. Jiggled his foot.

VP Shunt said, "There is a man in the Yemen I need to contact."

Willie cleared his throat, nodded. Sal held the gun to his lips, blew im-
aginary smoke from the barrel. Grinned.

VP Shunt placed his call. Said, "Sheikh Saleh, *Assalumu Alaykum*, a
long time."

He listened, his eyes on Willie and Sal. The two men, dressed in black
tracksuits with red stripes up the side of the pants and the arms, staring
back at him, listening. He saw Willie glance round at Sal leaning against
the door. Saw Sal nod, then Willie bend forward. Rap on the desk. VP
Shunt frowned, held up his right hand. Willie clicked his tongue, sat
back.

"Sheikh Saleh," said VP Shunt, "Sheikh Saleh, I am pleased that the
ruling went in your favour but my purpose in making this call is not
about weaponry of the modern kind, not about rifles or hand grenades,
what I am contacting you about is in the tradition of sword-makers because in a suitcase on the floor beside my desk is a rhinoceros horn of
large proportions, proportions not to be found in Africa today and of
an age, I have been led to believe, that makes it extremely valuable. I am
talking here of a jambia handle that would be the envy of every sheikh
across the Yemen.

"I am talking here of an opportunity that will not occur again in your
lifetime or in mine. But in this matter we have to act speedily and deci-
sively. I ask you to accept my word as a guarantor that what I am looking
at, what I now have my hand on, what I can feel beneath my fingertips is
an item worth the asking price. An item worth more than the asking price,
Sheikh Saleh. For you, an item equal to your status.

"Now, Sheikh Saleh, I am unfortunately in a situation here that is both delicate and urgent. A situation that is regrettable and could have been avoided. However, my world is a world of situations and I have known worse occasions than this. That said, I must add, Sheikh Saleh, that my clients are anxious men. Nervous men. They wish to settle this matter and go home to their families. They cannot take my word or yours even, they will not entrust me with this matter, so you see I have here what I would call a dire situation. They want cash and at this hour there are only a few people I know who can perform such a transaction. My clients have named a price which is high, fifty thousand US high, non-negotiable.

"Exactly, I know, time is against them but these are wily men, Sheikh Saleh, these men are conducting an auction. Even as we speak others are raising this capital to make their bids. The reserve is as I have indicated, the bid is yours. My advice, for what it is worth, would be to go up ten. A mere ten thousand on top would secure it.

"Now, Sheikh Saleh, in this instance, and given our long association, I am in a position to act as your agent. After all, what, Sheikh Saleh, is money between us but an internet transaction? At the moment of that transaction this horn is yours. You have thirty minutes, Sheikh Saleh. If the money is through in thirty minutes this unique horn is yours."

01h34

Willie sat breathing hard. White flecks of spit lodged in the corners of his mouth. A moment before he had stormed about the office, shouting. He had pounded his fist on the desk. He had brought out a gun and pushed the barrel into VP Shunt's cheek and told him he would die.

VP Shunt made another phone call.

"Jayendra Pillay, Jay, my old friend," said VP Shunt, "I know this is a bad hour, I know this is not the hour to bother friends, who prefer to spend this time of the night in bed asleep next to their wives or lovers as I do, but this is a deal you would want to know about.

"I am seated at my desk here in my office with a view over the lighted city towards the harbour, a view that I seldom see at this hour. Here with me are two desperate men. Two men who have created a situation that I have been asked to fix. The situation these men have created concerns a large rhinoceros horn valued at US$50 000 I am reliably informed.

"Now, Jayendra, Jay, I have made calls to people who would treasure such a horn. I have explained the situation. I have explained the urgency. The people I have spoken to are people for whom this sort of money is do-able at any hour of the day or night.

"But we have been sitting here for thirty minutes and the two worried men are now running out of patience. They wish to conclude this deal. They wish to conclude it as speedily as possible. Consequently I have come to an arrangement with these two men. The arrangement is this: they will take a down payment of R100 000. Tomorrow at a place and time of their arranging they will meet me to conclude the deal with the payment of a further R100 000 from which I shall have deducted my fee. You can see the advantages here. A discounted price and no complications with foreign exchange.

"Jayendra, Jay, my old friend, in ten minutes you could be here. I know that in your safe there lies a fund to cater for such emergencies. In ten minutes you could be wheeling to your Mercedes Benz a suitcase, a rigid, brown, innocuous-looking suitcase containing a rhinoceros horn worth much more than you will have paid."

09h45

VP Shunt, at breakfast with Geraldine, thumbed on his cellphone, said, "Captain. What a pleasure." Listened. Said, "I have heard the news. Extra-ordinary, quite extraordinary, Captain. These killings are a scourge. They give the city a bad name. Here we are a major tourist destination. Tourists flocking in from every city on the globe, and soon football enthusiasts will be joining the stream, meanwhile we are faced with gang wars. Turf murders. Street battles.

"We wake to bodies in the river, the lovely Black River a dumping ground for gangland assassinations. At least that is what the radio is reporting. A killing there a month ago, one last week, and now a double shooting in the small hours of this morning. Two men in tracksuits. Execution-style. According to the news.

"I would not like to be in your shoes, Captain. All the paperwork, all the sheer grim horror of such crime scenes.

"I can remember as a boy fishing on the Black River with my father near Valkenberg where the reeds are thick. Not often, perhaps only a couple of times, father and son, standing on the banks fishing some sunny after-noon in the mid-1970s. The mountain grey and bold against the light, the city drowsy in the bowl. Sometimes, Captain, we caught mudfish there, once even a steenbras swimming up on the tide. When the tide washed in that high. Idyllic Sunday afternoons as I recall them. Although occasionally you could hear the inmates of Valkenberg. My father always said it was the cries of seagulls.

"But to business, Captain."

VP Shunt stretched over to squeeze Geraldine's hand, smiled at her.

"Captain," he said, "Captain, let me run you through the situation. We now know the provenance and yes, it would be a gesture of public spiritedness to return the horn but consider this: the rhinoceros is a museum exhibit. It has been long dead. It is the work of a taxidermist. A recreation of the original. Yes its horn has been cut off with a power saw but museums have people who could make a prosthesis that when it was glued to the stump would fit so exactly, would look so exactly like the original that no one would know the difference.

"The public will stare at the rhinoceros and marvel that such a beast once roamed where we now live and those people will believe that this rhinoceros, the whole of this rhinoceros with its replica horn, was once a living animal. It is something they want to believe. That is why we have museums, to create a world of make-believe.

"But that, Captain, is all our palaces to the past are. Fantasies. So it does not matter if this rhinoceros gets its horn back or not. Schoolchildren will be none the wiser. They will still look at the beast with its long horn and smear the glass case with their sticky fingers and the older boys will make smutty jokes, but they will not know that what they are looking at is a fake.

"Consider this, too, that rhinoceros has no value. It is not a tradable item. The museum will not sell it, has no plans to auction it on eBay. In their inventories, on their balance sheets it carries no monetary value. So they have not lost anything.

"Now," said VP Shunt, "I know a Chinese merchant and a sheikh from the Yemen who would be interested in what you have in the suitcase. Already they have made arrangements to pay US$50 000, although considering the provenance and the age of the horn, we could probably increase this by half again.

"This sum we could divide, Captain, less a commission to the minister who asked for my assistance. At the moment the minister stands to receive nothing.

"This minister gets commissions and fees and sundry disbursements from various public and private projects but in themselves they are not major investments, they do not in themselves shift his status onto the ladder of extremely wealthy men.

"Consequently he would be pleased to know that when he is disturbed by distant relatives at midnight and has to make phone calls to stop his wife from pleading for his intercession and his wife's cousin from crying and his wife's cousin's daughter from weeping and wailing because his wife's cousin's daughter's husband has done something completely unthinkable and now has a large rhinoceros horn in a suitcase, when the minister has to make phone calls because of circumstances such as these, he expects that his efforts will be appreciated.

"Understandably he will not expect to be appreciated by receiving a fee in lieu of from the emergency fund Captain Jayendra Pillay of the SAPS keeps ready in the vaults for the sort of operation you were called upon to conduct at the last minute in the early hours of the morning. Heaven forbid.

"The minister is an honourable man. He is in favour of the public good. He is a signatory of the social contract between the state and the citizenry.

"That said, the minister is an influential man. Influential men have a certain position in life. A position that requires affirmation. Showing appreciation in this instance would be beneficial, Captain."

VP Shunt paused. He could hear Captain Pillay slurp at his tea.

"Captain," he said, "the minister is also a man facing a family tragedy. A relative is dead. Murdered. This man might have been an embarrassment in the family circle, but he was still family. The minister will soon be a man in mourning.

"These are some of the considerations one must bear in mind, Jayendra, Jay, my old friend."

A sea breeze from the open door ruffled Geraldine's hair and VP Shunt brushed strands from her face. She looked so demure in her white towelling gown.

Again he smiled at her. Lovingly caressed her cheek. Said to the police captain, "What do you say, my friend? All it will take is a phone call."

PETER CHURCH

Peter Church typed his first novelette on his mother's Royal typewriter at age eleven. He took a breather from a two-decade-long career in Information Technology to write his first novel, *Dark Video* (2008) and is currently working on the sequel, *Take 2*.

Of thrillers, he says: "I love the balance and timing of a thriller – the build-ups, the let-downs, the counter thrusts, shocks, surprises and revelations. It's like having your foot on the pedal of a fast car. I want the reader to escape from their everyday into my world."

Which is exactly what Church achieves in his short story, The One.

And Church, who lives in Cape Town, with his wife and three children, likes to slip a little technology into his writing. "Internet, cams, cell phones and IPods are intriguing tools to dabble with."

And what's all this about Goldfish? "My son bought the CD. He slipped it into my shuttle and now he can't get it back. Ooh ah woo ah ooh-ooh-ooh. Hypnotic, it's music to get calm to ..."

THE ONE

PETER CHURCH

I RECEIVED FOUR DIGITAL PHOTOGRAPHS THE DAY I ARRIVED HOME from a week in Greece.

My holiday was over, money spent, no photographs to preserve moments, no memories deemed worthy.

Now someone was sending me pictures from *their* holiday.

Taken on my camera!

I stroked the mouse across its pad, recognised the location of the third image: Beacon Island, Plettenberg Bay. Shot into the sun, the panorama spanned from the beach to a corner surf break, the silver light, the unbroken sand, a reliable timestamp of morning.

A door banged and I looked up from the computer. I imagined Alison had come back. We'd broken up three weeks ago. She was supposed to come to Greece with me.

I tensed my back, listened carefully.

Bottles chinked in garbage bags – the neighbour, I'd never met him, depositing weekend excess.

Alison hadn't come back; she wasn't coming back. Get that into your head, I told myself. I'd discovered her key pushed under the door; she hadn't even bothered to enter. The apartment on my return was hot and airless, untouched since the day I left. I sat back and plucked at my shirt. My clothes felt like they were gummed to my skin.

The first two images were snapped from the window of a car, blurred flashes of passing countryside, irrelevant digital records, best deleted.

I clicked on the last thumbnail: a girl on a blue striped towel. She wore a pale yellow bikini, her body untanned, the sugar-white sands contrasting with the colour of her towel. Her eyes were closed, a hint of a smile, barely perceptible.

As if she knew something.

Her costume fabric blended with her skin, so she looked naked, sex airbrushed out like a nude Barbie.

I pushed my chair back and walked to the kitchen, flicked on the kettle. Magnets spotted the fridge door, the notes and pictures they'd once held tight, removed by me on the day I'd departed. Tomorrow I'd be back at work.

I returned to the lounge and pulled up the blinds. In the flats across the way lights were going on. None of the occupants recently returned from Greece, I thought. If only my apartment faced the other way, I'd be looking at the sea.

I returned to my desk, switched on a bullet-shaped lamp, its warm copper glow spreading homeliness across the impoverished room. The picture of the girl in the pale yellow costume blinked at me. I thought I'd meet a girl like that in Greece. Erase memories of Alison. Anything but … Everywhere I went, I'd wished Alison there. I'd converse silently with her, about borrowing her dark glasses to protect my eyes from the intense sunlight reflecting off the white buildings, about water so blue there was no sky, about stray cats that rubbed against my legs. I'd touch the pillow where her head should have been.

The kettle clicked off. I stepped around my unpacked suitcase, walked to the kitchen, opened the fridge and lifted out the carton of milk I'd bought on the way back from the airport. A withered cauliflower skulked on the empty racks. I found a box of Five Roses in the pantry, fished a chipped mug out the basin, warmed it with water from the kettle. The tea in Greece had been insipid broth. I added the tea bag and fresh hot water.

No sugar.

I poured a sachet of Alison's sugar replacement into the tea, returned to my desk.

I sipped my tea, sat down, looked at the picture of the girl.

Who was she?

Like a surgeon with a scalpel, I selected the magnify button and dragged the cursor across the screen, to her face, her breasts, and into the shadow between her legs. I wondered if she'd swum yet, if she shaved. I wondered what she'd think about some stranger dissecting her body.

I knew the photographs had been taken with *my* camera. No one else would have configured their memory card to wirelessly transmit to my email address every time they encountered a WiFi hot spot.

Someone had stolen my camera from my rucksack at OR Tambo in Johannesburg, en route to Greece.

I tried to imagine the photographer's identity. Had I seen him? And the girl? Was she his girlfriend? Did she know he was stealing her image with my camera?

I downed the tea, the residue bitter. Outlook Express beeped its completion of the email download. I saved the girl as my wallpaper and hibernated the desktop.

The picture of the girl filled the entire screen.

Alison. I had to stop thinking about her.

I remembered the night of our break up. At first she'd said nothing. When I'd persisted, her words lashed me like a whip. It was completely unexpected. Earlier that night, she'd danced wildly with an inebriated friend of mine, hanging onto him like a desperate lap-dancer, and moving so extravagantly that one of her boobs slipped out. I'd watched quietly from the couch.

"I've already bought the tickets," I told her later.

"I can't go."

I swallowed, hoped she'd explain: a death in the family, fear of flying, an unexpected work assignment.

"I don't want to go to Greece with you. It's over," she said.

I focused on the fine blonde hair on her upper lip, to avoid her curled mouth, thin lips.

"Then I'm not going either," I said, looking away.

"Suit yourself." Her mouth tightened.

But I did go to Greece, the remnants of our conversation played over and over, the finer points of her verdict most unforgettable – I was a conformist, dull, weak, with no imagination, poor taste in music.

"Music!" I'd protested, watching her finger make a gash in my auction-acquired sofa. "I love music," I'd continued.

She'd held her hand to her ear. The room was dead.

"Only the sound of your voice." She stood up, patience expired, sneer replaced by snarl, pulling stuffing from the hole in the couch. Over her shoulder she'd imparted: "I hate this flat."

My vision blurred. I blinked my eyes, curled my hand around the empty tea mug, and stared at the reposed suntanner.

No music played, but the room wasn't silent – I heard my breathing, the hum of the hard drive, water dripping from the tap in the kitchen, injections of background traffic and domesticity from next door.

I rubbed my face, the spikiness of two days' travel, and stole a glance in the mirror – greasy hair had grown unevenly in patches down the back of my neck. Luckily, my appearance had escaped Alison's assassination.

The faint smile of the girl in the picture seemed to sense my discomfort. I wished she would open her eyes.

I'd accepted the loss of my camera as fate and refused to buy a cheap replacement. The pictures of my holiday would have looked ridiculous – a dull man with his heart ripped out, an empty space where his girlfriend should have stood.

I stared at the photograph of the girl, feeling a strange tingle of anticipation, like a secret spy, her instant in time unknowingly shared with me.

She seemed to be reading my horoscope: dry your tears, have some fun.

* * *

I didn't receive another photograph from my stolen camera for two years. I'd forgotten about the original pictures taken at Plettenberg Bay. The girl on the striped towel that glowed on the screen of my sleeping desktop had become decorative, no longer noticed, like the Port Elizabeth seascape I drove past on the road to work each day.

Then a new batch of pictures arrived in my inbox.

I was sitting on a recently purchased velvet sofa when the computer beeped; I'd started to revamp my lounge, piece by piece, new curtains, new carpet, now a new sofa.

I remembered it was Friday. My girlfriend of a year's standing – a new record – had broken up with me that morning. She said she'd met another guy with better prospects. *Prospects.* As if she inserted two names into columns of a spreadsheet and ranked future potential against rows of criteria. He'd come out a few points better than me.

I was sad, but not broken. She'd helped me forget about Alison.

And I feared she might be The One and that I'd never sleep with another girl in my life.

Her toothbrush and creams were left in my bathroom, and a pair of her panties that I kept in my cupboard. I still had a pair of Alison's.

I inserted one of my ex's CDs into the drive of the computer, but the first track reeked of failure and I killed it, sat down to inspect the latest delivery of pictures in silence.

They revealed a set of urban objects – a building, a street, another street, a parking bay, pedestrians, then the inside of a poorly lit building. I magnified a number plate on a car in a street scene – CA, the code for Cape Town.

The strange excitement I'd felt two years earlier resurged. I viewed the pictures, as if I were a physic delving into another person's life.

I wondered what had happened to the girl?

I stood up, stretched, and checked my watch. I had no plans for the evening. Despite the recent bad news, I felt oddly invigorated.

I wondered why my camera's new owner hadn't taken a photograph for two years.

* * *

A few days later I received another photograph. I think it was Monday or Tuesday.

A single shot.

On the weekend I'd dated a girl with stocky legs who'd reminded me of a ballerina I'd known at university. I don't like to rush into sex. She'd come back to my flat after a bottle of Chenin Blanc and had been very willing.

I clicked on the attachment. Got goose bumps on the back of my arms and a sudden chill down my spine.

A girl, standing, back to the camera, legs slightly apart, the light dim, in the background a thin curtain and beyond that, a landscape of flats and nightlife. She was nude. A wispy red negligee lay on a used bed, on the bedside table was a silver champagne bucket.

It was the same girl who lay on Beacon Isle beach. I cleared my throat, the room silent; in the distance, the engine of a heavy truck roared.

I fired up Ben Harper's *Another Lonely Day* on Media Player and used the magnifying glass on the picture, the resolution sufficient to inspect the taut skin on her legs, but not the label on the tangled underwear pooled at her feet or the hotel logo on a crumpled towel alongside.

I stood up abruptly, paced to the window and pulled up the blind, sniffed the air. Rain imminent.

What's going on, I thought? There must be a message.

I turned and stared at the screen, her round buttocks central to the display.

What did the photograph mean?

Was it posed?

I leaned forward, took a step, then another, towards the screen. I imagined an extra dimension. As if I could reach out and touch her. Place my hands upon her body.

My cellphone rang. I felt stupid, with eyes slit, hands groping towards an image on the desktop – trumped by the illusory power.

'Hello?'

It was the girl with the stocky legs returning my call. I pressed replay on Ben Harper and raised the volume button, asked her if she wanted to come around, but she said she was already in bed. I didn't ask if she was alone. And it was Monday. Or Tuesday.

* * *

Two weeks later I received eighteen pictures.

It was Friday and I didn't have a date for the weekend. The girl with the stocky legs had reunited with her boyfriend. Apparently they'd been going out since high school. She didn't tell me this the day I'd slept with her.

Earlier I'd compiled a CD comprising favourite songs from my youth: U2, Credence Clearwater Revival, Dire Straits. Even Billy Joel. Songs I hadn't heard in years.

I boiled some tea, inserted the bootleg CD and settled down to examine the attachments. I flipped through a slide show of roads and buildings, most taken from a car window. The cars in the street displayed CBS number plates: Mossel Bay. The compositions were random, a man stepping off the curb onto a zebra crossing, two businessmen in dark suits, lampposts bent like old men, a red robot, a row of shops. A number of images depicted the entrance to a building, the sign above the door partly obscured. Inside the building, the dim lighting indicated he'd disabled the flash. It was a bank, I was certain – the sad people inside, the bored security guard, the revolving door with green and amber lights, a counter with a pen tied on with a chain.

I guess it was pretty obvious, but it wasn't to me. Cape Town, Mossel

Bay. He was heading up-coast in my direction.

The music started to irritate me. I recalled the boy who'd listened to that music. He was dull and unimaginative.

I navigated backwards through the images. Why would someone be taking pictures of a bank?

* * *

I don't often read the newspaper.

I'd endured a weekend on my own. On Saturday afternoon, I'd trawled through Walmer Park, flicking through autobiographies in Fogarty's Bookstore, sat through a movie, its name I'd forgotten before the show ended.

I brought home the left-over popcorn and flicked through the TV channels – finding an interesting programme, scanning for something better, finding nothing, forgetting to return to the original.

Sunday was worse. The wind blasted onshore, made escape from my apartment impossible. I played Led Zeppelin to drown out the whine, loudly, until the neighbour banged on my door.

I opened *The Times* on the lounge floor.

On page seven was a small article about a bank robbery, hardly news. Police believed there was a pattern – a lone thief who followed the same modus operandi every week: quietly approach a counter, threaten the teller with an unseen weapon, exact a stuffed envelope of cash and breeze away. Yesterday was Mossel Bay.

The following evening, the celebration picture arrived. Earlier I'd watched *Rescue Me* on TV, the episode ended with a song called *Trouble*. I Googled the artist, downloaded the song, played it over and over.

I sucked in my breath as the picture emerged, developing from top to bottom on the screen: same girl. This time lying on a bed, smiling at the camera.

Her hair fell back on the pillow as if posed. Her hands held onto the bedposts, her breasts reduced to small round contours, the nipples perfect semicircles within.

The lower half of her body was covered in two-hundred-rand notes.

And her eyes! Rich, dark hazelnut.

My cellphone rang: my ex-girlfriend – she of the record one-year relationship. It hadn't worked out with the new boyfriend. Prospect is just that.

"Should I come around?" she asked. I took a two-hundred-rand note from my wallet and held it to my nose. In the background Ray LaMontagne sang about being saved by a *wo-man*.

"What for?"

"Pick up my stuff." Her voice dropped to a whisper. I pressed the note to the screen, edged up against it.

"What?" I still had her underwear. I still had Alison's. If Alison called, what would I say?

"My things. A toothbrush …" The voice was tinny. It didn't fit with the brown eyes that sparkled at me.

"Uh. I'm sorry. I chucked them out."

I placed the cell on my desk, breathed in and out against the money, ran my tongue across my wrist.

What would she sound like?

I had a theory about my camera's missing two years.

The photographer had been in jail. Ray LaMontagne repeated his ominous message. *Trouble.*

* * *

"Is there a reward out for the bank robber?" I tried not to whisper. I'd started dating an attorney's daughter, she was used to the good things in life. She liked my taste in music.

"Which bank robber?" the voice asked after a pause.

I'd stepped out of my offices and onto the street, but the lurking smokers' ears were tuned. I crossed the street.

"If I know a bank robbery is about to happen. How much will I get?" I hadn't prepared properly. But I'd remembered to disable caller ID on my cellphone.

There was silence.

"Who is this speaking?"

"No matter."

A big truck rumbled past, emitting noise and smoke pollution, a queue of disgruntled cars tailing behind.

"Sir. It's your civic duty to report a bank robbery. If you've got information …"

I looked at my watch. A salvo of cars hurtled past in the opposite direction. I was surprised at how much traffic travelled down this road at lunchtime.

"What's your name?" I asked him. Across the road, I noticed a girl from the offices below us, sucking on a fag. She hadn't seen me. Her expression contorted and hardened as the smoke emerged from her nose. I didn't know she smoked. She doused herself in perfume – I'd been in the lift with her once. To think I'd considered asking her out on a date.

"Visser. Sergeant Visser. Who're you?"

"Sergeant Visser. Is there a reward? Yes or no?"

"Lemme put you through to someone," he said.

I hung up, waited for a gap in the traffic and hurried across the road. I waved at the hard-faced cigarette girl slumped against the wall, one hand in her pocket. She seemed to straighten up when she saw me, smiled.

"I like your new haircut," she said. She had surprisingly nice teeth.

I snatched a glimpse of myself in the glass window.

* * *

Each Friday, I waited for the next parcel of pictures.

A couple of weeks passed.

My mood was slightly gloomy because I'd broken up with the attorney's daughter. She may have been The One for me. I've realised that relationships cannot be frozen, that each day they evolve, and if your feelings develop too slowly you get left behind.

I'd sensed she was getting bored with me. Alison had lamented my character; the next girlfriend, my lack of prospects. What would the attorney's daughter find?

So I told her it wasn't working for me. I wanted to break up first. She lived with her parents so there wasn't any packing up to do.

I downloaded the latest set of images; they took forever. He'd increased the resolution. I magnified the prints. The signage was clear: Nedbank. The number plates showed EC – Port Elizabeth, my hometown. I zoomed into a frame and recognised the signage of a cellphone shop near Greenacres.

I pushed my chair away from the desk and ran a hand through my hair.

Wait a minute...

I lunged forward, flicked through the sequence, stopped at the plate-glass window of the cellphone company.

No reflection.

Shit!

I felt a bead of perspiration run down the back of my neck.

I walked to the kitchen, put two slices of white bread together with a chunk of cheese and returned to my desk. I took a bite and changed directories. I'd saved pictures of the thief's girlfriend in a separate folder.

I flicked back and forth.

Shape, colour, size ...

Her hazel eyes, her smile, the fall of her hair, the hue of her complexion, the roundness of her breasts, the tightness of her buttocks.

I could take the visual discourse no further.

I wanted to touch her.

Smell her perfume.

Feel the warmth of her skin.

* * *

I drove once up the road, turned and drove back down, mentally confirming the objects from the last set of images.

No doubt.

Saturday morning. I parked three cars' distance from the Nedbank entrance and inserted the Goldfish CD into the front loader. I could see the entrance and the concrete steps leading up from the sidewalk to the bank.

I looked at my watch. Eight o'clock. I took off my jersey and tossed it onto the backseat.

Last night I'd dreamt about Greece. I'd fallen asleep floating on a lilo at the shore's edge. The wind had picked up, blown me out into the Aegean Sea. I'd woken, known I should have jumped off the lilo – with its label *not recommended as a flotation device* – and swum for the beach. A dark-haired lifeguard was blowing a whistle. I'd decided to ignore him. Do my own thing. Keep on floating.

A car hooted at a scruffy teenager wandering carelessly across the road. I snapped out of the trance; someone called Monique sang hauntingly on "This is how it goes". I cupped my hands around my nose and breathed in and out, considered a walk, decided not. Condensation formed on the front window, I wiped my sleeve against the glass.

I had no plan.

This is how it goes.

I leaned back, conscious of the thumping in my chest. I felt thirsty.

No expectations.

This is how it goes.

Goldfish skipped from track two to three. I like new music. Any music. Whoever said I didn't …

I waited and watched, my vision like a time-lapse camera, the motion of cars and pedestrians steadily increasing. I wound down the window.

Crack!

What was that?

I looked towards the entrance of the bank. A lady in a floral print dress flopped to the cement. I heard screams.

Crack! Crack!

I thought: two.

A siren blurted out, drowning the screams. People scattered like pigeons disturbed in a square. I looked about frantically. Where could she be? People were running, shouting.

A man emerged from the bank, limping badly, clutching his thigh. He hobbled through the throng, creating a passage like an ambulance through rush-hour traffic. A man in a black leather jacket brushed past him and sprinted away in the opposite direction. A small boy clamped his hands over his ears. The sirens seemed to confuse everyone. The thief limped towards my car.

I leaned across and opened the passenger door.

"Get in," I said.

Face contorted with pain, lids hooded over pale blue eyes, a dark wet patch on his faded blue jeans. He slipped into the seat without argument. I pulled the door closed, turned the key in the ignition and spun the wheel into the traffic.

I turned off the music. The saxophone riff was incongruent with the scene. It should have been Led Zeppelin with screaming guitars.

I crossed two lanes and turned right up a one-way, checked the rearview mirror. No flashing blue lights. The thief groaned. I thought he'd smell of gunpowder; he smelled of cologne.

I turned back against the traffic, slowed, allowed cars to pass. Checked the mirror again. Everything looked normal.

"You okay?" I said. I wondered where his gun was.

He didn't answer. I glanced across at him. His head lolled against the window, his jacket open, his checkered blue shirt was drenched in blood.

He must have been shot more than once.

The thief moaned, then sighed deeply, his hands fell into his lap.

I stopped at the robots. He looked as if he was sleeping, his head resting against the window. I checked the car alongside, two teenagers in conversation; no one seemed to notice. I turned left onto the William Moffett freeway. As long as I kept turning left, I knew it would be okay.

I picked up my cellphone and thumbed through the call register, found the number I was looking for, hit the green phone.

The giant fig tree appeared to my right, I kept left, followed the traffic down Main Road.

"Can I speak to Sergeant Visser?"

He came on after a pause.

"I'm the guy who called about the bank robber."

"Yeah?" He didn't remember.

"Is there a reward?"

The phone went dead. Maybe he thought it was a prank.

I drove steadily past the avenues, twelve, eleven, ten, took a cautious right into the police station parking lot. It was deserted.

I redialled.

"Yeah?" Visser answered.

"Sergeant Visser. Can you step outside? I'm in a red 1998 Cressida."

I took a deep breath and switched on the music, backtracked to "This is how it goes".

The thief had slipped lower in his seat. His hand moved and startled me. I picked it up and let it fall. There was no resistance. I noticed a message – *Room 1217* – written in thin black Koki pen on the back of his hand.

Ooh ah woo ah ooh-ooh-ooh.

I replaced the hand carefully on his leg, slipped my hand inside his jacket pocket and removed a fat manila envelope.

I looked through the windscreen at the station door. Nobody was coming.

I leaned across and patted his other pockets. Empty. A flourish of red blood stained my white T-shirt; I reached for a jersey on the back seat and pulled it over my head.

I wet my sleeve with condensation from the window and rubbed out the writing on his hand. Then I redialled the station.

"Visser?" I said. "You best get out here."

* * *

I stepped out of the getaway car before Sergeant Visser arrived. I didn't want any tragic heroics. A black garbage bin stood outside the station. I removed the lid and slipped the envelope down the side of the bags, then waited alongside my car.

"What the fuck you playing at, man?"

He looked and reacted as I had anticipated. He rubbed a hand across his thick gut, a white vest underneath, and swaggered towards me, stopped, hand dropped down to his belt, like a gunslinger of the Wild West.

"Sergeant Visser," I greeted him with both palms open and facing forwards. "Can I show you something?"

I walked around the front of my vehicle, opened the passenger door and the thief fell out.

"What the …!" Visser bellowed.

He unclipped his pistol, pulled it out, waved it at the thief, then at me. I raised both my hands.

* * *

I wasn't overly concerned when they impounded my car, or that most of my Saturday disappeared in a lot of waiting and a little cross-examination.

"Did he point a gun at you?" an inspector asked. He sat behind an empty table. A calendar on the wall was two months out of date. The room reminded me of a janitor's office, missing only the bucket and mop.

I eyed out Sergeant Visser who shifted uncomfortably on his seat alongside the inspector.

"The thief?" I checked.

The inspector nodded, smiled, he seemed to be on the ball.

"I thought he had one, but I didn't actually see it," I replied. No need to take any chances.

"But you thought he was hijacking you?"

"I heard the siren. Shots. My door burst open. There wasn't time to think."

"Of course," the inspector agreed. Visser nodded too.

The inspector removed a note from his pocket, unfolded it and recited a number.

"Is this your car licence number?" he said.

"Sounds like it," I replied. I can never remember my number.

"It belongs to a white Fiat," the inspector stated.

"Oh," I felt my cheeks redden.

Visser left to check my number plate. He returned with the correct number.

"That's mine!" I confirmed.

The inspector looked at the note again.

"A witness who saw the getaway car wrote this number down," he said, and looked straight into my eyes.

I shook my head, held his gaze. He seemed to be drawing the truth from me.

"I have no idea," I replied honestly. A thought struck. Imagination. "Perhaps the accomplice?"

"Accomplice?"

I described the switch-over: a well-dressed accomplice, black leather jacket, how he'd crossed the thief's path, how a packet was passed.

"A packet," the Inspector leaned forward. "Like a Checkers packet?"

"Could be. Could've been," I answered.

"With an envelope?"

I shrugged. Visser's eyes blinked.

"Yes. I think it was a Checkers packet," I confirmed.

The inspector nodded, looked at the note.

I produced a credible description of the accomplice based on an English teacher I'd had at school: ginger hair, goatee beard, lollipop glasses. He'd been harsh on my English essays – said they'd lacked imagination.

"Perhaps he drove the Fiat," I said. On a roll.

I wondered if they'd allow me to fetch my Goldfish CD from the car.

* * *

"You need a lift?" Visser said, lighting a cigarette. The inspector had left for a big rugby match scheduled in the afternoon. Visser's breath smeltled ⸒ liquor and the hand holding the cigarette trembled.

" I said. But I didn't move. I held the Goldfish CD in my hand.

᠆honed about a reward," Visser said.

he said.

arrogant. Like: "Fuck you, you risked your life for ᴏ the club." But this may have been prejudice.

I nodded. Slowly. Repetitively.

Said, "No problem." Silently mouthed the words: "Let me put you through to someone else." Stepped back from the counter.

"What did you say?" he said, a hint of aggression, fat rolls on his neck bulging.

"Nothing."

He relaxed, the jaw sagged, a face resigned to disappointment.

"You sure you don't need a lift? You'll get your car back next week." He looked down at the newspaper in front of him.

I left the station walking backwards, watching him.

He looked up; I waved with the CD.

Outside I checked my watch. Three thirty. I opened the black bin and slipped out the envelope, shoved it down the front of my pants. I hailed a minibus taxi bound for the beachfront.

I wondered if she'd enjoy Goldfish.

Room 1217. I know of only one twelve-storey hotel in Port Elizabeth.

TIM KEEGAN

Tim Keegan, Capetonian by birth and by inclination, started his working life as an academic historian with a PhD from the University of London. After spending some time in Britain and the United States, he returned to South Africa in the 1980s. He left academic life in his forties to turn his attention to writing full-time. Apart from several books of history, he has published three novels, *Waiting for the Moon* (2005), *Tromp's Last Stand* (2007), and *My Life with the Duvals* (2008).

"I do not regard myself as primarily a crime writer," Keegan admits, "but I consider foibles and weaknesses as central to the human condition, and criminality as an ideal vehicle for examining human life in extremis."

Keegan's detective novel *Tromp's Last Stand* is a rollicking romp with security-professional Jake Tromp through the city streets of Cape Town, but in *What Molly Knew* Keegan uses the measured prose for which he is best known. Here he focuses on an act of violence as a way of prising open the dynamics of a tragic family.

What Molly Knew

TIM KEEGAN

AT FIRST MOLLY RETIEF DIDN'T KNOW WHO IT WAS ON THE OTHER END of the phone. Tommie had never phoned her before, as far as she could remember. He sounded agitated, his voice shaking. Sarah's dead, he said. What do you mean, Sarah's dead? It can't be. But it was. Molly had never hidden the fact that she didn't like her son-in-law. She blamed him for everything that had gone wrong in her family. She liked to think they'd all been happy before he came along.

"Somebody shot her," he was saying. "In the back of the head. She's just lying there in her dressing gown on the kitchen floor. The police are here now."

That's all there was. What more was there to say? Molly wasn't sure what she should do now. What do you do when your only child is dead? She sat for a moment by the phone, running her fingers over the eczema on her arms. Sarah was all she had left after her first husband had been killed in a car crash near Laingsburg twenty or so years ago. She felt as if the world had ended, much the same as she'd felt when Neville died. All the anger and pain that existed between mother and daughter, the gulf of misunderstanding and mistrust, charge and recrimination, was like a balm, a reassurance, compared to this. They had been held together by their differences. They'd lived out their unhappiness and their guilt and their shame in mutual embrace, scratching each other's scabs, never allowing wounds to heal. But they always had each other. And now – what now?

Molly did what she always did. She turned on the kettle, got down the

125

tin of Five Roses tea bags, got the milk out of the fridge. The cat purred from her spot on the kitchen table, as if this were a day like any other, waiting for the saucer of milk that was her due. Why should you change the habits of a lifetime just because your reason for being had come to an end?

While she waited for the slow kettle to boil, Molly took the carpet sweeper out of the broom cupboard and began doing the rugs in the hallway. Housekeeping would keep her busy until eleven, when she allowed herself a break in front of the telly. That's how every day went.

As she was pouring the water into the chipped teapot, she felt a sharp pain in her ribs. She clutched her arms together under her breasts as she sat down at the table. She knew it was Tommie. Who else would kill her? Sarah had no enemies. She had nothing anyone would want to steal. And who could get into a third-floor flat in a secure block in Goodwood? She thought of phoning her husband Rollo at the Autoglass place in Milnerton where he was workshop manager. He should know. But she didn't phone him. She didn't want to interrupt him, especially now that they were short staffed. What could he do anyway? He never got on with Sarah. As a girl she'd resented his presence, the speed with which her mother remarried after her father's death. She'd got it into her head that Rollo was a rival, someone who was out to ruin her and her mother's lives. She never understood how little choice Molly had. Molly was always caught in the middle, trying to keep the peace, accepting the battering she took as the price she had to pay.

And then along came Tommie Nobrega, the psychologist, with his theories and suspicions. Sarah was a nurse aide in the clinic where she met Tommie. Of all the men her daughter could have fallen for … The horrid little man was determined from the beginning to poison her mind. She got it into her head that she'd been victimised, abused, interfered with, and it was all her mother's fault for allowing it. Recovered memory, he called it, as if you can make things up and suddenly it becomes real. All because of her resentments against the man who had always stood between them and destitution. Alright, Rollo wasn't perfect: he drank too much; he stayed out at night playing darts at Wally's Bar in Koeberg Road; he'd visited prostitutes in his time, had girlfriends. And he had a temper, used his fists when he was boozed up, used foul language. The neighbours had sometimes called the police in. But what was she supposed to do? Move out and starve? Go and live in a shelter? At her age?

"It's always the husband," agreed Inspector Duvenage. "Mr Nobrega is definitely top of the list, just between you and me. We reckon he had the opportunity. It happened between seven when she was seen picking up the paper downstairs, and nine when her neighbour came in to see why her door was wide open and found her lying there. The husband says he left at seven thirty to go to work. The neighbours say they heard nothing, though we're still busy going from door to door. No forced entry. That's the thing. The security gate is always closed. So whoever did it must have been known to her."

"I'm sure it's him," said Molly. "I never liked him. He filled her head with hate. She only married him to punish me. I never understood what I did to deserve it."

Molly stroked the cat sleeping on her lap. She looked drawn, worn out. Her brown, thinning hair showed streaks of grey. She was wearing a pinafore over her shapeless lavender jersey. She always wore the pinafore when she was doing housework.

Inspector Duvenage took a sip of tea, holding the cup with his fingers gripping the rim. He checked the ring-bound notebook he held in his left hand. "Mrs Retief," he said, clearing his throat. "I need to clear up a few things with your husband. I presume Mr Retief is at work?"

"Yes. Why?" The colour rose to her cheeks. "There's nothing my husband can tell you. I know Tommie will tell you lies, Inspector. He's trying to shift the blame. He's been telling lies about us from the beginning. That's why my daughter didn't speak to me. He turned her against me."

"I suspected he might be making things up. They do, you know, when they think they're cornered. But still, I think I should talk to him. Your husband, I mean." He scratched his head, looking at the notebook with a frown. "You say your daughter didn't talk to you, ma'am? Was there any particular reason for that?"

"No, not really. I mean, she was never easy. But it was Tommie who came between us. He seemed hell-bent on destroying us all. Now he's got his way. It's wicked, that's what it is. Wicked!"

She offered Inspector Duvenage another Marie biscuit from the glass plate she'd arranged them on. He declined. He was looking around the room, almost unnaturally clean and tidy, nothing out of place. Modest, but comfortable; old furnishings, pictures on the walls, a few ornaments carefully placed on the mantel. A room used only for entertaining, perhaps. Not that much entertaining went on here, by the looks of her. One of those stay-at-home women, in her fifties, with not much of a life outside these walls. Seemed like a family in which you didn't expect things to go wrong.

In Inspector Duvenage's experience, there were two kinds of investigations: Those, the everyday ones, where it's difficult to sympathise with the victims, people for whom life is cheap and death routine. And then there were those where violent death is as far from the victims' expectations as it can be, normal, good people living normal lives in homes like this one, whose existence is overturned in an instant for reasons that no one can fathom. It was at times like this that he found the job a strain, when he felt he had to nail the culprit just to calm the jangling in his nerves that didn't go away when he got home at night. He knew that all citizens were equal in the new South Africa, but he couldn't help but feel some people's pain more than others'. That's just the way he was, and the newspapers and television people seemed to think the same way, to judge by the posse of reporters and cameras outside Sarah Nobrega's flat in Goodwood when he'd left.

"Mrs Retief, why don't you tell me all about your son-in-law? Where did they meet?"

"I hate it when you call him my son-in-law. I never thought of him as part of my family."

Rollo Retief was a big, balding man with grey sideburns and rolls of fat under his puffy eyes. He breathed heavily and smelled of cigarettes and he needed a close shave. His round face was lined and his skin was yellowish, parchmenty, with little veins near the surface of his large nose. Yellow teeth, yellow fingers too. He didn't look healthy. Nearing retirement age, assumed Inspector Duvenage, and not a moment too soon. Nor was he pleased to see the cop, the way he stared at Duvenage as if he was to blame for wasting his time with enquiries when all these people with their broken car windows wanted same-day service. High crime rates made for good business in Rollo Retief's line of work, but clearly didn't do much for his temper. It was obvious his staff were wary of him, glancing at him with surreptitious looks through the glass partition of his small office to make sure he wasn't watching what they were doing.

"I'm sorry to hear that, but I don't know what I can do to help you," Rollo said when Inspector Duvenage told him of Sarah's death. The inspector was surprised to discover that Rollo Retief knew nothing about it, that his wife hadn't got in touch with him.

"I suppose you'll want to go home, to be with your wife, Mr Retief," he said.

Rollo shook his head. "I would, except we're run off our feet here. It's a terrible thing to happen but life must go on. We're short staffed, you know. The buggers come and go. The turnover's terrible."

He sat behind a desk piled with folders and files. It was an untidy place, with dirty cups and glasses and dust on the shelves. Not the sort of office to give clients confidence in the way the business was run.

"When last did you see Sarah, Mr Retief?" asked Inspector Duvenage, pulling the notebook and the blue Bic out of his inside pocket.

"I never saw her. Not since before she was married. She wouldn't have anything to do with me. Or her mother, either. You know she didn't even invite her mother to her wedding? She brought that man over to the house when they first got engaged, just to shock us, then there was a big fight and that was that. They sometimes spoke on the phone, she and Molly, but it always ended with a screaming match and Molly in tears for the rest of the day. Sarah was sent to torment her mother. Ever since she was little. The trouble I had from her! Her mother thinks it's because her father died, but that doesn't explain anything. Some of these kids these days are just naturally bad. Her mother won't tell you anything about it, but the boyfriends and the drugs! Molly always had her head in the sand over that girl. She doesn't know but I paid for more than one abortion. And then she goes and marries that man! I suppose you've seen him. Figures, doesn't it? She was bound to come to a sticky end after that. Thank God they didn't produce any children, that's all I can say!"

"She was a nurse, wasn't she?" asked Inspector Duvenage. "I mean, she couldn't have been such a bad case."

"Ja, well …" he shrugged, as if that meant nothing to him.

Not the friendliest, thought Duvenage. A man of fixed opinions, not to be swayed from his antagonisms by the girl's death. He felt sorry for the wife, putting up with this Sad Sack of a man, who presumably took his sourness home with him at night.

When Rollo came home, he wanted his supper ready, whatever time it was. It was after ten when Molly heard the Mazda turn into the drive. She hadn't spoken to anyone all day, not since Inspector Duvenage had been there before lunch. Except for Mrs Henning from next door, who came over to say it was on the radio, and was there anything she could do? Molly said no, it was very kind but she was coping, and didn't let her in. Trust Mrs Henning to know Sarah's married name. She seemed to know everything. Rollo didn't like Mrs Henning, who'd phoned the police before and was always snooping.

Otherwise, it was a day like any other for Molly, except that there was a big hole inside her that ached and ached. She'd thought of phoning her sister in Saldanha, but what could Lettie do? Lettie was married to a warrant officer in the navy and lived in a navy house, and thought herself superior. She'd say how sorry she was, but wouldn't really mean it, and that would be that. Her own sons were both qualified and gainfully employed and successfully married, one an electrician, the other an accountant, and that was all that mattered to her. Molly could do without Lettie's smugness right now.

She'd made chops and mash and gravy, the way he liked it, put it in the warmer, and waited in front of the telly. She always laid the table meticulously, just for one, with the linen tablecloth always clean and the pepper and salt shakers and the paper napkins in their container within reach. He came in, smelling of whatever it was he drank and wheezing heavily. He sat down at the table and looked closely at the food in front of him, as he did every night, with a frown, looking for faults.

"You heard anything more about Sarah?" Rollo asked after a while.

"No. The policeman said he'd phone or come by if he found out anything more."

Molly sat opposite him and watched him as he ate, ready to fetch whatever he wanted from the kitchen. Sometimes he wanted water, sometimes a beer or the bottle of brandy and a glass, sometimes tomato sauce or chutney. She sat stiffly on the edge of the chair, gauging whether he was in one of his moods or not, relaxing after a while when she was satisfied he wasn't about to explode.

Rollo ate without speaking, smacking his lips and clearing his throat as he always did, shaking his head now and again. Then he said, the fork hanging in the air in front of his mouth, "Jeez, that bastard!" He chewed and swallowed. "I'm sorry to say it, but I knew there was going to be a bad end to all this from the moment she brought him here to show him off to us. You don't marry someone like that if you come from a normal home. I know you cared for that girl, but she didn't deserve you, and if you knew what's good for you you'd be relieved she's gone to her maker. She wouldn't have stopped until she'd destroyed the both of us." He shovelled another forkful into his mouth and chewed away noisily, shaking his head again. "With all her lies. She wanted us both in prison, and you know it. Now at least you can get on with your life without that girl spreading shit about us."

Molly knew better than to say anything. Not that there was anything she wanted to say. She weighed up what Rollo had told her, and thought maybe he's right. He usually was, and even if he wasn't, there was no point disagreeing with him. It wasn't her place to argue with him. After all, he had her interests at heart. He always did have, and even if he didn't express himself with any kindness, he meant well deep down.

"That's what it's all about, Molly," he said as she put the tinned pears and custard in front of him. "What goes around comes around. She only got what she asked for. At least now you can sleep at night without worrying about her, without putting up with her lies and deceit. You're free of all that now. There's that to think about, once you get over the shock and all."

He was in a strange mood, oddly placatory but belligerent at the same time. Disturbed by what had happened today, but unwilling to yield an inch in his self-righteousness about it all. I told you so, so don't blame me for any of this, seemed to be his attitude.

"That husband of hers can rot in prison for all I care," he added, as if to himself, stirring the custard in with the syrup from the tin, as he always did.

Molly felt tears rise to her eyes. She held a tissue to her face, not wanting him to see her in this state. She hadn't felt like crying all day, but now, at such a time, there they were, hot tears welling up and spilling out. She stood quickly and went into the kitchen, busying herself with coffee cups. Rollo didn't like to see her crying. It upset the natural order of things. He didn't like to think there was unhappiness in the house. He had enough on his shoulders without having to put up with his wife getting in the way, demanding attention, implying there was something wrong with the way they led their lives. There were things he expected from a wife, and crying and complaining and carrying on weren't amongst them. When he came in late from the bar was the worst time, the time when things were most likely to go wrong, when she had to be on her best behaviour. Not a good time for tears.

"It hasn't been on the telly, has it?" Rollo called from the sitting room. "The cop said there was a camera crew there, outside the flat."

"I don't think so," Molly called back, trying to sound normal. She wouldn't know. She never watched the news.

Molly was always relieved when Rollo got home and there wasn't a fight. It made everything alright again, whatever the rest of the day had been like. Only today hadn't been an ordinary day. It was the day her only child had been killed, shot in the back of her head in her kitchen, by her own husband. Molly had been holding it in all day but couldn't hold it in anymore. She sat at the kitchen table and let the tears flow silently down her cheeks. When she took the coffee in, hoping he wouldn't notice her raw face and swollen eyes, Rollo was asleep.

Inspector Duvenage phoned the next day to report progress, or the lack of it. They had collected lots of evidence at the scene, but were still looking for the murder weapon. They'd taken Tommie in for questioning, but so far he was sticking to his story.

"The man is clever," he said, "and he knows how to sound convincing. After all, he has a psychology degree from UWC and knows all the tricks." The inspector counselled patience. He was sure they'd nail him sooner or later.

Then a man called Comrade Titus phoned to say there was to be a memorial event at the Congregational Church hall in Goodwood on Saturday afternoon at three o'clock, and the family would be welcome. Molly wrote it down and sat and looked at the piece of paper. She didn't know what to make of it. She wondered what Rollo would have to say. If he decided he wasn't going, she could hardly go by herself. Molly and Rollo hardly ever went out together, only to the movies sometimes or to the Wimpy or the fish and chips shop for supper over weekends. Not that often, really.

Molly didn't know what she'd wear. She had an old felt hat with a veil she hadn't worn in years, and a pair of good shoes she never wore either. Her floral dress wouldn't do – something more sombre was required. Perhaps the navy woollen two-piece suit, if it wasn't too warm.

"Titus?" Rollo was sceptical, as she knew he would be, when she told him that evening. He sat at the dining table, an angry scowl on his face, looking at the piece of paper he'd taken from Molly.

"Who's he? You didn't ask him who he was? Why didn't you ask him? I suppose he didn't leave a number."

"He was in a hurry. I didn't have time to ask."

"I can just imagine. And what's a 'memorial event'? Is that what he called it? And why's it in the church hall? Funerals are normally in churches."

"It isn't a funeral. They haven't released the body. I think they'll cremate her. The inspector said it's up to the husband. He's next-of-kin."

"Well, I'm not going – that's for sure."

"You don't think we shouldn't just show up, just for a short while? It might be my only chance to say goodbye to her."

Rollo snorted, stuffing pork sausage into his mouth, washing it down with a Castle straight from the bottle, but didn't say anything more.

On Friday morning, Molly did what she always did on Friday mornings. She went to have her hair done at Mary-Jane's on Voortrekker Road, followed by a cake and coffee at Nino's. She saved all the spare cash she had left over after the grocery shopping and spent it on herself. It was her favourite morning of the week. She always felt pampered and special having her hair washed and set, listening to the hairdresser, fat, unnaturally blonde Marcelle, carry on about her mother and her child and her boyfriend and all the small dramas of her life, feeling reassured that other people's lives were also far from perfect, but that they, too, somehow managed to struggle through.

Marcelle knew not to pry into Molly's life. She knew her life at home was difficult. The telltale signs were there often enough. It sufficed to ask every week how Rollo was, getting the same answer. "He's fine. Nothing ever changes with Rollo." "And Sarah?" "She's fine too."

"Did you see that terrible story about that woman in Goodwood who was murdered by her husband?" asked Marcelle, who always read *Die Son*, because it provided her with talking points that kept her going through the day. "Shot in her head, she was, in her kitchen. My cousin lives in the same block of flats, and she says she's not surprised. She says the husband is one of these illegals from Mozambique. They say he's half-Portuguese, but he's more black than white, to judge by his appearance. Can you imagine it, he's living there in a respectable block of flats in a white area, dressed up in ANC gear all the time, with all these blacks coming and going, having meetings and things? And with a white wife who always looked like there's something wrong with her, with these dark rings around her eyes. She's married to one of *them*, that's what's wrong with her! What do you expect? My cousin says people heard him threatening to do things to her, and now it's happened. So why am I not surprised, hey?"

Molly said nothing. She felt her fists balled tight under the sheet, her nails digging into the soft flesh of her palms. A moment later Marcelle said, "You alright, Mrs Retief? You don't look so good."

Molly was feeling faint and wanted to go home. Come over all funny, she said, looking anxiously at her white face in the mirror. They called a taxi and Marcelle helped her in, saying she should see a doctor just in case.

When Molly got home, the phone was ringing in the hallway. She sat down heavily and picked it up. It was Inspector Duvenage, just checking in, he said, reassuring her they weren't going to let up until they'd nailed the culprit.

"We're getting some useful information from neighbours," he told her. "You know how it is. Leave them for a day or two to jog their memories and they come up with all sorts of stories. Shake the tree a bit and who knows what falls out. They know nothing when you first ask them, nothing out of the ordinary, just ordinary neighbours, but two days later – then they remember all kinds of things. Did you ever hear they fought a lot, Mrs Retief? Did you ever see her with bumps or bruises?"

"No, I didn't."

Molly didn't want to hear anything more about the subject. She felt a headache coming on. She just wanted to take a couple of aspirins and lie down.

On Saturday morning, Rollo went down to the bar at ten thirty, as he always did. "You better get my suit ready if we going to this thing," he said as he went out the door.

Molly was full of nervous energy after he said that. She got out the suit, a pin-striped, double-breasted thing that probably wasn't in fashion anymore, and a good shirt and the ironing board. She took out his good shoes and polished them, and found a decently sombre tie and sponged it. She then took out her navy outfit and made sure it was clean and free of musty smells and moth holes. It was once in a blue moon they ever got dressed up like this. She rushed through her housework, fixed lunch and then sat and waited with the cat on her lap for company. He'd be smelling of drink when he got in. Pray God he wouldn't fall asleep and forget all about it. Or that there wouldn't be a rugby match on that he'd decide was more

were no hitches and they arrived at the hall on time. Molly
. She felt Rollo's hackles rising, his breathing getting louder as

they parked the Mazda. The first thing they saw on entering the hall was the large ANC banner hanging from the table in front. A steady, echoing buzz of voices arose from the twenty or thirty people there, almost all coloureds and Africans, several in ANC Youth League T-shirts. At the front, surrounded by his friends, sat Tommie, his back to them. Molly feared Rollo might create a scene or decide to turn around and head home. He stood and stared with that look on his face that warned there was trouble brewing. Then they saw Inspector Duvenage sitting at the back against the wall, well out of the way. He nodded to them.

They sat down, on plastic chairs spread around from the piles stacked against the walls, feeling self-conscious and out of place. Rollo was not one to put up with situations that made him feel uncomfortable. Molly knew she'd take the brunt of his anger once they were home, he'd let rip later, but that was a small price to pay. For her, being here was important. It wasn't her life, but it was Sarah's, and she couldn't turn her back on her now that she was gone.

A young man came up to them, introduced himself as Comrade Titus, and said there were chairs for them in front. Rollo said they were staying put, at the back, out of the way. He was restrained, but Molly could tell that there was real anger in him, violent anger.

The proceedings began. Comrade Titus welcomed them. Heads turned to look at them, two old white people staring back. She looking embarrassed and anxious, he scowling and displeased. Two men and one woman at the head table stood up and spoke in turn, about Sarah, what a committed partner she was for Comrade Tommie and a committed member of the branch too, about the good work she'd done amongst the victims of violence and the homeless. They talked about Tommie as if he was a victim too, about his family who had fought the Portuguese, although his father was Portuguese himself, and about how he'd joined up to the struggle against apartheid oppression in South Africa. Then people were invited to make contributions from the floor. Molly didn't follow much of what was said after a while, keeping a nervous eye on Rollo, who looked red and puffy in the face as if his blood pressure was going through the roof again.

When it was finished, Rollo was out of the hall while everybody else was still slowly getting to their feet. Molly followed him. They drove home without saying anything. Rollo gripped the steering wheel tightly and chewed his teeth. He went through at least two red traffic lights as if his life depended on it. People hooted at him, but he wasn't in a mood to take heed. As she let herself into the house, Rollo sped away, back to the bar, she knew, to calm his nerves and let off steam. He wouldn't be back till late, she was certain of that, and then very likely his temper would come out and she'd have to put away the breakables. But she was quietly pleased she'd been there, reclaiming part of her daughter for herself, making it known Sarah had a mother.

Molly didn't know why she went out into the unkempt back garden. She might have been looking for dill or parsley left from the lot she'd planted in what had once passed as a vegetable patch. What she found was something else, which explains why she could not recall later what she was doing there. It was a scrunched-up envelope pushed into the compost heap behind the shed. Only a bit of white was visible under the pile of brown lawn clippings that Rollo dumped there when he mowed the lawn. She didn't know why she pulled it out, what on earth she thought she was looking for. Perhaps it was just the incongruity of it, a fresh-looking bit of white paper underneath grass that had been there for weeks, moist and mouldering, disturbed by the cat that had climbed up and rummaged in the warm mulch. Almost as if someone had deliberately pushed it down out of sight, only to be revealed because of a cat's curiosity. She picked it up, shook off the dirt, straightened it out. It was Sarah's handwriting. No question about it. Addressed to Rollo Retief, just the two words on the front of the envelope, the Rs sloping forward and the ls backward. The envelope had already been torn open and there was a letter inside on crinkly airmail paper, a single sheet that had been crumpled into a ball in someone's fist before being reinserted in the envelope and disposed of.

Molly looked around, frightened someone might be watching her. She put the letter in her pinafore pocket and rushed back inside. She sat down at the kitchen table, trembling, and held the thin paper open flat on the tabletop as she read it.

> *Rollo* (it said) –
> *You know what you did to me as a child and yet you keep*
> *on denying it. This can't go on anymore. My own life is at a*
> *standstill until I get closure on this issue, which still haunts me*
> *and makes my life a living hell. My husband knows all about*
> *it. We have decided that you should be confronted and made to*

own up to everything or else we are going to the police. I have
already written a thirty-page statement. So, we are coming,
Tommie and me, on Saturday morning to your house at ten for
an intervention, where you will have an opportunity to admit
the wrong you did me and ask for my forgiveness, failing which
I will have no choice but to go to the police and lay a charge.
Please make sure my mother is present, because she has to know
the truth as well.
  Sarah Nobrega

Molly sat and stared at the piece of paper for a while, not knowing what
to make of it, thinking maybe it isn't what it seems to be, maybe there's
an explanation. Then she noticed the date written in the top right-hand
corner – two days before Sarah was killed. She got up, took out the frying
pan, found the matches she kept for blackouts, put the letter in the pan
and lit it. She watched it catch fire, those poisonous words decomposing
into blackened fragments, curling up, breaking off, dissolving into ash.
She lit another match until there was nothing left of it. She shook the pan
out in the garden and washed it in the sink.

Molly set about making supper, cutting up potatoes and tomatoes and
carrots for the lamb shank stew. When she'd laid the table and cleaned up
the kitchen, she sat down in front of the telly and waited for her husband's
return, much like any other Saturday night. Of all the nights of the week,
Saturday was the most fraught, the night there was most likely to be a
scene. She knew she might end up locking herself in Sarah's old room,
as she had often done in the past. But whatever happened, she knew that
tomorrow he'd apologise, say he'd had too much to drink, and then they'd
get on with their lives.

MICHAEL WILLIAMS

Williams began writing "crime radio plays" for Springbok Radio while a student at the University of Cape Town and had his first novel, *My Father and I* (1986), published when he was twenty-five years old. His first musical – *Siddartha, Birth of a Dream* – was produced at Kathmandu's Royal Nepal Theatre. He has written libretti for several symphonic operas – *Enoch, Prophet of God, Sacred Bones, Buchuland,* and *Poet & Prophetess* – premiering in opera houses in Pretoria, Windhoek, Cape Town and Umeå, Sweden, as well as a number of operas for young people based on African mythology. These have toured to townships and schools throughout South Africa.

Of the ten novels he's penned, three are "Jake Mulligan Mystery" novels – *Who Killed Jimmy Valentine?*, *Hijack City* and *The Eighth Man*.

As General Manager of Cape Town Opera, Williams says, "Writing crime fiction is a good antidote to the drama of keeping an opera company alive in Africa."

His keen sense of story shines through in the chilling tale, *Boys*.

Boys

MICHAEL WILLIAMS

THURSTON PETERSEN KNEW THERE HAD TO BE A FRIEND FOR HIM SOME-where in this world; a ten-year-old boy who liked spitting in his hand and giving himself a hard-on. A boy who also thought the world was fucked up. Someone who would understand about Thurston's plans to run away from his parents and about the terrible dreams he had at night. The faces of boys staring at him from a dark hole, their sad eyes filled with fear, their hands pleading with him. In his dreams his teacher made him do what he didn't want to do. The dreams always made him wet his bed.

And why was it that when he woke up in the morning, with sun streaming through his window, the morning chatter on the next-door neighbour's radio, everything was all right again? Why was it so easy to forget everything the next morning and pretend none of it had happened?

Thurston never understood why he always lost his friends. They would come and go through his life like the taxis speeding along the highway from Strandfontein, here the one moment and disappearing into the streets of Mitchell's Plain the next, never to be seen again.

His uncle living in the backroom always had something to say to him, "Why don't you go play with your friends, Thurston?"

As if he had a room full of boys he could choose from! As if friends were as easy to pick up as empties! As if friendship was something every-one had! Thurston knew that somewhere there had to be a boy who liked to swim in the brown waters of the quarry, who enjoyed the feel of skin against skin, and the drawing of secret patterns in the sand and drinking green cooldrink mixed with sherbet and saying fuck and crap and shit and *jou ma se poes* whenever he liked. He couldn't be the only boy in the whole of Mitchell's Plain without a real friend.

His teacher said the best place to find friends was at the Blue Moon Café. Thurston wondered how his teacher knew where to find boys. He didn't question him. Teacher was always right.

So he went to the Blue Moon Café and hung around at the entrance, hands in his pockets, one foot up against the wall, looking, he hoped, as if he was waiting for a friend. At last, when he had the courage, he sauntered into the café, staring longingly at the cooldrinks stacked in the fridge and watched as a boy took out a can of Fanta Grape, split open the lid and drank the cooldrink as he walked up to the till. How he envied the way the teenager slapped a ten-rand note down on the counter as if there were hundreds more of them in his back pocket. Thurston watched, jealous of the teenager's confidence, hating how easily he swept the change into his wallet. He turned away when the teenager looked at him as if he was a pile of shit.

Thurston searched through the change in his pocket for a two-rand coin to feed to the Destroyer. The teenager was there already, putting his money in the slot.

Standing beside the video game, watching, was a boy – the teacher had been right once again – a smaller boy, perhaps eight or nine years old. Thurston walked to the other side of the video screen and pretended to be interested in Kung-fu Jack's high kick to the head of the Destroyer. He sneaked a look at the boy across from him.

Eyes like blue glass marbles.

He had seen him before. The boy was at his school but they had never spoken to each other before.

Thurston thought of smiling, but the corners of his mouth wouldn't turn into a smile. He was too afraid he would be laughed at, too afraid the boy wouldn't smile back.

They both watched the game in silence. The teenager jerked the stick to spin Kung-fu Jack into a full frontal attack: fists flying, knee kicks, head butts, finger jabs. Then the teenager swore and slammed his flat hand against the screen as the Destroyer killed him.

"Hey, Mansoer, you break my machine, I'll break your head," the shop-keeper shouted, looking up from the newspaper sprawled open on his counter.

"*Jou ma se poes*," said Mansoer under his breath and winked at Thurston.

Thurston knew he should smile now. The boy with the marble eyes was looking at him, waiting for him to speak, but he didn't know what to say. His tongue lay thick in his mouth. Mansoer scratched in his wallet for more change.

"Can I play?" the small boy asked.

"You got money?" asked Mansoer.

"No."

"Well, tough shit."

"I've got two rand," Thurston blurted out, holding up the coin to the small boy as an offering.

"Thank you very much!" said Mansoer, snatching the coin from his hand and feeding it into the machine.

The Destroyer jerked into life. Eyes of fire emerged from the black screen. A tongue snaked its way out of a cavernous mouth filled with razor-sharp teeth. Loud plastic music filled the shop. Red lights flashed a warning. The game was on. Kung-fu Jack lived again.

"That's his money!" the marble-eyed boy shouted. "You took his money!"

"Mansoer, leave the *laaitjie* alone. Mansoer!" The shopkeeper smacked the counter with a sawn-off broom handle. "If I have to get up from this chair and come over there, you'll be bloody sorry."

Mansoer kicked the machine and sneered at Thurston, "You fucking moffie," he said sauntering out of the café.

Thurston was alone with the boy with the glass-blue marble eyes.

"You play," offered Thurston quietly. "I'm no good at these games."

"Okay."

Thurston pretended to watch the screen but he stole glances at the boy. Could this be a new friend? Someone he could play with? The boy looked ordinary enough – his cinnamon-coloured skin, his black hair curling around his ears and those eyes, eyes bluer than any sea or any sky he had ever seen.

The Destroyer destroyed. The boy was not very good at the game and the machine died and was silent. Game over.

He looked up at Thurston and shrugged apologetically. "He gets me every time. You got any more money?" he asked.

"At home."

"Shall we get it?"

Thurston nodded. "Okay." He swallowed the word, knowing he should smile now, but there was nothing to smile about. The boy wasn't really his friend. Not yet.

"Let's go past my house first," said the small boy. "I can steal some empties from the old lady next door. She'll never notice."

"Ja, okay." Then Thuston said, "But why don't we go for a swim first? At the quarry."

Thurston was surprised by the smile that broke across the boy's face as they left the Blue Moon Café.

"Ja, that's cool. It's so hot. Good idea."

"What's your name?" asked Thurston shyly.

"Lance Cooper, but everyone calls me Coops."

"Let's go, Coops," he said, giddy with happiness that the boy had offered him his nickname.

"Hey, where do you think you two are going?" shouted Mansoer as they walked quickly across the street. Mansoer pushed himself away from the wall and started jogging across the road after them. Thurston did not want to play with Mansoer. He had made a friend. Coops. This afternoon it was just Coops and him. He had to get away from Mansoer.

"We'd better run; he's following us," said Thurston, looking back and seeing Mansoer following them. "We'll split up. You go that way and then I'll meet you at the quarry. He'll never catch us." As Thurston ran he felt the wonderfully warm feeling of friendship. He and Coops were a team. They were doing something together and shutting out the rest of the world. Having a friend was so much fun.

*   *   *

The old slate quarry had a swimming hole so deep that none of the neighbourhood boys had ever touched its bottom. Thurston played with Lance Cooper among the rocks until they were both sweating. He liked his new friend, he liked how soft he was to touch and how his eyes – those blue-blue eyes! – grew wide when he showed him how big he could make himself. He was only sorry that he accidentally hurt the boy by touching him too much. His new friend started crying and wanted to go home and everything was going sour.

That was when Thurston said they should go for a swim.

"It will be all right with a swim. Everything will be all right after a swim. Come on, come feel the water. It will be fine. Please don't cry anymore," said Thurston.

Coops liked that idea. It was hot and the water was cool.

"Let's see if we can touch the bottom," Thurston said, climbing up the rocks.

The boy did not go home; he followed Thurston and climbed up the side of the quarry. Perhaps it will be okay after all, thought Thurston.

Thurston knew that the swimming hole was as deep as sin – he had warned other boys never to swim there – yet it was Thurston who, after Lance's third failed attempt to touch the bottom, had suggested the stones, a few flat, round stones in the pockets of his gym shorts.

"When you get to the bottom you take the stones out and you'll shoot up to the top," Thurston said, offering a stone.

"Will it work?"

"Of course it will," he said, stuffing stones into the boy's pockets, until they bulged into hard blocks on either side of his thin legs.

They stood on a ledge above the swimming hole looking down onto its still, brown surface.

"There's an old car down there," said Thurston.

"A car?"

"An old Chevie."

"What colour?"

"Brown."

Lance laughed. Thurston seldom made jokes.

"You going to jump?" challenged Thurston. "Or are you shit-scared?"

"You'll follow after me?"

Thurston nodded.

"See you later!"

The last words that Lance Cooper would ever speak echoed faintly in the quarry as he jumped, arms flailing, his small, slender body falling rapidly through space, entering the water as cleanly as a pin, and disappearing.

The brown water of the swimming hole was always still. Warm, too, like bath water. Thurston knew that once Lance began sinking, his ears would ring with the pressure. He knew the water would become increasingly cold. The darkness would seize him in an icy grip that would force the breath from the boy's body. Then the thought of being alone in a liquid tomb would hurry the onset of panic. Lance would experience a desire for light, air, sky, so overwhelming that he would turn frantically, kicking furiously, his lungs contracting, his body rejecting the darkness and striving to break through the water, up, up, up into longed-for sunshine.

Would the thought of his mother and her warm hands tucking him into bed flash through his mind as he lost consciousness? Would he think of his father? A favourite pet, perhaps? Or would he think of his new best friend?

Thurston sat on the ledge, dangled his legs over the side, and observed with interest a slight disturbance on the water's surface – was it air from Lance Cooper's lungs? Thurston wondered idly what drowning felt like, the fear, the futile clawing, and the deadly intake of water.

He emptied his pocket of stones. He held the last stone and rubbed it thoughtfully between his fingers. He threw it up into the air, watched its arc, its rapid fall, and the water below swallowing it as swiftly as it had done Lance. The brown water soon become still again.

Thurston stood up and clambered down the quarry wall to where his clothes lay. He never considered jumping in after the boy. It was time to go home. Supper would be on the table and he dared not be late. He knew the punishment that awaited him if he was late. He dressed hurriedly, looking once over his shoulder at the water.

Had Coops reached the bottom? he wondered.

* * *

The local police made some effort to find Lance Cooper. The station commander of Philippi sent one of his constables to interview the child's parents and a few of his friends at school. Yes, they had sent Lance off to school, said the distraught parents. No, they had not accompanied him to the school, but his teachers reported that Lance had been at school that day. He was an average pupil, said the principal and no, he didn't think there were problems at home. After school his friends had seen him walk towards his house and no, none of them had played with him, or had seen him ever again. Coops was a lonely boy. It seemed he didn't have many friends.

When it was Thurston Peterson's turn to be interviewed he shook his head in response to all the questions put to him. He stood before the policeman, smiling, concerned and eager to help. He was fascinated by the policeman's revolver; once his father had allowed him to hold a similar weapon. He remembered the grave weight in his hand, the oily feel of the handle, the black hole of its caw.

"So, Mr Petersen, you are the teacher of the Grade Four class? Is that right?"

"Yes, that's right."

"Lance Cooper was not in your class?"

"No. It's a big school."

"Did you see Lance after school on the day he disappeared?" the policeman asked, for the twentieth time that day.

Thurston's head moved slowly from side to side.

"Do you know if there was any problem with the other boys in the playground? Any bullying? Is there anything you might think of that could be a reason for his disappearance?"

Another slow shake from Thurston.

"And you don't know where he could have gone?"

A slow, sad shake.

"Well, if you remember something, you will let us know?" ordered the policeman, standing up and wondering, now that it was almost four o'clock, whether he shouldn't go straight home and not bother about returning to the police station.

He would file the report tomorrow. Pass the case on. Forget it soon enough.

"If I think of anything, of course I'll let you know." Thurston fingered the policeman's card, then asked, "Have you ever killed anyone with that?" pointing at the revolver on the man's belt.

"Yes, I have," said the policeman, startled by the question.

Thurston Peterson asked then, as if in awe, "What did it feel like?"

Postscript: Each month an average of fifteen children are reported missing in the Cape Town area alone. Ten of these fifteen are usually found, but in each month five children between the ages of three and fourteen disappear. They are misplaced. Lost. Absent. Gone. In the Western Cape Province each year sixty children disappear without trace. Their faces appear momentarily, if at all, in local newspapers, on notice boards at shopping centres and police stations, and then they are forgotten, erased, by adults engrossed with their adult society, which has little time or patience for the inconvenience of missing children.

JANE TAYLOR

In 2006 Taylor won the Olive Schreiner Prize for her detective novel *Of Wild Dogs*. She's penned a successful play, *Ubu and the Truth Commission*, as well as an opera libretto, *The Confessions of Zeno* – both with artist-director William Kentridge and Handspring Puppet Company. As a scholar and cultural theorist, she works in a range of media in visual arts, performance and literary studies, and holds the Skye Chair of Dramatic Art at the University of the Witwatersrand, Johannesburg.

"In detective fiction," Taylor says, "comprehension is teased from the incomprehensible. The crime story variously withholds and releases information in order to lead and mislead; to reward or to frustrate the reader. From the point of view of law and order, crime is outside of society. A divided world exists, with good and evil on either side of a boundary line. However," she adds, "it's also possible to imagine a world which holds all within its generous embrace, including criminality, the deviant and the perverse."

The Labourer is Worthy of His Hire, a carefully crafted narrative that threads between these two world views, reads like poetry.

The Labourer is Worthy of his Hire

AUGUST 2008

JANE TAYLOR

WHEN IT FINALLY CAME, IT SEEMED AS IF IT HAD BEEN ABOUT TO HAPPEN all along.

Every African had become a foreigner.

I, who had waited all my white life to discover whether I belonged or not, seemed to have been given a reprieve. For now at least, the vengeance that was being enacted was against black Africans. They were under attack in our midst, yet this time the scythe had left us standing. So it was in part out of a sense of relief and gratitude that I found myself delivering six blankets and a box of groceries to the back door of the local church on the fourth day of the attacks against strangers in the city.

I had intended to do this drop in the afternoon, but through bad planning which was entirely my own fault I was delayed by rush-hour traffic at five thirty in the evening. That is often the way. Darkness and light were already slanting on alternate crimson and puce-coloured shafts against the thick grime of the urban sky. The church was not far from where I live in the northern suburbs, and it had, over the past several years, changed entirely in character. At sunset there were the familiar clear-throated bells I associated with my childhood, but the traditions of modest piety had been displaced by energetic celebration. At any time of the day, the precinct of the churchyard itself was filled with rich and ecstatic singing, mostly, it seemed, in French. The great polyphonies of spontaneous choirs poured from the simple oak church doors, and statuesque men and women wearing indigo and orange swathes of cloth gathered in interested communion along the avenue of jacarandas, some loitering beside four-wheel-drive vehicles, some sitting on their haunches in the dust, grateful for the welcome shelter of the old trees.

I had heard all of the usual stories: these migrants were the real cause of the new crime wave; they were dealing drugs; they were stealing jobs from honest South Africans. I had no real experience to go on in making a judgment, and I was rather pleased to have a way of examining these assessments at first hand. Perhaps the encounter would give me an opportunity to understand who it was that had moved into my city.

So it was with some curiosity that I made my way to the church, with the simple donation bundled in the back of my car. It was not a tithe – nowhere near – but nonetheless I trusted that the gift would help to assuage my guilt when later that evening I was compelled to watch the latest news report of xenophobic violence. The grim apocalypse that had been cast abroad the night before, still repeated itself in my mind's eye. The scenes showed what we were willing to do to strangers in our midst. One kind of man douses his neighbour with petrol. Yes. But another man touches the flame to the flapping tail of a soaked shirt.

At the church a young African lay preacher was on duty, and he received the unwieldy carton of canned goods and boxed milk. His attitude toward me seemed rather skeptical, not entirely trusting, but he was helpful enough and pleased to receive the delivery. I left him navigating his way into the church with the cardboard carton and returned to my car to retrieve the folded blankets. The meagre solace of soft cloth against my cheek comforted me as I entered the vestry. The man had disappeared, and so I returned to the body of the church and left the blankets on a pew at the rear. There was almost no light in the building and I didn't linger. We have in recent months become accustomed to minimising fuel usage. Those of us with electricity remind ourselves to turn off the heated towel rail after a morning bath.

As I stepped out onto the rough gravel path, I noticed him sitting alone on the stump of the sawn-off limb of a vast pepper tree. The last light in the sky turned him into a silhouette. He beckoned to me and I wandered over toward him. There is a moral authority that belongs to a man of the cloth, even a lay preacher, and so, despite the lateness of the hour, I felt compelled. Astonishingly, he was drinking from a half-jack, and he held the bottle out to me. The lawlessness which I felt abroad in the city seemed to have entered even this haven.

"No thanks."

He grinned as if with foreknowledge. I don't like to be considered smug, and his expression made me want to explain myself to him.

"I'm busy working. I have to get back to my writing, and if I start now, I'll go on drinking when I get home, and my evening will be shot."

Language is a curious thing.

He looked at me intensely with an expression of suspicion. Then he nodded.

"A writer?" It was a question. He formed his fist into a simple ball, with thumb and index finger holding an invisible pen, as he waved the hand with a flourish in front of me. "What do you write?"

"Stories," I replied. "Mainly short stories."

"Oh. Not poetry?" he looked disappointed. "In my country I used to write poetry."

"Will you go back? To your country? To writing poetry?"

"No, I don't belong to my country anymore. I don't belong to poetry anymore."

Thrusting the half-jack of liquor between his lips, he drew off a huge gulp which made him gasp. "Perhaps I belong now to short stories." He smiled disarmingly at me. The anxiety of mistrust in our early encounter began to dissipate, and I became interested in this elegant young man, with his high forehead, narrow chin and broad cheeks. I tried to locate his accent. Was it the Cameroons? The question rose up inside me. I then tried to decipher him by reading the characteristics of his features. What did I know about the Cameroons?

In recent days it had become impossible to ask a black man in South Africa where he came from, and I reckoned I would just have to wait until he was ready to tell me.

He caught me glancing at the half-jack in his hand and held it out to me once again after wiping the neck against his sleeve. I accepted and noticed that it was cane spirits. The rush of cold heat burned into me as I pulled at the bottle like a calf. I was beginning to surrender myself. I don't remember whether we exchanged names, but in my own mind I remember him as Claude. How could I find out about him, about why he was here?

"If you were a short story, what would that story be?" I asked him.

"Ah, well." He looked away. The defined line of his jaw now echoed the horizon behind him as he stared out across his shoulder towards the North. He seemed to have separated himself from me, as though taken up again by the continent that lay behind him. Perhaps he had been waiting to tell it to someone, because he then looked back at me with the intensity of a child.

"This is the real story. There is another story, also, about how I got here, how I come to be working at the church. But this is the true story of how I first left my home."

I felt a great sense of oneness with this man who was about to disclose the history of himself to me, a complete outsider. He was about to tell me how he ended up as a refugee in Johannesburg. His inflections were French but he spoke flawless English with a slight American accent.

"I was just a boy, in my second-last year of school. I enjoyed the mission school. I especially enjoyed reading: the wars of Caesar, the French Revolution, the battles for liberation in Africa. But in that last year at school I fell in love. It was no ordinary affair. I fell in love with money."

Claude's cane-scented breath felt like ice against my ear.

"How do I know it was love? How does one know such things? I felt incomplete without it. I couldn't imagine a future apart. I spent long hours at my school desk dreaming about what we would do together over the weekend."

I was about to smile when I realised from the look on his face that he was speaking in earnest.

"My friends always seemed to have more than I did, and they could get things and do things. They had cellphones. My best friend even had a computer. But I didn't want those *things*. I wanted the money. It became an obsession. Do you know what it is to have an obsession? I sometimes would just say that word, and it comforted me to think of myself as a man obsessed. That idea made sense. Nothing else engaged me. I lost interest in reading, I stopped eating regular meals. I began to dream of having more money than you could ever imagine. There were drug dealers – they had money. There were traders – they had money. The Big Man Mbangos, with their funeral parlours – they had money. Such men inspired me, made me believe that one day I would be like that. I had decided early that I would not be satisfied to climb the ladder just three steps up like my father had done.

"Then a rich man arrived in our area, what you would call a stinking rich man. I had never seen anything like it. He wore a black suit, and a yellow shirt. On his head he always had a brown cowboy hat made of real leather and he carried a fat briefcase. I asked my friend who he was. My friend laughed: 'That's Mr Wages,' he said. 'He works with the church. He's from the United States.' That's what we called it; not 'America' or 'the USA.' We all, in my crowd, called it 'the United States.'"

"Mr Wages?" it was a question.

"That's not his real name. It's what we called him because he always had piles of cash," was the answer.

"After school I managed to follow Mr Wages about. He carried his brief-case everywhere with him. When he crossed the busy street he held it close against his body, as if it were an infant. 'That must be where he keeps the wages,' I told myself. In my head I began to calculate how much money such a bag might carry, and I tried to use x-ray vision to see what kind of currency it was. If dollars, there was no limit to what it could be worth. I watched him go into shops. He drank coffee at the European coffee bar; he bought a stack of CDs from the music vendor; he picked up a mask carved out of black wood. Everywhere he went he seemed to convert money into objects. I stopped myself from feeling sorry about what I was planning to do by reminding myself that this American was going around my country handing out dollar bills on each street corner.

"It seemed as if Mr Wages believed that God was protecting him because I never once saw him with a bodyguard, even though he carried that money around with him all over town. Over the weekend I watched an American movie about a bank robbery. That was when it occurred to me that the only way I would persuade the man to give me his bag was if I had a gun. Guns were not easy to get hold of in my neighbourhood. We were still a quiet country. I had to find out from friends at school how I could get in touch with a man who could sell me one. 'Alain,' they told me. He was a cool guy, thought he was a movie-star gangster. That was the man I needed.

"Of course, the dealer just laughed at me. 'What, little sparrow,' he chuckled, 'do you want with a gun?' He was smoking a Gauloise cigarette, and jeered openly in my face. In order to win back my honour, I had to tell him the whole story. Finally, we made a deal. If I would identify the man, he would let me be his accomplice. He even let me borrow a pair of his gloves, though both of us knew that I didn't need them. We would do the robbery together, and he would split the money with me. I was, you remember, only sixteen years old.

"That Friday night we met near where I knew Mr Wages was working. I was wearing the gloves. In the end I was pleased of this because Alain instructed me that I had to go up to the American, and shake him by the hand so that it was clear who he was. I knew I would be sweating. The gloves would be my shield. They could hide my identity and my intentions. Then we discussed the plot.

"'Wait until the target is walking in an alley or somewhere alone. Snatch the bag while I challenge him with the gun. Nothing can go wrong. As soon as he sees the gun, he'll give it up. They always do.'

"Alain let me hold it, by the way. The gun, I mean. I held it in my hand and it felt as if it had always been there, as if my hand was meant to hold the gun."

Claude paused, looked out into the dark sky. I could see that he was no longer looking at me.

"'The Lord trieth the righteous,' the Bible tells us. Also, it tells us that we will not be tried beyond our endurance, but I was. It was a stupid and childish plot and the man who had become my partner was stupid, and I now understand, childish. There are many childish men who never ask themselves 'What if?' I didn't know that then. The simplest solution for a man with a gun is to use it.

"That's what I know now. I was hiding behind a bin when Mr Wages entered the alley. He had a broad chest and big arms, and when Alain stepped forward, I realised that he would be no match for the American without that gun in his pocket.

"Mr Wages looked right at him – stared at him, face to face. It was not, I think, a hostile stare from the American. For a moment I thought that he had recognised Alain, but perhaps he had only recognised his intentions. Perhaps that was the deciding moment, because before I could run forward, Alain had his gun pointing directly at the man's face. Mr Wages tried to raise the briefcase with his hand, and a crimson patch opened in his glossy black throat, as if he had suddenly grown the wattle of a ground hornbill.

"'The wages,' he said, 'the wages,' as he collapsed like a bull onto his knees.

"Alain turned back to me. His face was filled with the crazy frenzy of a hyena. 'The fool,' he shouted. 'The stupid old man doesn't know he's already dead. He's trying to bribe me.'

"A soft noise was bubbling from the mouth of the man who was becoming a body.

"Alain snatched up the briefcase and ran out of the alley and across the main road where big transport trucks were streaming past like bullets. I pursued him over the highway to the big tree. I only just made it. My ears were ringing and I had to pause on the curb to steady my nerves. Sometimes I still hear the whine of those trucks as they charge down the road at me. As I hunched over gasping, I could see Alain where he had sheltered himself behind the tree trunk. Just as I arrived he tipped the contents out of the briefcase by inverting it and shaking it. Sometimes you will see someone shake a child like that if they won't stop crying.

"The bundles were coughed out of the throat of the bag, and wads of money scattered onto the ground. Alain snatched one up. Flipping the stack with his thumb he let out a cry – you know that terrible cry you hear when a dog is run over. Then he ran like a madman into the bush.

"Cautiously I approached the tree, keeping my eye open for a snake. I had heard that some men keep a snake in their bag to protect their possessions. Then I looked at the bundles of money. I had never seen real American dollars before, although I had seen them in movies. I knew they were green, 'greenbacks'. I picked up one bundle. The money looked alright, and it had the face of Abraham Lincoln on it. I recognised him. I had studied about him in school. But some of the bundles on the ground looked strange. I examined what I held in my hand. I turned the bundle over. On the other side of the 'banknote' were some words printed in red. It took me a while to understand those words I remembered from the Bible. Mr Wages, you see, was a preacher, a missionary from the Baptist church. That's was why he came out here, giving up his air conditioning for our red dust and yellow heat. It was his calling."

The dark had now enfolded Claude, who all but disappeared. I could just make out his profile in the glow from the tip of his cigarette. His voice was more of a presence than he himself was. An orange glow from the city radiated off the hill below us, and I heard two gunshots in the distance. Sitting there beside this lean traveller, I did not know what to make of his story. Was this why Claude had fled his home? Was he a hardened killer? Was he a petty criminal, a misguided fool? I could make no meaning of the encounter, and despite our time together he remained a foreigner to me. Claude seemed to intuit my uncertainty.

"You don't believe the story?" He reached into his pocket. "Here," he said. "I have proof. One of the bank notes."

He thrust a piece of paper into my hand, and flicked on his Bic cigarette lighter. In the dim light I could see a picture of Abraham Lincoln on a green background.

Claude peered at me through the darkness, watching my reaction. "Turn it over," he said.

I did so. There in red letters was the familiar legend:

The wages of sin is death. (Romans 6:23)

After several moments he commented. "Once I thought it was meant for me. Perhaps it's meant for you."

My white hand gleamed like wax in the small pool of light. Somewhere in the distance I heard another three gunshots. They now seemed closer, and the banknote between my fingers began to blur as an uncontrollable shaking possessed me.

MICHAEL STANLEY

Long-time friends Michael Sears and Stanely Trollip are the writing team Michael Stanley. Taking time out from varied careers, in academia and business, they have enjoyed a number of flying safaris to southern Africa, with Botswana a favourite destination. Their many adventures include tracking lions at night, fighting bush fires on the Savuti plains in northern Botswana, and being charged by elephant. On a memorable plane trip the door popped open over the Kalahari, scattering navigation maps across the desert. The idea of leaving a murdered body in the veld for hyenas to destroy – as a perfect way to get rid of a body – came to them on one of these trips after which they wrote their first novel *A Carrion Death* (2008).

"But the intriguing thing about a perfect murder," they agree, "is that it never can be perfect. The intricate plotting of a murder mystery seduced us both, and resulted in our debut novel." Look out for the sequel *A Deadly Trade* (2009), also featuring Detective Bengu, nicknamed *Kubu* meaning "hippopotamus" in Setswana.

Kubu, both endearing and astute, has a very different sort of puzzle to unravel in *Neighbours*.

Neighbours

MICHAEL STANLEY

THERE WAS TROUBLE ABOUT THE FENCE AND TROUBLE ABOUT THE DOG, but the worst trouble was about the goat.

Part of the problem was that no one in Gabane liked Nonyane. When he took over the small trading store in the village he insisted on cash. To the well-off customers it was: "Dumela, Mma Molotsi. How is your sister? And your fine mother?" But for most he would add up the items, announce the price and hold out his hand for money.

Kutsi was a friendly man and there was much sympathy for him over the issue of the fence. He had needed additional street frontage to fit in a large double gate for the delivery truck that was his livelihood. To achieve this he had erected the fence at an angle to the road, before Nonyane came to the neighbouring land. A small wedge of the next property was thus included by Kutsi's fence. Enough for the gate and the large garage he built for his truck.

Nonyane, however, spotted this infringement almost immediately.

"Rra Kutsi. There is a problem with your fence. It is not in the proper place. This section of it is on my side. And so your goats and fowls are on my side also."

"Rra Nonyane. Good day, and I hope you are well?" As there was no response he plunged on. "I am well, although you did not ask. It is true that the fence is a little crooked. The man I paid to put it up was not too clever. He overcharged me, too. However, all the land belongs to the village and is given by the chief – as you well know – and the chief has accepted the arrangement. I have had no complaints before."

Nonyane was unimpressed by this argument. "Why would anyone else complain? It is my land that has been stolen." Kutsi's mongrel, Bina, trotted over to the two and immediately started barking at Nonyane, jumping up and down and dancing from side to side. Kutsi laughed and walked away, leaving Nonyane to continue the argument with the dog.

Nonyane, furious about the fence and Kutsi's rudeness, took the matter to the local kgotla. When next the elders met with the chief to debate matters of importance to the village, Nonyane made his complaint. It was a conundrum. Kutsi had certainly taken more of the street frontage than was fair but no one had objected. Could it not be argued that the layout was now altered by tradition? It was so argued. And what of the garage? It would be very expensive to move. Still, by what right did Kutsi take the extra land in the first place? He could have asked the chief for more land, but admitted that he had not done so. The matter was argued back and forth by the elders at the kgotla while Chief Nkosi listened.

Nkosi was a wise man. He knew that a peaceful life required compromise. That right and wrong, like beauty, sometimes lay in the eye of the beholder. He also knew that the time to intervene was when all the others had had their say. He held up his hand for quiet.

"Is it not so," he asked, "that the use of the land in the village is my gift?" There was nodded agreement. "I have given land use to Kutsi, and I have given it to Nonyane. So this is what I shall do. I will take back the wedge of Nonyane's land that Kutsi mistakenly fenced and give it to Kutsi." He held up his hand again to still the excitement of both sides. "But for this favour, I shall require a fine goat. And this goat I shall give to Nonyane in compensation for what he has lost. It is my wish that Nonyane and Kutsi live beside each other in peace."

Everyone thought this a wise decision. Although it was not in his nature to be generous, Kutsi was careful to give the chief a fine goat, not his best but still a good specimen. Anything less would be an insult, not to Nonyane, but to the chief. Nonyane feigned disappointment with the outcome, but actually he was quite happy with the goat. It was plump, had good confirmation, and an attractive, groomed coat. Things were peaceful between the neighbours for a while.

*   *   *

Unfortunately Bina was not happy, and the goat was not happy. Bina had taken a dislike to Nonyane and barked whenever he came near the fence. It was particularly irritating for Nonyane to be barked at by a dog standing on what he still felt was his land. The goat wanted to join the rest of his herd on Kutsi's side of the fence. It was forever trying to break through the fence, bleating its disapproval at the enforced separation. To make things worse, Bina now regarded the goat as an intruder and vigorously fended off its advances with barks and snarls.

Then Bina started barking at night, for no apparent reason, racing up and down the fence. Sometimes Kutsi could see a light late into the night. It was very suspicious. People who worked hard and feared God went to bed early and rose early. They didn't wander around late at night causing other people's dogs to bark. Indeed, why was Bina so set against Nonyane? What was it that Nonyane did in the early hours of the morning? These were good questions, Kutsi thought, and he put them to Nonyane when he came to the fence to complain about the noise.

"Your dog keeps me awake all night. He barks for no reason." Nonyane lent across the fence, momentarily reoccupying part of his stolen land.

"What is it that you do there late at night? Sometimes the light is on when I call the dog in."

"The light is on because the barking wakes me up! What I do – when your flea-bitten dog permits it – is to sleep! Are you an idiot?"

"Bina never caused trouble before you came. He doesn't like you. Why is that?"

"Perhaps he barked at the people who lived here before. How would I know?"

Kutsi shrugged. "Dogs bark at strangers. That is what they are for. It is the way of dogs."

Nonyane clenched his teeth. "We will see about that," he said.

At this point the goat made a foray at the fence, almost knocking into Nonyane.

Kutsi smiled broadly. "He knows where he ought to be," he said turning away. He added over his shoulder: "It is the way of goats."

A few days later, the morning after a night of prolonged barking, as Kutsi reversed his decrepit delivery truck from the garage, he saw Bina lying near the fence. Immediately he knew something was wrong. The dog always bounded up to the vehicle as he left, but today there was no such exuberance. He jumped from the truck and walked over. Bina was lying on his side with his tongue hanging out. He was dead.

"Thobela. Thobela, come here," Kutsi shouted. His wife hurried from the house, two children in tow.

"Look what has happened to Bina," he exclaimed.

"Someone has poisoned him," Thobela said.

"Bina would never eat anything I didn't give her."

"It's Nonyane," Thobela cried, pointing across the fence. "He hated the poor dog. He is certainly to blame for this." She picked up a handful of sand and threw it over the fence towards Nonyane's house.

"And what about the children?" she asked, pulling them close. "This man is a bad man. I'm scared for the children. Maybe he will kill them for muti. Aai, I am afraid!"

Kutsi shook his head. "He is a pig, but he wouldn't dare touch us."

They buried the dog at the back of the garden. Kutsi read a verse from the Bible, where Noah had the animals two by two. Thobela held the crying children. Then they threw earth into the grave and covered it with stones.

Kutsi vowed that he would get even.

*　　*　　*

The next day Nonyane came home, and there was no sign of the goat. It infuriated him that the goat still wanted to return to his enemy. He had fed it for nearly a month, but it had no loyalty. He checked the fence. Sure enough he found a place where the goat could have forced a way through. The man who had built Kutsi's fence without any geometry skills, also had very little engineering expertise. The wires were not tensed; the fence was not taut.
He stormed to his neighbour's house. Thobela opened the door in response to his angry banging. She shrank back. "Rra Nonyane, what do you want? We are having our supper." But the man forced past her into the kitchen where the family was gathered around the table. He glared at Kutsi.

"Where is my goat?" he demanded.

Kutsi looked at the food in front of him, untouched, awaiting the saying of grace. "How should I know where your goat is? Why should I care?"

Nonyane looked at the food. "What is it you are eating?" he demanded.

Thobela replied. "It is stew," she said. "Goat stew, if you want to know."

Nonyane could hardly speak. "He came through the fence, didn't he? Or you stole him!"

Kutsi looked at him. "I bought half a goat in town. Some is in the fridge. Some is here in the stew."

"You are eating my goat!"

Kutsi shrugged. "I don't know whose goat it is. I bought the goat in town – paid far too much for it, especially if it was yours. Now you must go, so that we can thank Jesus for our food and satisfy our hunger."

Nonyane glared at him, his face full of anger. He turned and left. Kutsi looked satisfied, but Thobela was scared. She ate very little.

The next day, his deliveries done, Kutsi came home and demanded lunch. Thobela was busy cleaning.

"What do you want?"

"Some of the goat. It was good. I like goat."

His wife took a container from the fridge and threw some stew in a pot and started to reheat it.

"Is there no pap? I can't eat it like that." He opened the fridge and helped himself to a beer that was barely cooler than room temperature.

"I'm not starting to make pap now. There is none left over," Thobela said sullenly.

"I'll have some of the vegetables." Kutsi pointed to the jars of green beans that Thobela had preserved. He had obtained a special price for an overly large parcel of beans.

"They are for a special occasion!" But Thobela opened a jar and dumped some on the plate with the stew. She shoved it in front of her husband.

"Where did you get the goat?" she demanded.

Kutsi finished a mouthful. "What's the matter with you? I bought it. I got a good price for the half. Why don't you eat some?" Thobela shook her head. She didn't want to eat that goat.

By his second beer, Kutsi was brooding about his dog. He wasn't satisfied. He wanted the matter investigated at the next kgotla. He drained the beer and went to see the chief. There he related the story of Bina and asked to present his case to the kgotla.

"Your visit is most convenient," the chief said. "Only this morning Nonyane arrived to complain that you had stolen the goat I had given him. And that you ate the goat in a stew." Kutsi was about to protest, but was silenced by the chief's raised hand. "Now you say he killed your dog and threatened your family." He stood up, angry. "You will appear at the kgotla tomorrow afternoon, and we will listen to both of you."

Kutsi left the chief and finished his afternoon's work. But that evening he started to feel unwell – his mouth was dry, and he had some difficulty focusing. I never get ill, he thought. It must be related to the death of the dog.

Nonyane has put the witchdoctor onto me. I will tell the chief tomorrow.

The next morning he felt worse. Still the dry mouth, and his vision had deteriorated – he was seeing double. Still, he had no fever and had much to do, so he took several aspirins and set off for the day's deliveries before he was due at the kgotla at four o'clock.

*   *   *

Chief Nkosi was not happy. His elegant solution to the Nonyane-Kutsi conflict had dissolved into chaos. Nkosi shook his grey head. He would have to teach the two a lesson on how neighbours should behave.

By three o'clock people started to gather for the kgotla. It was traditional for relatives of those appearing in the proceedings to gather and provide support. Besides, the elders might even call on them to provide information for the deliberations. Having come to the village from the North, Nonyane didn't have any relatives to support him. However, Kutsi's family was there in force. The family had lived here for generations and were plentiful. They sat in front of the elders, umbrellas unfurled to ward off the fierce sun.

There was one other dispute before the kgotla, and the chief heard it first because he feared the disagreement between Nonyane and Kutsi would take a long time to resolve.

As the arguments in the first case wound down, Thobela became increasingly worried. Kutsi had not yet arrived. She stood up and looked around, but he was nowhere to be seen. A few minutes later, Chief Nkosi asked Nonyane and Kutsi to come forward. Nonyane did so, but there was no Kutsi. It was very rude and disrespectful to keep the chief waiting, so Thobela was embarrassed for her husband. Perhaps his delivery truck had broken down on the way back from Mochudi. She dialled his mobile phone. There was no answer. Eventually she stood up and approached the chief.

"Chief Nkosi," she whispered in his ear. "Kutsi does not answer his phone. I worry something must have happened to him. You know he has always respected you. I must go and look for him."

Angrily Chief Nkosi ended the kgotla, ordering Thobela to have Kutsi come and see him. Thobela walked home with the embarrassment of her family on her shoulders. What had happened to Kutsi?

As she approached the house, she saw Kutsi's truck parked outside. How could he have forgotten, she wondered.

She pushed open the door and gasped. Kutsi was lying twisted on the floor, his face contorted, mouth open, his head lying in vomit. Thobela screamed and rushed to him.

"I can't breathe," he gasped, his hoarse voice difficult to hear.

She screamed again and again. Within minutes neighbours had gathered and an ambulance was called. Kutsi was soon on his way to the Princess Marina Hospital in Gaborone, nearly twenty kilometres away, with the paramedics doing what they could to keep him alive.

The doctors were puzzled. Kutsi continued to deteriorate even though his pulse, temperature, and blood pressure were normal. His breathing became more laboured, and he could barely speak. He had great difficulty swallowing the medicine they gave him.

"It's Nonyane. He's a witchdoctor. He's cursed me," he whispered at the doctors. He was barely audible. "It's Nonyane." That was the last thing he said.

* * *

The next morning the village turned out to pay their respects to Kutsi and to sympathise with Thobela, who cried and wailed in sadness and fear. Later in the day, when it was cooler, Chief Nkosi arrived with some of the elders. When she saw him, Thobela screamed that it was Nonyane who had killed her husband. Had Kutsi not named him with his dying breath? She told how Nonyane had barged into their house just as they were about to say grace, accusing Kutsi of stealing his goat and eating it.

"Kutsi bought half a goat from the Ever Fresh Butchery," she shouted. "You can ask Thebe there. He bought it from him!" She turned and pointed at Nonyane's house.

"Nonyane is evil! At night he is making muti there in the house. That is why Bina barked at night. That is why Nonyane killed him. Now he has cursed Kutsi and killed him too! You must arrest him. Put him in jail." She started to cry.

A ripple of support ran through the throng. Several men suggested waiting for Nonyane to return in order to beat him until he confessed to whatever witchcraft he had used. Chief Nkosi sensed the growing swell of anger and demanded silence.

"It is only I who can punish Nonyane if he has done something wrong. You all know the game we played when we were young. We tried to guess what type of bird was calling in a tree. And often we were wrong because it was a drongo, which is very clever and makes the calls of other birds. So before we punish Nonyane, we must shake the tree to make sure what bird is in it."

The crowd murmured, appreciating the wisdom of Nkosi, but still wanting action.

"We will have a kgotla in two days," Nkosi continued. "Then I will tell you what I have found out."

*   *   *

Chief Nkosi realised the situation was not one for him or the kgotla to resolve, so he telephoned the policeman son of his friend Wilmon.

"Detective Bengu," he said after being put through to Assistant Superintendent David "Kubu" Bengu's office in Gaborone. "I am an old friend of your father. He has told me many times how clever you are at catching people who have done wrong." He quickly summarised what had happened over the past week. "I need your assistance. My people are angry because they think one neighbour has killed another. They want to beat Nonyane, maybe kill him. But it is the anger of Kutsi's wife that stirs them, not proof that Nonyane is guilty. I do not know whether he killed Kutsi, but if he did it is no longer my responsibility, and the police must take over. I have called a kgotla in two days and want to tell them what actually happened. I wish for you to come and see for yourself and decide what should be done. I will be at the customary court building in the morning."

"Yes, certainly I will do what I can to help," Kubu replied. Although he thought it would be a fruitless effort, he agreed – mainly because of the chief's friendship with his father – to visit the village first thing in the morning.

*   *   *

Kubu set off early in a vain attempt to avoid the traffic on the Gabane road. It's busy all day, he thought, as he swerved to miss a minibus taxi that shot onto the road from the pavement. But it only took him just over half an hour to get to the village, where he soon found the customary court enclosure nestled below the hills at the top of the main road. Kubu wondered whether the buffalo head sculpted on the gate was a warning about the chief's temperament. He found some of the tribal elders seated under a tree.

"*Dumela*. Greetings. I am looking for Chief Nkosi," Kubu said as he approached.

The man closest to the tree stood up. "I am Nkosi."

"*Dumela*, Chief Nkosi. I am Assistant Superintendent David Bengu. Everyone calls me Kubu. You spoke to me on the phone yesterday."

"Welcome, Kubu." The chief's eyes twinkled. "I can see why you have such a name." He glanced at Kubu's considerable bulk. "We are fortunate to have a hippo in our midst. I have known your father for many years. How is he?"

"He is well, as is my mother. I am very fortunate."

Over a cup of strong tea, without biscuits to Kubu's disappointment, Chief Nkosi told Kubu everything he knew about the Nonyane-Kutsi affair.

"Nonyane was not happy when he found Kutsi's fence on his land. Then Kutsi was suspicious that Nonyane may have used muti to kill his dog. Next Nonyane's goat disappeared, and Nonyane is certain that Kutsi stole it and ate it." He shook his grey head sadly. "It is not like it used to be. When neighbours were friends and helped each other. Now they fight. And maybe they kill each other."

Kubu listened to the details, and then took his leave.

"Chief Nkosi, I understand you have a difficult problem. This man Nonyane seems to be a suspect, but the evidence is circumstantial. It isn't clear how Kutsi died. But I will do my best."

Despite the extra drive, Kubu decided to make the Princess Marina Hospital his first stop. He wanted to question the doctors about what Kutsi had said, and he wanted to link up with Ian MacGregor, the forensic pathologist. He needed to be as well informed as possible before he met Kutsi's wife.

The doctor and one of the nurses confirmed that Kutsi had accused Nonyane of witchcraft, but that he had said little else, saving his strength to breathe. After that Kubu sought out Ian in his laboratory attached to the hospital. He found the pathologist in a pensive mood.

"Let's get some coffee," said Ian, by way of greeting.

The reception area of the hospital had a vending machine which produced a foul brew, in Kubu's opinion, but Ian commented, "At least it's wet and has caffeine." Despite black looks from the staff, Ian filled his pipe and sucked in the moist tobacco aroma, making no attempt to light it. At last he was ready to talk.

"It's puzzling, Kubu. Nowadays one always suspects Aids when a youngish man dies, but there is no wasting, and anyway they did an HIV test which was negative. The early symptoms looked like a stroke, but that isn't consistent with what came next. A snake bite was a possibility, but they examined the body and found no fang puncture marks. The doctor did a pretty thorough job." He shook his head. "Could be some sort of rare disease, but I doubt it. It all happened too quickly."

Kubu nodded, impatient.

"Well, what do you think killed him then?"

"You can't rule out witchcraft."

"Witchcraft!" Kubu exploded. "You're not serious."

"Oh, yes. Kutsi thought Nonyane himself, or some witchdoctor, had cursed him. There are many cases where a powerful curse has lead to death. There is no physical cause, just the victim's belief that he will die. And he does."

This was exactly the scenario Kubu and Nkosi wanted to avoid. "What about poisoning?"

Ian shrugged. "Yes, that's a possibility too. Nothing obvious, though. No almond smell or anything like that. And the symptoms don't indicate any common poison. But the desert is full of rare plants that hardly have names. Who knows what one can find out there? Maybe I'm missing something." He seemed to be about to say more, but sucked again on his unlit pipe. "I'll do a full autopsy. Perhaps then we'll know more."

Disappointed, Kubu clambered to his feet. "Well, I'm going to drive back and visit the widow. She's the one making the claims about Nonyane, so I'd better see if she has any real evidence against the man."

"May I tag along? I'd like to see his house, where he was eating and such like."

Kubu was surprised, but Ian was his friend and the company was welcome.

*   *   *

Kubu and Ian found Thobela with her family and her children around her. She seemed calm and took them into the kitchen for coffee and privacy. She offered them homemade bread with jam, but to Kubu's disappointment, Ian refused firmly, if graciously, for both of them. At another time, Thobela would have been embarrassed to have a senior official and a white doctor in her kitchen, but now she was beyond that.

"Why do you not arrest this evil man? He sits there in his house watching us. Perhaps I am next, or the children. What will you say then?"

"Mma," said Kubu, "I am a senior officer in the CID, and this is the chief police doctor here with me. You can see how seriously we, and the chief who asked for us, are taking this case. I believe it will be solved in the next few days." Kubu wondered if there was any chance of that happening. Then he asked Thobela about their friends, enemies, family. She kept coming back to Nonyane. Ian took his coffee and walked around the kitchen, stopping to look at various items. But he touched nothing. At last, when there was a break in the interaction with Kubu, he ventured a question.

"Mma, would you tell me exactly what Rra Kutsi ate on the day before he became ill?"

She gestured to a row of boxes of cornflakes – their breakfast since Kutsi had discovered an extra carton loaded onto his truck – and mentioned the leftover goat and the vegetables for lunch, and the pap and wors they had shared for dinner. Ian asked if anyone else in the family had felt unwell, but she shook her head.

"Was there anything that only Rra Kutsi ate or drank?"

She thought for a moment. "The leftover goat stew and the beans. Two beers at lunchtime and two more in the evening." She hesitated. "Maybe he had something in the morning when he was doing deliveries. He was sick of cornflakes. And you have to throw out the weevils."

Ian was looking at the jars of preserved goods supporting the cornflake boxes. Something stirred in his memory.

"The beans. Were any left over?"

Thobela pulled a container from the fridge, still a quarter full, and put it on the table. Ian unscrewed the lid and carefully examined the contents, but nothing seemed untoward.

"I'd like to take this with me," he said.

"There's nothing wrong with the beans," Thobela said. "I made them myself. And how could Nonyane know which jar Kutsi would eat? How would he get into the house?"

Ian had no answer for this, and Kubu took up the questioning again. Shortly after, they left with the remains of the beans but little else to show for the visit.

As they drove off they noticed that Nonyane's windows had been shattered. It seemed the people were already taking matters into their own hands.

*   *   *

Ian returned to Gaborone in his own car and Kubu continued to investigate. Thebe at the Ever Fresh Butchery had no recollection of Kutsi buying half a goat, so Kubu asked the police in Gabane to investigate any other butchers there. No doubt they made jokes behind his back about why he would be looking for only *half* a goat, but that did not bother him at all. Next he visited Nonyane at his store. It was empty; no one would shop there now. Nonyane closed up and took the detective to his small office at the back. He emphatically denied any involvement with Kutsi's death, but he came clean about the dog.

"It made me crazy. Always barking, even in the middle of the night. And Kutsi did nothing. He didn't care. Eventually I could stand it no longer. I consult a man sometimes. On matters of love. You know how it is. Well, he said he could help me. He gave me some muti, said I must mix it with meat and give it to the dog. Then it would stop barking at me. When it killed the dog I was very upset, but this man just laughed. 'Well, it's not barking at you, is it?' he said. I won't ever go to him again."

Kubu left, worried. He believed Nonyane. Why admit poisoning the dog if he had poisoned Kutsi too? But what then had caused Kutsi's death? Could someone else be behind it? What about the grieving widow who was so keen to lay the blame next door? She would have no trouble slipping something into Kutsi's food; no one else could be sure who would eat what. His mind was turning over this new possibility when he heard from the Gabane police.

"Can you believe our luck, Detective Bengu? The very first butcher we visited said he traded Kutsi half a slaughtered goat. In exchange for a live one. And Kutsi said something strange that the man remembered. He said that he'd exchanged the goat for a dog."

Perhaps the issues of the goat and the dog are resolved, Kubu thought. But that is not what the chief and the kgotla will want to know about tomorrow. They will want Nonyane's head, and failing that, they may want mine.

When he got back to Gaborone, Ian was waiting with a new twist.

*   *   *

This time the whole village turned out for the kgotla. There were not enough seats so people stood around at the back. Thobela sat surrounded by her family and friends, a big gathering under a sea of colourful umbrellas. Nonyane sat alone. He looked very scared in the midst of the hostile crowd. Kubu sat next to the chief, with Ian at his side. He had insisted that Ian come to tell his story himself. Assuming his strange idea with its roots in his training in Scotland could be confirmed, of course. If not, Kubu meant to arrest Nonyane on suspicion of murder. Not because he believed the man guilty, but because he had to get him away from the crowd which could easily become a mob. He had asked the chief to delay the kgotla, but Nkosi had refused. "You must tell us what you have found. The people are too angry to wait." So here they sat, waiting for Ian's cellphone to ring.

At last the chief spoke, and the crowd quietened. At a leisurely pace he outlined the whole history of the conflict, starting with the fence, then the dog, then the goat, and culminating in Kutsi's horrific death. "Now the police will tell us what actually happened," he concluded with a confidence Kubu couldn't duplicate.

Kubu hauled himself to his feet and wished he had eaten a better lunch. He had to face the crowd on a half-empty stomach. He began with the story of the goat in full detail. It would be best to show that Kutsi, too, had been at fault. Then he told what had happened to the dog. There was an angry growl from the crowd. It seemed to them a small step from poisoning a dog to poisoning a man.

It was then that Ian's cellphone rang. Kubu sighed. At least now they would know one way or the other. He waited while Ian listened to his phone. Then Ian nodded, and Kubu let out the breath he hadn't realised he'd been holding.

"Dr MacGregor is the chief police doctor for all Botswana. He will now explain the poisoning of Rra Kutsi," he said and sat down.

The crowd was puzzled. Why was this white man telling the story instead of the important detective? But Ian had lived for many years in Botswana, and he spoke excellent if accented Setswana.

He nodded to the chief and to the crowd and began with a list of his qualifications. What he would say would count for little if they didn't believe him.

"When I was a young man," he began, "I trained at a small country hospital in Scotland, like the one at Mochudi." He described where one might find Scotland. The people were listening now, caught up in the story. "One day a man became very ill after eating a can of fish. This man was poisoned by a very bad poison which comes when food goes rotten in a most unusual way. The food can be sealed – in a can or in a jar – but there are seeds of a germ that can grow unless they have been killed by long boiling.

These germs even grow in the dark or where there is no air. This is how Rra Kutsi died." He held up his cellphone. "I have just this minute heard from our laboratory where the test was done. Rra Kutsi died of botulism – the poison made by these germs – which was in the jar of beans he ate with his lunch."

There was chaos. Everyone spoke at once. Thobela screamed that there was nothing wrong with her food. The chief and other elders stood up and told the gathering to be quiet. At last it was possible for Ian to answer questions.

Thobela's brother jumped to his feet. "Is it not possible for someone to put this poison in the food? Someone who hated Kutsi? Like Nonyane."

Ian shook his head. "How could he do that, Rra? The jars were sealed." He looked at Thobela, and she reluctantly nodded. "And how was he to get into the house? Also, this is not a poison you can find or buy. It is rare. You would need a laboratory to make it."

"What about witchcraft? What about a curse?" Thobela's sister pointed to Nonyane. "Kutsi said that man cursed him!" But Ian answered everyone's questions with firm confidence, and eventually the mood shifted. Thobela started to cry quietly, accepting that her beans, boiled, but not for long enough, had led to her husband's death. Not Nonyane. Not witchcraft.

At last there was quiet, and Chief Nkosi summed up: Kutsi had died by accident, and Nonyane was innocent and free to go. Kubu noted with relief the nods of acceptance from the crowd.

When they left after the profuse thanks of the chief and the elders, Kubu gave Ian a slap on the back. "Well, you left that till the last minute, Dr MacGregor, but you came through in the end." Ian started to answer, but his cellphone interrupted him. He listened for a few minutes, thanked the caller and hung up. Then he turned to Kubu with a broad smile. "That was the lab. They've confirmed that Kutsi died of botulism. And it *was* the bottled beans that were contaminated."

Kubu gaped. "But didn't they tell you that earlier? The call at the kgotla?"

Ian shook his head. "That was some chancer trying to sell me life insurance. But I knew I was right." For a moment Kubu was stunned. Then he started to laugh.

*   *   *

It was a month after the funeral, and Thobela was alone, the children at school. When she opened the door in response to a firm knock, she was

startled to see Nonyane. He was dressed smartly in a dark grey suit, matching felt hat, polished black shoes. He was holding a cardboard carton with
both hands.

"What do you want, Rra Nonyane?" asked Thobela.

The man looked down at the cardboard box. "I have come to offer my
condolences, and pay my respects, as a good neighbour should. I regret
that Rra Kutsi was not my friend. Nevertheless I am saddened by his passing on." He paused. "May I come in?"

Thobela hesitated, but in the end this man had not harmed Kutsi, and
she was curious about the carton. She led him to the small lounge, pointed
to the couch, and sat opposite him in the farthest chair.

Nonyane sat with the box on his lap, looking around the room, at a loss
for words.

"You have a fine house," he said at last. "Rra Kutsi was a good provider."
His embarrassment made him uncomfortable. "I am thankful that the fat
detective proved me not guilty of your husband's death. It was a very bad
time for me too, you know. It is very frightening to be accused of witchcraft and having rocks coming through your windows."

Thobela nodded, but said nothing.

"I brought you this." He opened the box revealing a nondescript puppy,
just weaned. He placed the scrawny, now yelping creature in Thobela's arms,
where it set about testing her fingers with milk teeth. In spite of herself, she
smiled and cradled it. "The children will be pleased," she said. But her face
darkened at the thought of her fatherless children and all their expenses.

Nonyane seemed to pick up the thought. "Is there any money now?"

"A little. There is the truck – I can sell that – and this house. That's all."

Nonyane nodded, and there was silence again. "Please ask me if you
need a man to help you with something. I am right next door." He rose to
go, and Thobela saw him out. At the door he turned back, put on his hat,
and took her hand.

"We are neighbours who are both alone. May I call again? When it is
convenient?"

Thobela did not smile, but she did not pull back her hand. After a moment she nodded.

"Yes, Rra Nonyane. When it is convenient," she said. Then she closed
the door and returned to the lounge. The puppy was wagging its tail, una-
shamed. Next to it was a small, yellow puddle.

DIRK JORDAAN

Dirk Jordaan is a journalist at the Afrikaans daily paper *Beeld* in Johannesburg. Apart from editing, he also writes about motorcycles. His debut novel, *Die Jakkalssomer* (Summer of the Jackal) (2007) features Captain Div Pelser, who works with a unit of the National Prosecuting Authority. The novel was shortlisted for the magazine *Insig*'s fiction award for 2007 and was a finalist in the language and cultural organisation ATKV's annual Quill Awards for 2007 in the category Suspense Fiction.

"To me," Jordaan says, "it was a natural development to start writing crime-thriller fiction, as I constantly imagine plots and especially action sequences. It's my way of escaping reality! But crime fiction also gives me the opportunity to investigate moral issues and our innate longing for balance in our lives and surroundings." With a growing readership, the Afrikaans 'crime-thriller' has now definitely come of age.

His story *Masterclass*, is another take on the "perfect crime". After all, isn't this what every killer hopes for? To get away with it?

Masterclass

DIRK JORDAAN

The rolled-up newspaper hit the front door with the sound of a far-away, muffled gunshot.

Duncan Penwright opened the campus cottage door and, as dictated by a thousand other mornings, retrieved the paper – to be gutted and spread on the kitchen table. He sat down with a full coffee mug and lit his first cigarette of the new day. It was still quiet outside, the pale frost-covered lawns not yet disturbed by the shoes of students rushing to their first classes, and making it just in time. Somewhere beyond the old buildings and bare jacaranda trees, the capital was stirring, shaking off the grey winter dawn.

He reached for the coffee mug, but froze, his hand on the ceramic ear as icy crystals slowly spread up through his body. His stomach tightened, the muscles in his neck contracted. He almost had to force the cigarette to his lips on which he drew deeply.

"Good God!" he muttered. On the dirty white paper in front of him was the face of one of his students. A slightly blurry, monochrome portrait shot, taken somewhere to be used on some form of identity document. "He's dead!"

He reread the short report. Vasily Fyodorov had been murdered early the previous evening. But the frosty hand that gripped Duncan, somewhere just below his heart, did not squeeze because of that statement of fact. It was the way the post-graduate student had met his end that rocked him.

"It's just as we discussed the day before yesterday!"

The story reported that the cause of death seemed to be a single stab wound to the neck. Vasily had been killed in the park on the far side of the station, the report said, and the police were considering the possibility that he was lured from the station to the more solitary space by someone he knew. A train ticket in his coat pocket indicated that he, like most students, used that mode of transport daily to commute between home and campus.

Duncan stood up. His legs felt shaky but he started pacing the room. The knowledge that the murder was too much of a coincidence overwhelmed him. During their last weekly tutorial they were supposed to have discussed the group's final dissertations, but the dozen or so students had other plans. They had goaded Duncan into a light-hearted free-for-all. And he fell for it, as easily as a sophomore could be baited into a date with a senior.

Duncan Penwright enjoyed moments like those. He relished exhibiting his knowledge of matters criminal. As a leading academic in the field of criminology, he was regularly called upon to testify in court numerous times. His photograph was sometimes included in press coverage of high-profile murder cases. In fact, for a while he'd featured on *The Pretoria News*'s dial-a-quote expert when it came to crime. But it was in the front of a classroom where he felt most at home. Where he could see the lively interest in the students' faces. Especially some of the women's, who were transfixed by his superior knowledge, experience and, none less than any of the above, his fiery eyes and closely cropped grey beard. The classroom was where he could impress. Even more so in the informal, intimate surroundings of the lounge where they held their tutorials.

It had started with the question that came up annually: "C'mon, Prof, with all your experience, how would you commit the perfect crime?"

"Crime or murder? Perfect? What is perfect? Do you mean perfectly and neatly executed or," and here he paused slightly before emphasising, "by not being caught?"

He had smiled at them. "I assume you want to know about the latter. Well, in that case, what do you think?"

Their suggestions meandered around shootings, stabbings, poisonings (both orally and intravenously), stranglings and bumping people off various high places or pushing them in front of large vehicles. One student even mentioned snakes and poisonous spiders, something that seemed extremely out of place in their civil urban surroundings. Duncan's replies were witty and deadly, he thought. He let their imaginations run, before reminding them that forensic evidence would bring about the demise of all the killers in their examples. Evidence including blood or skin samples on the murderer himself. "Or herself," he had smiled towards the blonde Catherine, sharing a sofa with Yuri Kravchenko. He could see her pale knees pressed together under her skirt. She had smiled back. Catherine Norman, his student assistant, had a mind sharper than a pathologist's blade. And she was different. She did not lay an obvious trap for his attention – he liked that about her – no flirting or scheming, no parting of the legs, no flashing of inner thighs in classroom for him to notice as he stood at the whiteboard.

"Most violent crimes leave something, or a residue of something, on the perpetrator. Like abrasion marks on the hands after a strangling. And poisoning – well, these days almost no poison is untraceable. And getting hold of it isn't easy, which means the police are able to track it back to the user.

"So, you see, it's not that simple. You could possibly get away with murder, literally, if you pushed somebody off a desolate cliff," (grins all round) "but, as always, motive and opportunity will mean the dirty deed will be traced back to you. Not to mention eyewitnesses. You have to make sure there's no one around.

"But personally, I admire the methods used by silent killers. Like the perfect stabbing." He had strolled over to the mantelpiece and lifted his own regimental sword from its rack; a singing sound cut through the atmosphere as the long, slightly curved blade left its scabbard.

"The Spartans used it in battle and the Japanese ninja practised it to perfection. A single, deep downward stab between the clavicle and scapula in the shoulder. That would either damage the heart or sever the aorta. The way of the assassin!" he declared dramatically, priding himself on the fact that he was more than a criminologist. His military past kept him interested in warfare and he was still a keen student of weaponry.

He first demonstrated the downward thrust, before holding the sword in front of his chest to show the route it would take inside the chest cavity.

"And the beauty of it is that all the bleeding is done internally and it's lethal. You can do it in the lobby of a hospital and your opponent will still be beyond salvation."

He had swung the sword in the air, feeling its perfect balance once more, striking a dashing pose before seemingly emerging from his reverie.

"But," he wrapped up the discussion, "do you really want to know the best way?" Nods all round. "Get someone else to do it." They laughed.

"No, I'm serious! Get someone else, without him, or her, knowing that he did it on your behalf. No matter what method he uses, you're free! That's the perfect murder. Right. More torrid tales of morality and mortality next week."

Duncan stopped next to the kitchen table and picked up his packet of cigarettes. Someone, one of that dozen, had taken his advice to heart. Had listened too well.

But who? And maybe he was mistaken. It could be a coincidence. But he had to know.

He looked for the investigating detective's name in the newspaper report and went to his study to call the police. After introducing himself as the student's tutor and assuring the man that he would assist in any way possible, after all, he was also a fine criminologist, he fished for information. His worst fears were realised. Vasily had been killed by a deep wound in the shoulder which had led to extensive internal bleeding. The murder weapon was gone, the police were busy dredging the river in the faint hope of finding it. There were no footprints on the winter-hard ground near the corpse, which was found on a park bench. The park, where thousands of students had shared lovers' benches over countless summers.

He put down the phone and slumped behind his desk. It could still be a dark and unfortunate coincidence. But his stomach rebelled against that notion. He knew. After all these years of study he knew the criminal mind. And someone had taken advantage of him. He lit a cigarette and closed the newspaper still lying open on the table.

Who could it be? He had to start somewhere. By using a process of elimination.

Duncan grabbed a notebook and pen and started by writing down all the students' names. All his suspects. The cops have no chance, he thought. But he had. He had an advantage – inside knowledge. And he'd been there when the crime was planned, so to speak.

He would have to revisit the discussion. The tutorial blazed in his mind. Who had been really interested? Who had asked pertinent questions?

Catherine, as usual. He visualised the room. And Yuri, he realised, sitting next to her. The others participated and put forward their crazy ideas, whilst Yuri did not. He had, however, uncharacteristically asked most of the questions. He had initiated the discussion, for heaven's sake! Yuri, usually quiet and slightly stubborn-looking in a Slavic, peasant-like way. The Russian expatriate had a bit of a history – if he remembered correctly. He rushed back to his study and called the head of student affairs.

His colleague refreshed his memory. Yes, Yuri had been involved, and admonished, for a fistfight on campus. He had attacked a fellow student. Also a Russian. Something about a girl. ("Isn't it always?") But that was not all – and this was news to Duncan – Yuri had been arrested once for hitting a local in a pub after being provoked. By some trivial comment, something to do with being called a "Ruskie". The man ended up in hospital. Duncan thanked the colleague after assuring him that Yuri did not necessarily have anything to do with the murder, "But," he stressed, "we will have to look into everything, you know".

His feeling of dread increased. Yuri and Vasily were compatriots, thus Yuri could easily have lured Vasily to a desolate spot. Opportunity, in other words. Motive? Yuri's punch-up had most probably been with Vasily. (How many Russians could there be on campus?). And with passion at play, the motive may well have been jealousy.

And Duncan Penwright himself had shown the young man exactly how to kill. He thought of his ridiculous demonstration with the sword. The sword! What if …

Duncan dressed hurriedly, grabbing his hat, scarf and wide-brimmed hat, although his carefully matching apparel was useless against the cold in his bones. He rushed to the office, unlocked the wooden door with trembling hand and threw open the connecting door to the lounge. The sword rack was empty.

It felt as if he barely made it to the swivel chair behind his desk. The young fool! Yuri had let jealousy and anger consume him! And he had involved him, Duncan Penwright! It slowly dawned on him. There was more. His own fingerprints were on the sword. If the police did manage to find it, he would be implicated. Yuri most probably would have worn gloves. He was definitely smart enough. It was his sword, his fingerprints wouldn't be out of place, but nevertheless. Maybe that was the young Russian's plan all along.

Duncan knew he would have to call the police and explain everything.

But some force held his hand in his lap and he did not reach for the telephone. What if they find the sword afterwards, he thought, and there was no real evidence to implicate Yuri? That would make it appear as if he had tried to pin the murder on the student. Just like the case of Foster McCarthy, some years ago, who'd awoken suspicion the moment he had called the police in an effort to blame someone else – right after killing his wife. And look where he ended up …

Duncan realised he had to corner the young man. Had to force him to admit to the murder and then he could hand him over to the authorities. It was up to him. Thank goodness he had thought about this, had worked out what the student's plans were.

He heard muffled noises in the outer office and stood up. It was Catherine. "Morning," he greeted through the open door. She looked up from behind her own desk. She looked pale, startled. "You heard?"

"Yes, Professor. It's terrible."

He nodded. And it's even worse than you can imagine, he thought.

"I want to ask you something, Catherine. About the other day at the tutorial." He paused. He had to be sure. "You sat next to Yuri. He asked the questions about the perfect murder, didn't he?"

Her eyes showed white around the pale blue irises as she answered, "Yes, Professor, if I remember correctly. Why?"

"Nothing really."

"You don't think he had something to do with this?"

He shook his head. "No, no. Not necessarily. But can you get hold of him for me? I need to speak to him. Oh, and please cancel my twelve o'clock class with the third years. And go home. We all need to get over this."

"Yes, of course." The girl looked even more shaken, startled than earlier.

Duncan closed the door behind him and returned to his desk. He felt braced, more sure of himself. He was right. And he would resolve all this. Swiftly.

Time wore heavy boots. Duncan realised he had not eaten breakfast and soon he threw his empty cigarette packet in the dustbin. But he could not leave to go to the cafeteria, he had to wait. His thoughts swirled around the case like tea leaves in a pot after stirring. At last he heard movement in the outer office, then a soft knock on the door.

"Come in!"

The swarthy Yuri looked like a boxer, square-shouldered and strong.

"Morning, Professor. You wanted to see me?" His English was good, but his accent heavily dragged down by the guttural sounds of his native tongue.

"Yuri, come in." Duncan suddenly felt at a loss as to how to start breaking down the young man's defences.

"You," he hesitated, then opted for a different word to *heard*, "*know* about Vasily?"

Yuri nodded.

"I want to talk to you about it. You see, the problem is this. We discussed ways of murdering someone the other day, and he was killed in just such a way. Do you realise that?"

The frown between the dark eyebrows deepened, but the young man did not reply.

"Well," Duncan steepled his fingers in front of his chest, "it therefore could have been someone in your class. Do you understand?"

Still no response. Duncan sighed.

"Yuri, is there something you need to tell me?"

"No, Professor. Why?"

"Are you sure? You see, I know that you and Vasily fought over a girl. In other words, you had motive."

Yuri's eyebrows raised. "Me? No, Professor, no!"

"But Yuri, you also had opportunity. You are the prime suspect." The young man shook his head furiously.

"Yes, you are! But let me explain. I'm on your side. You are a good student, Yuri. You rose above your circumstances. You are making something of your life. Don't throw it all away now. I haven't called the police yet. Just cooperate and I will help you. I'll support you. You are a good man."

"No, no! I did not have anything to do with it. Vasily was my friend."

"Was, yes. But recently that changed. I can help you." I've got him in a corner, Duncan thought. "If you don't come out with it, you are on your own." He reached for the telephone.

"No!' The young man was next to his desk in two quick strides. "Stop!"

Duncan's right hand retreated.

"Yes?"

"It wasn't me! You can't call the police. I will be deported."

"No, I don't think so, I'm afraid. Justice will have to be done right here."

"I cannot go to prison, and I cannot be deported. I can't go back there!"

Duncan saw the fear in the dark eyes.

"I understand how you feel, but you used my sword. In other words, I'm involved, and I won't allow you to get away with it! Be a man, stand up for yourself and admit your mistake!" As he said it, he found the truth in Yuri's eyes. "You've done it before, haven't you? That's why you can't go back! You're wanted for murder in Russia, my God!" He was shocked. With all his experience, Duncan had misread the man. "Damn Russians! We couldn't trust them during the Bush War and you can't trust them now," he thought.

The student lowered his eyes. "You don't understand, you don't understand," he growled softly.

Duncan felt the anger rise: the man is a coward. "We have to put an end to this," he said firmly and reached for the telephone again, this time with full intent to use it. Yuri rushed forward and grabbed his arm.

"Let go, you young fool! Stop!"

He snatched the phone with his other hand, but Yuri was, quite unexpectedly to Duncan, on top of him. They wrestled for control of the device. His chair toppled over and Duncan landed heavily on his back, the air compressed from his lungs. Yuri pinned him to the ground and tore the telephone out of his hand.

Duncan saw bright pinpricks before his eyes, first felt a hand around his neck, then something else, the telephone cord. Tight around his neck. He tried to say something, attempted to scream, but couldn't. He heard the other man's breathing, then the dustbin as it skittled over the floor as he kicked it. Darkness crept into his vision and his lungs were on fire. At last his legs stopped their shuddering and the young Russian let go of the black electronic cord.

The inspector trod heavily up the stairs and ground to a halt in front of the dean. His breath was like the steam of a train waiting to depart. "He's gone, Professor. He fled."

He turned to Catherine, pale and thin next to the old academic. She was shivering, her arms folded across her slight chest. "Miss, you are sure he was the last person to see the professor alive?"

She nodded slowly.

"It's him," he continued confidently. "Eyewitnesses said he only grabbed a couple of personal things and fled. He looked quite spooked, apparently.

Don't worry, we'll get him." He turned away.

The dean put his hand on her arm. "Go home, my dear. Try to get some rest."

Catherine nodded once more, turned away and walked over the dark lawn in the direction of the station.

Before passing through the turnstile, she stopped, seemingly thinking of something. Then she turned around and walked back to the tramp standing beside his fire in a drum. He greeted her and smiled. He held up both hands, as proof that he still had the two gloves she had given him. She smiled back and opened her briefcase.

Catherine took out her notebook, pressed it against her thigh and tore out the page on which she had written her prescribed questions to Yuri in the tutorial lounge, as well as a couple of pages underneath – so that no imprint of her handwriting would remain. She crumpled the pages into a heart-sized ball and tossed it into the fire.

The fools, she thought. Both young men in love with her, available to do her bidding. With the jealous Vasily blabbing on about Yuri's dark past in an attempt to gain the upper hand it had not even been necessary to activate Plan B, to plant the bloodstained sword she had used. Both the professor and Yuri had been true to their nature. She stared at the flames, and saw there the academic being carried out his office on a gurney under a grey blanket, his left hand sticking out from under the cover. Welts on his fingers where the telephone cord had cut into the flesh. She remembered the feeling of that hand on her inner thighs, pushing up under her skirt.

He won't force himself on anyone ever again. Duncan Penwright will not ever violate another young woman, Catherine thought, before turning towards the station entrance to catch the 7:15.

MESHACK MASONDO

Masondo currently works as a publishing manager with Macmillan SA. He writes in Zulu and speaks many languages, including English and Afrikaans. He's much degreed with an MA dissertation to his credit on the subject of the detective novel in Zulu. He's won a number of awards, including the Nasionale Boekhandel Award for African Language Literature for *Inkunzi Isematholeni* (Future leaders are the young ones of today) in 1998. Of his three detective novels, Masondo likes *Iphisi Nezinyoka* (The Hunter and the Snakes) best. First published in 1987 with the seventeenth impression published in 2007. This first novel was penned while Masondo was still at school and published several years later. As a prescribed setwork, it has sold over one million copies.

Of the Zulu detective novel, Masondo says, "While based to an extent on the English model, the Zulu detective novel adds its own themes – related to social problems caused by the meeting of modern life and Zulu traditional customs – to the 'classic recipe.'"

"The Hunter and the Snakes" will soon appear in English as a new version of the isiZulu novel, and features characters you will meet here in *The Love of Money* – Detective Themba Zondo and Sergeant Thulani Zungu.

The Love of Money

MESHACK MASONDO

MAGWEGWE BUTHELEZI, SHAREHOLDER AND CHIEF OPERATING OFFICER of Rogue Private Investigators, one of the big private investigation companies in Johannesburg, had worked till ten o'clock. He left the office situated at the railway buildings in De Korte Street in Braamfontein, at half past ten. He was dog-tired after the long day, and thirsty.

Magwegwe got into his car. He drove slowly down De Korte Street, unusually quiet at this time of night, and stopped at the Alba Hotel, as he did most evenings. The bar, with no more than a handful of patrons in it, was hardly full. Magwegwe bought himself a drink and moved towards the corner, where he sat alone, deep in thought and not wanting to be disturbed. But of course, moments later, his peace, if you could call it that, was interrupted.

"One move and you're dead!" he heard the voice shout. The patrons, and Magwegwe, turned their heads towards the doorway from where the voice was booming. A tall man with a thin body, his head and face covered with pantyhose, stood there with what looked like an AK-47 in his hands.

"Take out your wallets and put them on the table!" the stranger ordered. "Put them together! Quickly! And no heroics, or, ratatat, I'll blow your brains out!"

At first there was no movement. Then one by one the patrons stood quietly, making sure their hands were up and seen, and placed their valuables on the table next to the till.

"I said be quick!" said the man, wildly pointing the weapon, as if he could lose his cool and shoot at any time. "Move over there, all of you!" The man pointed to the back of the bar. "And no one try stupid tricks now! Hands up!"

It happened exactly as the gunman commanded. He pulled out his bag. He helped himself, starting with the till and ending with the wallets. He worked quickly. Magwegwe felt cheated when he saw his wallet, together with the others, disappear into the gunman's bag along with the takings of the day.

The thief reversed towards the door, facing the patrons, still pointing the gun at them. Laughing and walking through the door, he said, "You have behaved well! So I too will behave well – if you stay still for ten more minutes."

Even when it was apparent that the prescribed ten minutes of "good behaviour" were over, nobody in the bar moved. It must have been twenty minutes later when, finally, the barman angrily picked up the phone. He slammed it down before he even attempted to dial a number. He paced in and out of the bar, swearing and talking to himself, threatening to tear the gunman to pieces if he ever saw him again.

Magwegwe tried to finish the dregs of the beer in his glass, but found he could not. He got up from the chair and slowly walked out of the bar into the steady rain that had been threatening all day. Heavy-hearted, he got in his car and drove home.

His wife, Popi, whom his many acquaintances described as beautiful, was watching television in their nice house and reading the newspaper. When Magwegwe walked in, Popi put down the paper and said with a smile, "Hi love. I've been waiting for you for too long now. When you phoned to say you'd be late this afternoon, it didn't cross my mind you'd be home close to midnight."

Magwegwe just threw himself on the couch saying, "Yes, my wife, but now I am home."

"Did you eat, love?"

"A little curry, in the afternoon," said Magwegwe nonchalantly, as if Popi's question was trivial and the words he spoke weightless, of little importance.

Popi sat quietly looking at her husband and asked, concerned, "Is there something worrying you, love?"

Magwegwe nodded, spreading himself on the couch, and answered, "Yes. I stopped for a few minutes at the Alba Hotel to refresh myself with a drink. Unfortunately a gunman robbed the bar. I am a victim, my sixty rand and my wallet were stolen. All my credit cards, everything in there."

Popi moved swiftly towards Magwegwe. "My God! You are not injured are you?"

Magwegwe replied feebly, "Nobody was injured, my wife. It is just that ..."

She sat close to him and stroked his beard. Magwegwe could not finish what he wanted to say. He stood up and paced around the room, shaking his head, his hands deep in his trouser pockets.

Popi persisted: "What is wrong, love?" Magwegwe stopped pacing and looked at his wife. He took a deep breath and sighed, "I know who the culprit is."

"What?" asked Popi.

"Even though the criminal had covered his head and face with panty-hose, I knew it was Taga Nxumalo!"

"Do you mean the very same Taga who works in your office, love?"

"Exactly."

"Maybe you're making a mistake ..."

Magwegwe shook his head. "I know how this sounds to your ears, my wife, but I have no doubt that it was Taga."

Magwegwe sat on the couch and continued, "I heard his voice. He thefula's when he speaks. You've heard the way he substitutes l for y in speech. It's that gap between his top front teeth."

Popi shook her head, surprised, and said, "Yes, I know the sound he makes! But this does not make any sense, love. Taga is doing a good job, which pays well. What would make him do such a bad thing?"

"I cannot answer your question, my wife."

"Did you report this to the police yet?"

Magwegwe shook his head, "No."

Popi tried to put words in Magwegwe's mouth, saying, "You are not *prepared* to report this to the police, is that it?"

"It seems as if you are correct there, my wife."

Popi stood up and put her hands on her hips. "Is your brain working properly, my husband? If it is true that Taga robbed you of your money, let alone the money he stole from others, how can you just sit down and do nothing about it? Taga Nxumalo is a thief! He deserves to be in prison!"

"You are correct there, my wife. The problem is I have no evidence to prove it was Taga. The court will not accept my argument without some sort of *prima facie* evidence. If I try to get Taga arrested, he will flatly deny he's involved. I have no proof to pursue my claim. Can you imagine? I will look like a stupid man who goes around accusing people of crimes they did not commit."

"How can he deny it, my darling? You recognised him. And the sound of his voice is like no other."

"Sometimes people are caught red-handed on the scene committing a crime, but the lawyers get them off the hook. This incident is nothing compared to that kind of evidence. I think it's better to just let it go, my wife."

Popi threw her hands in the air in despair. "If you do not report this case to the police, what are you going to do with it? How are you going to carry on working with Taga? And how are you going to get your money back?"

Magwegwe stretched himself. "I have no doubt that Taga will return my money tomorrow. If he does not, I will make a plan to get it back." He closed his eyes.

Popi stopped talking too. She rushed to the telephone, picked up the receiver and started dialling a number.

Magwegwe opened his eyes and said, "What are you doing?"

"I am calling the police," Popi answered.

"Magwegwe stood up and went to Popi. He grabbed Popi's hand and said in anger, "I do not like what you are doing, my wife."

"This is exactly what is needed! How can it be that somebody robbed you and in turn you are protecting him? You do not want to report him because you have no proof. No! That cannot be, love."

"But I told you, darling, I will make a plan. Please put down the telephone."

Magwegwe and Popi struggled for a short time, one trying to take the telephone receiver from the other. Magwegwe eventually managed to get hold of it, and Popi, furious, dashed to the bedroom and slammed the door.

Later, Magwegwe lay next to the sleeping Popi, on his back with his knees raised. He kept tossing and turning. Thinking about this and that, he could not sleep at all that night. In fact, Popi was right. It was wrong for him not to report Taga to the police just because he had no proof that he was robbed by him. But, he thought to himself, it is equally wrong to rush things. Was the money he was robbed of worth going to court over?

No! A measly sixty rand. The money was too little. Not worth all the fuss. Grappling with these thoughts, Magwegwe fell asleep.

When he woke, it was already time to go to work. "I know how you feel my love, but trust me," said Magwegwe, patting his wife on the shoulders when he was ready to leave.

"I hope you know what you're doing, my love."

"I know very well, darling Popi. There is only one thing you need to do. You must listen to what I say."

Popi knew better than to carry on arguing with her husband, so she kissed him on the cheek and Magwegwe left for work.

*   *   *

In his office, Magwegwe kept thinking about Taga. He hoped when Taga showed his face there would at least be some sign of guilt etched on it. But instead, Taga walked briskly and unexpectedly into Magwegwe's office and said, "Good morning, sir, and how are you?"

Magwegwe was surprised at Taga's upbeat mood and responded with the same enthusiasm, "Hi. I'm ok, Taga."

Taga pulled his chair closer to Magwegwe's desk, and sat facing him.

"If you try to get me arrested," he started immediately, "I will deny it flatly, sir," said Taga, pulling Magwegwe's wallet from his pocket and placing it on the desk.

"I know that very well. What surprises me the most is why you committed such a crime," said Magwegwe. He checked his wallet, the money and cards still there, and returned it to his pocket.

Taga smiled briefly, then laughed. "I simply did it in order to add a few cents to my meagre salary."

"Are you mad? How can you say that? This will only lead to a hell of a lot of trouble! Don't do it again! Do you understand?" Magwegwe shouted at Taga, as if he was his son.

Taga laughed again and said, "I have no intention of doing so."

Magwegwe pulled his diary towards him. He paged through the blank pages.

Taga cleared his throat, wanting Magwegwe to look at him. "I hope you didn't tell anyone about what happened last night, not even your wife."

Magwegwe knew before answering Taga that he was about to lie. He said, "No. I did not tell anyone. Especially not my wife."

"Why the hell not?" asked Taga, smiling as usual.

Magwegwe kept quiet for a long time before attempting to answer. "It is because …"

Taga kept quiet, waiting for Magwegwe to finish his sentence.

After a pause, Magwegwe continued, "It is because I have thought of doing the very same thing you did. This company is facing a financial crisis. Any cent we get in will make a difference."

Taga nodded his head to show that he understood Magwegwe, before saying, "But I cannot see you stooping to crime, sir."

"Do you think I'm joking?" Magwegwe asked.

Taga shook his head. "I'm sorry, sir. You don't look like somebody who would go to those lengths for money …"

Magwegwe reached out and grabbed Taga's wrist. "I am serious. What is it that you see in me that makes you doubt what I say? I would go to any lengths to save my company!"

For a few minutes neither of the men spoke. Staring into each other's faces, each tried to make meaning out of the faintly detectible expressions that could mean a thousand words, if only one knew how to interpret them.

"It's ok, sir. We'll make a plan," said Taga after a long silence.

That afternoon Magwegwe arrived home early.

"Wife of mine," he said to Popi, as she sat drinking tea from a pretty porcelain cup, "I am rushing back to the office. There is so much work to do this evening."

"And what about Taga?" Popi asked, placing his supper in front of him. "Have you reported Taga to the police yet?" Magwewe did not reply. He showed her his wallet, and without further discussion he left for work.

*   *   *

Magwegwe got home late that night. He knocked at the back door. Popi opened. She'd waited up as she always did. He walked into the kitchen in a happy mood, singing, dancing and patting his wife's buttocks.

"What is wrong with you? My husband, have you been drinking again?" She asked, though she noticed no smell of booze on him.

Magwegwe carried on singing:

"Vuka! Vuka ndod'uyosebenza!

Wake up! Wake up, man, and go to work!

Ngob'isihlalandawonye
Because the one who stays in one place
Sidl'amanzonzo aso.
Starves.
Vuka ndoda!
Wake up, man!"

"My love! Why are you so happy?" asked Popi.

"You married a real man, my wife! You know what? I do not sleep and expect everything to fall like manna from heaven. I work, my love!"

"What are you talking about? I do not understand," said Popi.

"You will never understand, my darling. But the day I die, you will cry tears of blood because you will know how hard I worked for you ..."

"My husband," Popi interrupted Magwegwe, "we will talk about all this later. But now there are people waiting for you in the lounge."

Magwegwe said, surprised, "Waiting for me?"

"Yes, love."

"It is very late now! Who are these people?"

Magwegwe, following his wife to the lounge, shook his head in anger.

Magwegwe smiled briefly when he saw Taga sitting on the couch. "Oh! It is you, Taga. I was worried about who might be visiting me in the middle of the night," said Magwegwe, relieved, sitting with his wife on the couch opposite Taga and another man with a wide body sitting next to him.

Taga smiled, as usual, and put his hand in his jacket pocket. He produced a card and showed it to Magwegwe. As Magwegwe fingered the plastic identification card, the muscles of his face seemed to collapse, and in a minute he was all goose flesh.

"Please, sir. From now on, call me Detective Themba Zondo. Taga Nxumalo is a pseudonym, a figment of your imagination. Do you understand?" asked this stranger, the very man whom Magwegwe had trusted as Taga, as a work colleague and even a friend.

"And I am Sergeant Thulani Zungu," said his barrel-chested colleague, pulling his card from his jacket pocket and presenting it to Magwegwe.

Magwegwe looked closely at the cards, as if he could not see clearly what was printed there, and said nothing.

"What is going on, love?" asked Popi.

Magwegwe was as silent as death.

"Do you know, madam, that a branch of Nation Bank was robbed two years ago? Your husband was poor then. All of a sudden he became extremely rich. He bought shares in Rogue, and your nice house, as you know … I got a job in the company and worked with him closely as a private investigator. I tried all the tricks in the trade to make him cough up about his past. Where did all the money come from, I wanted to know."

Popi looked at Magwegwe, who now stared up at the ceiling, as if asking God for help. "Tell me, love, tell me this man is lying!" She turned to Themba and said, "What are you talking about a bank robbery for? What proof do you have of anything like this?"

"What I do have is proof enough to have your husband prosecuted for theft and put behind bars for a very long time."

"I do not believe this," said Popi, confused and frustrated, turning to Magwegwe. "We need to talk to our lawyer."

"And I hope he is a very good one, madam," said Sergeant Zungu.

Themba Zondo smiled, as was his habit, and turned to Popi. "Madam, I will tell you how I nabbed him. Yes, it was me at the hotel bar last night. I robbed the patrons – all friends of mine if you'd like to know – of their money, their jewellery, their watches. I made sure your husband recognised me. I was trying my damnedest to impress Mr Buthelezi here."

"What are you saying, Detective Zondo?" asked Popi.

"I am trying to tell you that my plan worked like a bomb, madam. He trusted me. I had made a deal with his auditors too. I knew he was in trouble. The company is doing badly. So many security firms springing up all over the place, you'd think there was room for all of them with this crime wave, but no. Your husband needed money. And on top of that, I drained his account further …"

Mrs Buthelezi started stammering, "It is you who has caused our problems …"

"The only way to trap Mr Buthelezi was to get him to starve first."

Popi screamed, "Tell me, love! Tell me, my husband, that this man is lying! It is not you he is talking about."

Magwegwe was staring at the floor. The intense silence was broken as Popi screamed once more, "Talk to me, damn it! Talk to me! Tell me who you really are!"

Sergeant Zungu turned towards Detective Zondo, "It is getting late, Zondo. We can't spend the whole night telling folktales here. Let's move on."

Themba Zondo nodded, agreeing with Sergeant Zungu. "But I believe it will be a good thing to let Mrs Buthelezi know briefly what happened this evening, Sergeant."

Then Sergeant Zungu, looking very sorry for Mrs Buthelezi, began to tell her the truth. "The agreement between them was that Magwegwe Buthelezi would steal the money from the garage tellers and Taga would drive the getaway car …"

* * *

"Do not panic at the last minute, Magwegwe, you must just tell yourself that you will complete your mission successfully," said Taga. "There is only one petrol attendant. The owner of the filling station is inside. We'll definitely get a few thousand there, perhaps more if we're lucky. Here is the balaclava. Here is the gun. Get in there and do your thing in the blink of an eye!"

Magwegwe felt elated at that moment. He'd get thousands from a job that would take only a few minutes! Taga smeared Magwegwe's car's number plates with mud so that nobody could jot down the number if something went wrong. "It feels good to have a partner," Taga smiled.

Taga drove slowly so as not to draw attention to the car. When he stopped the car, Magwegwe got out, striding like a man with a purpose straight to the petrol station.

Although Magwegwe's car was parked under the trees in a dark place, Taga kept his eye on all the action. The lights were on in the petrol station, and very bright. Shortly, Taga saw Magwegwe running back, holding a bag in one hand and a gun in the other. Taga turned on the car engine and pulled off at high speed, skidding towards the approaching Magwegwe.

Magwegwe opened the door and threw himself in, pulled off the balaclava as the car slipped away into the darkness.

"He! He! He-e-e-e-e!!!!!!!!" laughed Magwegwe as Taga drove. "Whooooa, Taga-boy, we did it!" Magwegwe shrieked, throwing down the pistol.

Magwegwe opened the bag packed with money. "Taga, look at this!"

"Get a hold of yourself, sir. Keeping cool counts a lot in this game, Magwegwe," said Taga. "You have to learn how to stay calm, otherwise you might not be able to do this with me again. Problem is, you don't have the experience."

"Don't worry, boy. You're talking to a professional. I'm not new in this game. I'm an old horse, I've been around the track a few times, boy."

"Is that so?"

"Of course!"

Taga smiled, patting Magwegwe's thigh as he drove, and said, "I'm happy to hear that."

"I've done bigger things than this," Magwegwe said, the shake-up of the robbery having loosened his tongue. "I'll tell you something, once I robbed a bank single-handedly. No noise, boy! There was no noise after that," Magwegwe boasted.

"I am very happy to hear this, Magwegwe."

"Where do you think I got the money from to buy the shares for Rogue Private Investigators? Courtesy of the Brooklyn branch of Nation Bank, boy!"

"I am even happier to hear this, Magwegwe," smiled Taga.

"Which means we are going to work hard," said Magwegwe, glowing in the aftermath of their successful heist.

Taga looked at Magwegwe and laughed loudly saying, "Of course you are going to work, and even harder than you are expecting! For many years to come."

"Good to hear that, Taga."

Taga parked off the road. He switched on a small torch and they divided the money. Magwegwe took his share, put it in a cloth bag he'd brought along, and shoved the bag under his seat. Taga disappeared into the bush and Magwegwe drove his car along the main road towards home.

* * *

"I do not believe this, Sergeant Zungu. Am I dreaming? Is this is a bad dream?" said Popi turning towards Magwegwe. "Why don't you say something? Is all this true?"

Sergeant Zungu cleared his throat. "We have wasted a lot of time here already, madam. The whole episode was recorded." He turned to Detective Zondo. "Please, handcuff the gentleman and let's go."

In the presence of Detective Zondo and Sergeant Zungu, Popi searched everywhere in the car, and eventually pulled the bag full of the stolen money from the petrol station from under the driver's seat. Printed in large letters on the bag was *Nation Bank – Brooklyn Branch*. Popi read the inscription on the bag and turned to Magwegwe crying, "It is true! It is true! Oh God! Why have you forsaken me?"

Magwegwe laughed and spoke for the first time. "I love you Popi, but I love money too." Sergeant Zungu took the bag from Popi. Detective Zondo turned to Magwegwe, "You are charged with armed robbery, committed 20th August 2006, of the Brooklyn branch of Nation Bank. Anything you say, can and will be used against you in a court of law. You have the right to remain silent …"

JOANNE HICHENS

With degrees in art and psychology Hichens worked as a lecturer, an art director, a book illustrator, and a co-coordinator of an eating disorders unit at a psychiatric hospital, before completing a Masters degree in creative writing at the University of Cape Town. During a stint working as part of a City Improvement District team, she gained valuable insight into issues around "crime and grime".

This varied experience, plus being widely travelled, informed her writing of *Out To Score* (co-authored with Mike Nicol, 2006), youth-novel *Stained* (2008), and various articles and stories for newspapers, magazines, and anthologies.

"Crime-thrillers brings the cruel and the tragic to our attention, and underscore the absurd and fragile nature of life. I'm of the opinion that crime-thriller writing can be as open-ended as real life is; sometimes there are loose ends, an 'unorderliness' exists which can be shown through the writing. I tend to prefer writing the bad guys, which comes easier to me if they're verging on the psychopathic, or are at least somewhat over the top – as are the characters in my story *Sweet Life*."

Sweet Life

JOANNE HICHENS

1

THE WAY MABEL MARTIN THOUGHT OF HERSELF WAS INVISIBLE. LIKE the wind maybe. That's right, like the southeaster, the Cape Doctor. People put up with it: it had its uses, it blew away the pollution. But beyond that, people'd rather it didn't blow, and were glad when it was gone.

Mabel took the service lift – never the glass-fronted lift with the lights all the way around – and slowly, painstakingly, started the clean-up routine. Her job for the past three years at the Cape Grande Hotel was to make the beds, scrub the toilets 'til the bowls shone. Flush the vomit, scoop up used condoms, pull matted hair from blocked drains. She made the ugliness of hard, rich living disappear.

She lugged her trolley behind her, it rattled with cleaning materials as she dragged it from room to room. She heard the clink on clink of dirty glasses – the dregs of wine in them with smears of red lipstick on the rims – and of coffee cups and ashtrays and plates congealed with last night's room service. And already a pile of soiled sheets was heaped on the trolley. Even with the water shortages, she clucked, sheets were washed every day. Hardly creased, hardly rumpled the way some people slept so still, the sheets went straight to the laundry. Rich people didn't worry about water or electricity or how you were gonna pay rent at month-end for your cramped Wendy house in the yard of your uncle's place, living like a dog in a *hok*, in a kennel at the back. Life was luck. About who got the breaks.

2

In her recurring dream, Lucy Munro walks to the front of the auditorium, her breasts and butt jiggling for attention and a turn-on to every man in the place. Oh yeah, she has a body on her alright, she's not straight up and down stiff as a plank like her anorexic white-girl colleagues in the world of TV.

Lucy steps on to the podium to accept her Celebrity of the Year award – finally recognised for the great actress she is – plus one of those giant cheques worth a million bucks with her name on it, part of which she'll donate to charity, of course. She smiles for the cameras, tosses back sleek hair glossed with gel, fingers the gems glinting in chains around her neck, and delivers her thanks. With the applause, Lucy graciously bows her head and bends low, tantalises with her deep cleavage, those plump breasts the colour of cappuccino contrasting against the clotted cream of the shaped suit.

Then she walks towards the respected businessman of her dreams. He takes her in his arms, kisses her hard on the mouth.

At this precise moment in her recurring dream, Nic Mabuza, the stalker ex-boyfriend who won't let her go, storms into the auditorium. He grabs her from the arms of the other man and presses her against him so hard there's pain in her heart…

*　*　*

As she had every day in the Cape Grande Hotel this week, Lucy Munro woke at this point from her pill-induced stupor, her tongue thick and furry as a small animal trapped in her mouth. She watched her cellphone vibrating on the table, spinning a non-stop dance there on the glass top. Didn't need to check the screen to know it was bloody Nic Mabuza. The bastard Nic still calling constantly, the loser still desperate to possess her even though she'd ditched him.

Why don't you get the fucking message? It's over, Nic.

She reached for the glass of water on the beside table. Her throat parched, her brow sticky with the residue of last night's sex, she wiped sweat from her chest.

Lucy Munro has had it with being a presenter on nowhere programmes – eco shit and infomercials – was down in Cape Town for an audition for a local movie. At least have her talent recognised. And after the audition today, she'd kill a couple of hours at the Sex Expo. With over two hundred exhibitors she was sure to pick up something titillating to spice up the night – 'cause of course she was down here too, in the Mother City, for some no-strings-attached sex.

She hated the way Nic wouldn't let her out of his sight in Joburg, his insistence on Exclusivity with a capital E driving her nuts.

To hell with all that.

3

At ten o'clock that morning, as Mabel Martin approached suite 752, Ms Lucy Munro opened her door, came out screeching into the cellphone precariously trapped between her shoulder and ear. "Don't give me the bloody bullshit about how I belong to you, Nic. Don't you bloody get it? You come near me again, I'll get a restraining order. I'll tell the cops you're nothing but a thug. I've fucking forgotten you already. Nic you're history!" Pressing disconnect, eyes on the cellphone, she tripped over the tray she'd dumped in the passage the night before. She managed to right herself against the wall after the inelegant stumble.

"Why haven't you picked up this mess yet?" Lucy Munro snapped at Mabel, the scapegoat for Ms Munro's stupidity, tripping the way she had in those impractical stiletto ankle-boots of hers.

Mabel felt the hot blush creep up her neck, as if Lucy Munro in her designer clothes, going down for her leisurely buffet breakfast, her chin tilted up in that superior way, had the right to grind her into the dirt like she was shit on Lucy's heel.

"Sorry, Ma'am," Mabel said, "I'll do it now." She stooped at Ms Munro's feet, picked up a plate of leftovers, mumbled, "What a waste."

"Excuse me?" Lucy shot her a cold stare.

"I'll make haste, Ma'am," Mabel said, scraping the remains of a smelly half-eaten crayfish and dried-out sushi rolls into the black bag open on a frame at one end of the trolley. She watched as Lucy's muscled calves criss-crossed towards the lift, heard the swish-swish of stockings at the junction where her thighs rubbed against each other – a result of the too skintight skirt. Ms Munro huffed off in her red coat with the leopard-fur trim and black beret for the crisp winter weather, not deigning to look back, now raising her voice into the cellphone again: "Nic Mabuza is call-ing me non-stop. He won't leave me alone. He threatens me. Treats me like

I'm his property. What am I supposed to do, Detective Smith? Wait till he does something nasty? Do I wait 'til I'm dead? Then will the cops do something? Detective Smith, call me as soon as you get this message."

*   *   *

Maybe the odd guest would greet Mabel, with a nod of the head or a cursory mumbled good morning before rapidly padding off, footfalls absorbed by the carpeting. They might smile tightly, with no meaning, before closing themselves in the lift with a view, turning their attention to what truly mattered: the city below, the razzmatazz, the glitz, the tourist attractions – Adderley Street, Table Mountain, the Waterfront.

But it was a sure thing guests at the Cape Grande didn't think twice – they didn't think at all it seemed to Mabel – about leaving her a tip. Not even a few rand *footjie* on the dressing table, for cleaning their filth, for flushing their shit and *gemors*, for making things right, so they could *sommer* start all over again.

From the silence of no-man's-land, Mabel pushed in the key-card and walked into Ms Munro's temporary life. She closed the door behind her. The only sound the rhythmic hum of the air conditioning unit. The TV sound down, on the screen last night's repeat of *Generations*, one of the popular soapies Lucy Munro loud-mouthed she was auditioning for.

Mabel had read all about Ms Lucy Munro in *heat* magazine. How the council-flats girl made good, was on her way up, up, up. And read about her wild streak, too. She yanked off Lucy's pillow cases and sheets, where marbled on the undressed fabric was evidence of another *woes* night – spit drooled on the pillows and stains of semen on the mattress still damp and smelling of sex, that pungent odour she'd come to know working the job. Stale sweat and glistening discharge on sheets. And there were other smells; spilt coffee and acrid smoke.

And this morning, in Lucy's suite, were the remnants of the white dust of drugs on the glass coffee table, and a spill of red wine on the carpet, which Mabel attacked first, on her knees again, spraying carpet-cleaner and scrubbing.

Then Mabel pulled on fresh bed linen and fluffed out the bedcovers.

In the bathroom she picked up a crumpled dress from the floor and held it against her body, checked herself out. Nice breasts, long legs and a round bum like Lucy Munro. Even their skin-tone was similar. From neck down *she* could be on TV too. But her face let her down, though they both had oval shaped chins. Ja, if only her nose was a bit straighter, her eyes not so close set, then *she* could be the one booked in the room – not cleaning it. Ja, it was the details, the accidents of birth and fortune that separated Mabel Martin from the ones that got the *good parts*. Sure Ms Munro was moving up in the world, auditioning for movies and talking non-stop about what a big star she was gonna be, how she was gonna get a big part on one of those soaps like *Isidingo* or *7de Laan*, maybe even on *The Bold and the Beautiful*; Mabel couldn't even get a job as a cashier at bloody Shoprite. Her eye twitched as she ran a finger along the pink scar running from her hairline down to the outer corner of her left eyebrow.

She threw down the dress and stubbornly circled the dust cloth on the bathroom mirror, restoring the crystal-clear shine. She had a brain, if anyone cared to notice. She'd wanted to go to Technikon but with Daddy out the picture and Mommy drunk on *dop* since he left her, where was money for education? This was the only job she could get, had for years now, as she'd made the change from starry-eyed schoolgirl to woman.

Is this what life is all about, then?

She scrubbed the taps 'til they gleamed; refilled the plastic bottles of shampoo and conditioner; in the bedroom every visible stain was soaked up, every stray pube and sprinkle of cocaine vacuumed. Lastly, she replaced the mini booze bottles in the fridge. Thought about pocketing a couple. Ja, temptation was ever-present, like the Devil.

She switched off the TV. Wheeled her trolley into the passage. Closed the door.

She'd be back in the morning.

4

That night, Lucy pulled on sexy panties, lacy black and gold, adjusted herself in a matching bra, the gold trim scratching against her nipples and hardening them like marbles. She slipped on a camisole, then a slinky black dress over the lot and did a touch-up of the crimson lipstick.

Lucy Munro'd had a good look around the Sex Expo. You name it – tasty lubricants, incense, an erotic art gallery, quick tattoos – it was all there. She'd made a bee-line for the Collars'nCuffs stand; nice leather gear

there but nothing she hadn't seen before on their website. She'd bought
a few toys at Kinx, thrilled at how many different styles of dildo there
were to choose from! She couldn't decide between Dick with a Vengeance
and Power Buster so settled for a wireless remote-control number, and
a blonde wig. She'd hung around for a pole-dancing class; some of the
moves came in handy at her audition.

Now she pinned in place the wig she'd bought and pouted at the mirror,
looking like a black Marilyn. She swayed her hips, approved of her reflection, and hummed Soft Cell's "Tainted Love"; Lithe Soviet-block gals – the
Mavericks' Stars –had stripped to the classic hit on stage at the Sex Expo.

Catchy tune that one, all about touching and teasing.

Oh yeah, Cape Town was sexually liberated indeed and Lucy Munro
was smouldering hot, ready to burn up the night.

Her cellphone kept ringing with Nic's insistent redialling.

Sure, she'd run to Nic at first and all the things he could give her. Bling
on those manicured hands, diamond studs in his lobes spoke of his success as a nightclub owner. His tight abs from the gym workouts, his taut
body kept her interest.

But no more.

She ignored his calls.

You're one has-been lover, Nic Mabuza.

She couldn't switch off in case her agent called. She wanted the part
badly – not about to tell anyone the audition was for a porn flick, but hell,
how else was she gonna get a break into the big time? The flick *Anyone but
my husband* was a start and the director didn't expect her to do a thing she
hadn't done before. She flashbacked to when she was thirteen, and getting
gifts and cash for letting sugar-daddies *pomp* her.

She checked the details on her Samsung.

The message from Leatherman:

C u at Plush Bar ten p.m.

She SMSd him:

On my way.

Pushed send.

From BurninghotBabe.

Oh yeah, in bed, where it counted, she was sizzling stuff. Hadn't been
without a date since she'd joined the Collars'nCuffs site she could access
anywhere, thanks to her fancy phone. She threw the cell on the bed. She

breathed onto the dressing table mirror, drew a smiley face in the misted glass.

Fuck you, Nic Mabuza.

*   *   *

Lucy Munro knew the guy was Leatherman as soon as she saw him at Plush Bar. The guy, dressed in a pinstripe suit, drumming his fingers on the counter, looking around with a keen nervous energy. She hoped he wasn't a beginner. But what she could guess of his physique got her moist at once: well built, strong, and the tattoo she saw lurking at his wrist under cover of his sleeve was a clue he was into a certain type of intense experience. On the whole, a good-looking white guy with a close-cropped haircut.

Several Camparis later, plus the sexy slow-grind tones of Usher's "Love in this Club" getting the juices flowing, Lucy and "John", he said his name was, were chatting up some heat.

"You could tie yourself in knots just sitting on one of those Kama Sutra sofas at the Sex Expo," John aka Leatherman said. "And did you try out the bucking-bronco dick?" he asked. "Looked like a helluva a ride."

"You know," Lucy smiled, "in a moment of madness I nearly bought a pair of bunny ears and a pink feather boa! But they're so not my style."

"Oh yes, I know what you like," Leatherman said. "I am one lucky guy. You're way more gorgeous than you are on TV, you are one sexy lady, BurninghotBabe," he circled his tongue in her ear as they headed out the door, "and I can't wait to get you in bed and see how hot you really are …"

*   *   *

Back in the hotel suite Lucy switched MTV on low – dancers gyrating and thrusting and grabbing balls and butt. LL Cool J coming on now, the track "Baby" messing with their heads, putting them in the mood.

They drank champagne. Licked each other's lips. Touched tongue and teased.

"Let's order in," Lucy said.

"I'm only hungry for you, Babe. Wanna get straight to the games," he said.

"You're impatient," Lucy said as he came up behind her, ripped her dress, grabbed at her breasts. She heard her sharp intake of breath as he pinched her nipples. Slapped her hard across the arse. Bit her lip, drew blood there, the taste sweet on her tongue.

"Got me some new toys here. You into these?" He emptied his briefcase – handcuffs, collars, leather, ropes.

"Whatever you want to do to me, Leatherman, I'm yours. Just don't use any dildos on me, I can do that myself at home. I want meat."

He pushed her onto the bed. Cuffed her. Teased her more.

"*Now's* the time for patience," he said as he selected the silk ropes. "Shibari bondage," he explained, "used to be a form of torture way back in Japan. A load of fun in our circles though." He smiled, slowly starting to wrap the ropes around her thighs. "Targets the pleasure points. Promises a real intense time, Babe."

"I'm feeling a little light headed," Lucy tittered as with each knot he pulled the ropes tighter.

*   *   *

"Trust breeds lust," Leatherman said. "Relax, Babe …"

He expertly strapped her up, lifting her, lacing her up from under her thighs, across her pubic bone, working his way to her breasts; pulling immeasurably tighter with each knot he could tell the pressure at her cunt was intensifying.

"Oh yes, yes …" she moaned.

She was at his mercy.

So close to orgasm, he eased up on the ropes, gave her respite, but for only a second before he again applied pressure … slowly … slowly … tightening the ropes until she could hardly bear it.

She told him, "No, no, stop, I'm begging you …"

Sure he stopped, though she hadn't used the emergency stop-word they'd agreed upon, now had she?

He pulled out his state-of-the-art cellphone, said, "Give me one of those wide celebrity smiles of yours, Babe."

She opened her eyes. He snapped her pic. She squinted with the flash.

"Hey, Leatherman, put that thing away."

"Which hardware you talking about, Babe?"

He took a video clip of her writhing, her back arched as he tweaked the rope.

"Jesus, stop ..."

"You, Babe, are a notch on my belt," he said, standing naked in front of her, his cock hard as a lead pipe. "These few pics are simply a memento of an auspicious night."

She whimpered as he pulled the ropes tight. "No ... no, stop, really, I can't breathe ..."

"Babe, this is what it's all about; you'll pass out in exquisite pain." He held his hand over her mouth, half-covered her nose and lay on top of her, knowing that on the verge of losing consciousness she had no energy, or will, to bite into his hand. He shifted the ropes and fucked her to the beat of the hard rap right there in his veins, felt her breath grow shallow under his vice grip.

"You love it, Babe. Face it, you *hot-not* nympho, you love it!"

* * *

Lucy Munro gasped as he threw champagne in her face, bringing her round.

Some tune running in her head.

My tainted life.

Loving and teasing and hurting.

He stuffed a spongy red ball into her mouth.

She groaned, strained against the ropes, felt her eyes rolling wildly.

"I'm not done with you yet," he said.

5

Mabel knocked on Lucy Munro's door. No answer.

She knocked again, as she always did, three times, just to make sure – ever since she'd walked in on the old tourist and street boy having *poep-*sex just like she read about in *The Voice*. Like Sodom and Gomorrah.

She heard nothing.

She opened the door with her master key-card, shut the door behind her and pulled her trolley into the room.

Mabel gasped and felt her hand draw up to her mouth at the sight of celebrity TV-presenter Lucy Munro on the bed, tied up in ropes and spread like a star. Hands cuffed to the headboard, ankles tied on either side to the fixed legs of the bed. A blonde wig at an angle on one side of her marked and blotchy face.

"My God," said Mabel, as suddenly Lucy's eyes opened wide.

Mabel stood still a moment, then she pulled the red ball from Ms Munro's mouth. Lucy coughed and twisted her dry lips and rasped, "Thank Jesus you're here! It's about time!" Her voice was coming out a hoarse series of croaks. "Jesus, find keys for the cuffs, girl! I'm scheduled to fly back to Joburg today!" She had difficulty speaking, as if her throat hurt. "The stupid shit left me this way. That's the last time I pick up some arsehole S&M freak in a bar!" Ms Munro coughed. "Big stud of a man but how could he bloody leave me like this? Next time I'll stick with the escort service." Ms Munro tried to force her thighs together, grunted and fell back, opening flesh of dusky pink at her crotch as she couldn't help writhe in an attempt to free herself. "My God, what time is it? The taxi'll be here at eleven!" Ms Munro's voice a frayed rope of tension, her veins fat and blue where the collar – black leather with silver studs, just like a dog's – dug into her neck as she twisted. "Help me, for fuck's sake!"

Mabel looked at the torn crotchless panties, the *poes* pink between Ms Munro's thighs. Her rolls of brown flesh squashed between the ropes and goose-pimpled tits spilling over the top. All trussed up like a Sunday roast ready to be thrown in the pot. And Heavens, Ms Munro had one of her nipples pierced! She looked like a TV whore in one of those scenes Mabel saw on the pay channel when some pervy guest left a porn movie running!

"Hurry. Get a move on!" Lucy Munro groaned. "I have a plane to catch. I have to get back to the network. I can't stand this a moment longer."

The woman was in agony.

"Get this bondage shit off. Now!"

The woman was used to giving orders.

As she had all week. *Pick this up. Take my suit to the laundry. Make sure you stock the mini-bar with Cape Velvet.* Talking to agents and yelling at some man called Nic on the phone, strutting around in her underthings, as if Mabel wasn't in the room cleaning up after her.

"I'll get you loose as soon as I can," said Mabel, undoing the collar – the price tag still on it – seeing the raw chaffing there.

Then Mabel stepped back and stared and bit her lip.

"What the hell are you waiting for? Don't just stand there, for God's sake! Find the key, and there are nail scissors right there in my vanity case; c'mon, cut me loose!"

Mabel crossed her arms over her white apron. Scowled. "I'd appreciate the magic word," said Mabel. The "please" was what she now wanted to hear. "Ms Munro, where have your manners been this whole week?"

*   *   *

In the brief silence that followed, and as she blinked, one tear spilled onto Lucy Munro's cheek.

"Oh, come on," she said. "Please, with a cherry on top. Is that what you want me to say?" The heavy drop zigzagged down Lucy's face, through the smudged mascara towards her bruised jaw.

Mabel rummaged in the vanity case, found the pointy scissors and now came closer with them. She saw the stubble at Lucy's underarms, and a few stray hairs she'd missed while shaving. She sniffed at the sour smell of BO, of expended energy gone wrong. Lucy's armpits glistened now with the strain as she tried yet again to pull free of the cuffs so tight around her wrists her fingers were fat as cocktail sausages.

Like little boys swollen *tollies*, Mabel thought.

"He took photographs. What the hell is he gonna do with those?" Ms Munro groaned, half delirious. "Get me out of this get-up. I don't know what I was thinking! Help me, please!"

"You never even asked my name, did you, Ms Munro? I'm the one who cleans up your mess every day."

Lucy sniffed. "Whatever your name is, just get me out of here. Please. Thank you. I appreciate it."

*   *   *

Mabel had never stolen a thing. Yesterday an Omega ladies' watch was left unattended in suite 725, the day before a hundred-rand note on the dressing table in 742; Mabel'd wanted the pair of real diamanté earrings forgotten on the bathroom basin in suite 721, and though her fingers itched, she'd handed them in at reception.

But an opportunity like this was never going to happen again.

"If you want to have random sex, Ms Munro, you should know there's a risk when you pick up strangers."

Mabel put the scissors down on the bedside table next to the small key. She picked up the red ball. Gave it a squeeze. "You can get diseases, Aids!"

She quickly stuffed the ball back into Lucy's mouth and tied it in place with fishnet stockings. The look of panic in Lucy's eyes was quite something, her head shaking back and forth in tiny movements – and her stifled moans more than Mabel cared to listen to for long. First, Mabel pulled off Lucy's ankle-boots, satisfied, as she checked the size on the sole, that they'd fit her.

Then Mabel picked up the scissors. She imagined plunging the tiny blades into Ms Munro's belly. She'd have to jump away fast as the colour of life squirted there, like the way it splattered all over the place in the crime shows on TV.

She wondered if the scissors stabbed in Ms Munro's belly, between the ropes, would kill her. Or would she have to stab again and again?

"This sort of thing happens all the time in Cape Town," Mabel said. "Cape Town is the murder capital of South Africa and that's a fact, Ms Munro." Her brow furrowed. "Or is it the murder capital of the world? And no one ever gets caught."

Then Mabel plunged the scissors, instead of into Lucy Munro's body, into Lucy Munro's neck.

*   *   *

She bundled her bloodied uniform and the scissors in a bin bag. She'd take it along and get rid of it later. She showered quickly. She dressed in Lucy's clothes which were as perfect a fit as the boots. Mabel was the picture of style with Lucy's Dior carry-all slung over her shoulder, containing money and jewellery and the plane ticket to Joburg she'd found and a stash of those small liquor bottles.

Reception called. The taxi was ready.

The fancy cellphone buzzed again.

Nic showing on the screen.

Then an immediate SMS.

Pick up. NOW.

"Too bad, loverboy," Mabel said, switching off, popping the phone in her bag. Checking the passage was quiet, she wheeled the trolley to the scullery.

Back in the room, with a last glance at her new self – Holy Heaven, her legs looked decent in the stiletto ankle-boots! – she squirted perfume on her wrists and collarbones. Then she sprayed air freshener.

In a last gesture she bent and kissed Ms Munro goodbye, tasted the sweat and blood, not entirely unpleasant, on her brow, and remembered her manners. "Thank you, Lucy," she said. "You'll be found soon enough. When the *meid* comes to turn down the bed and put the mint on your pillow."

And quietly satisfied she'd get away with this – at least for a few days while the *domkop* police figured out it wasn't some random sex-kill gone wrong, if they ever did – she closed the door on Lucy's room smelling like Spring Garden. A cloying scent to cover up the smell of human spills. Some other *kiepie* would have to change the sheets.

She looped the do-not-disturb sign over the door handle.

Mabel Martin, the new look-at-me Lucy Munro – dressed in a cream suit, plus a red coat with leopard-fur trim, the black beret pulled down over her face, and big Jackie O sunglasses – made her way to the glass lift. She pressed the button for the ground floor and saw the bustling city at her feet. She waltzed through reception the way Lucy would, strutting in her boots, owning the sweet life. The doorman doffed his cap and opened the door of the waiting taxi.

"Airport, please," Mabel said.

All the way there, and once she'd hidden the evidence under the seat, she fingered the ticket. She knew she could do this, just like she'd seen her soap stars on TV get on planes and fly into a new life. She'd be a star for a few hours before she disappeared in Johannesburg and started afresh. She'd call herself Gloria, or Melody. Something with a nice ring to it, positive and upbeat, with the promise of a better future.

6

Ten thousand feet up, the hum of the engines as comforting as the hotel air conditioning, Mabel accepted champagne, or was it sparkling wine? Mabel had a brain after all and read the latest news in *The Voice*, about how the Europeans had hogged all the good names for their booze and cheese. She toasted her new life as she turned her back on her life discarded: her black and white portable in the room in her uncle's yard; her uncle who took his rights without asking; the outside toilet; her maid's uniform.

She smiled and sipped, enjoying the view from the business-class seat, the burst of sparkling-wine bubbles on her tongue. And the bumps, turbulence they called it, not nearly as bad as being in a minibus taxi hurtling along the highway to a dead-end job. Up here in the clouds she felt a thrill. She savoured the canapés, the salmon that melted in her mouth like butter, the meringues with coffee cream for pudding. A hostess asked for her autograph. And without batting an eye behind the sunglasses, she signed the in-flight magazine. So this was the luck of Lucy Munro! She held her hand to her nose and breathed in the scent of Opium.

Mabel wasn't worried. Not about what she'd do or where she'd go. She had Lucy's money, lots of it. She had bottles of booze from the mini-bar and the chocolate bars and peanuts. She'd find a cheap boarding house. She'd find her way.

As the plane circled, approaching Joburg, she saw, in glimpses through clouds fluffy as candyfloss, the mine dumps, then the vast tracts of township shacks. She saw the land divided into larger middle-income plots, then saw the land walled off by the rich, their cement-and-brick *droompaleise* with swimming pools that from so high looked the size of postage stamps.

She'd ditch Lucy's clothes and buy new things soon as she could. Stay a night at a Holiday Inn maybe. She'd make a plan. There was plenty of opportunity in Jozi, Egoli, City of Gold. She clutched Lucy's bag in her lap as the pilot announced the imminent arrival at OR Tambo International Airport.

Today, she thought, *is the first day of the rest of my life!*

*   *   *

Mabel saw the policemen just beyond the arrivals gate – one on a cellphone, the other staring at the legs of a hot blonde the age of his daughter, if he had one. She remembered straightening the do-not-disturb sign on the door; there was no way they would have found Lucy Munro yet.

Or had they?

Caught up in the snake from the plane, she kept pace with the departing crowd, hurried towards the waiting people with eager smiles and signs of welcome, there to meet tourists, business partners, loved ones. Mabel swallowed her fear, walked quickly in the opposite direction of the policemen, the adrenaline shooting into her fingertips as she saw, from the corner of her eye, one of them move forward.

She pulled the brimmed beret further down over her forehead, secured Lucy's sunglasses tightly on her face, hurried through the arrivals lounge with Lucy's bag, kept her head low as she pushed through the throng. Click-click-clicked with those stiletto heels, every second getting closer to the glass doors opening to the big city.

She felt a tug at her arm, a vice grip on her shoulder.

"Where the hell d'you think you're going?"

She could not pull away. She felt the lurch of her stomach as it jumped into her throat.

"I've left a hundred messages you haven't picked up, Lucy," the man whispered in Mabel's ear. "You remember me, don't you? Nic Mabuza the only man for you." He spun her around and clutched her close to him and simultaneously Mabel felt the pain at her chest. "It's over alright," he hissed. "You made a fool outta me. You're the one who's fucking *history*." Pushing her viciously to arms length, her sunglasses clattered to the tiles.

The last thing she saw was the look of horror on Nic's face – did he first see the puckered scar across her forehead or was it was her eyes set too close together? – before he quickly retreated, leaving the knife in her, and disappeared into the crowd. He left her there sinking to her knees, Lucy's life slowly seeping into Mabel's lungs.

She was unable to call out.

She turned her head.

Where are the police when you need them?

Her life bubbled up in her throat, warm, thick, choking. She tried to swallow back the blood pooling in her mouth. Blood – now that had a different smell from anything else she knew, a metallic smell, and a taste like rusty tin cans.

In a last effort Mabel raised one arm, stretched red fingers pointing out the escape route of the killer. And as she slumped down and her head settled on the cold floor, she smelled bleach on the tiles.